WE'RE ALL CRIMINALS

ALSO BY MIMA

The Fire Series
Fire
A Spark Before the Fire

The Vampire Series
The Rock Star of Vampires
Her Name is Mariah

Different Shades of the Same Color

The Hernandez Series
We're All Animals
Always be a Wolf
The Devil is Smooth Like Honey
A Devil Named Hernandez
And the Devil Will Laugh
The Devil Will Lie
The Devil and His Legacy
She Was His Angel

Learn more at **www.mimaonfire.com**
Also find Mima on Twitter, Facebook and Instagram @mimaonfire

WE'RE ALL CRIMINALS

MIMA

WE'RE ALL CRIMINALS

iUniverse books may be ordered through booksellers or by contacting:

iUniverse
1663 Liberty Drive
Bloomington, IN 47403
www.iuniverse.com
844-349-9409

ISBN: 978-1-6632-1338-9 (sc)
ISBN: 978-1-6632-1339-6 (e)

Library of Congress Control Number: 2020923088

Print information available on the last page.

iUniverse rev. date: 11/23/2020

Acknowledgements

I want to thank my mother, Jean Arsenault for all her help, love and support. Also, thank you to my readers and everyone who supports and encourages my writing.

Acknowledgements

CHAPTER

1

Freedom is the trademark of humanity. To those in a prison cell, confined to a hospital bed, or trapped in their figurative coffin, there is nothing more beautiful than freedom. We're all animals, and as such, it's in our nature to claw our way out of any trap we feel locked in because the light of freedom shines much brighter after it has been lost. We will fight for it. We will beg for it, and if we have to, we will kill for it.

No one appreciated freedom more than Jorge Hernandez. As a former Mexican cartel leader, he had managed to escape both death and prison, something he recognized as a rarity for his kind. Now in his 40s, he was blessed with a beautiful family and lived in Canada. As the CEO of Our House of Pot, Jorge had the monopoly in the legalized marijuana industry. To the outside world, he was a charismatic Mexican-Canadian businessman who is relatable and brought jobs to communities throughout the country. But to those who knew him, Jorge Hernandez was one of the most dangerous men in the world and did whatever he needed to get what he wanted.

It was the ultimate freedom.

"Paige, you would not believe what he say," He shook his head while leaning back in his chair as his dark eyes glanced around the home office. A lopsided grin appeared on his lips. "I thought this here, it cannot be true. I must be dreaming."

"What?" His wife's lips slowly slid into a smile while her blue eyes remained full of hesitation. "When you said the head of the police wanted to meet with you…"

"I know, but this here, it does not worry me," Jorge said with a shrug. "It is, how you say, *irrelevant* to me."

"I don't trust that…"

"Paige, this here, it is ok," Jorge assured her as he leaned forward on his desk. Staring into each other's eyes, they silently communicated. "You know me, I think the police are useless, I do not fear them. They are nothing."

"I hope you didn't tell him that," Paige calmly replied even though her eyes were showing signs of humor, as she pushed a strand of blond hair behind her ear.

"Of course, I tell him that!" Jorge boasted and let out of a loud, abrupt laugh. "This here, it is how I feel."

"Maybe not the best idea…"

"Hey, he put the words in my mouth, and I simply agreed," Jorge shrugged as he glanced at his bulletproof window. "Plus, he say my name wrong. He pronounced it the Spanish, not the English way, and you know how that pisses me off."

"He said that they were useless?" Paige appeared stuck on the first comment.

"More or less," Jorge nodded as he fixed his tie. "*Si, mi amor,* that he did."

"Only you could manage to do that," Paige shook her head.

With that, Jorge leaned back in his chair and let out another loud laugh.

"Paige, you do not even know half of this," Jorge continued to laugh and shook his head. "He openly admitted to me that they are fuck ups. That they aren't capable of doing their jobs and to this, well, I, of course, agreed."

"Of course…"

"Paige, you know me. I do not hold back," Jorge reminded her as his dark eyes twinkled, and he winked at her. "This here, it is not necessary. I believe we should always say how it is so, when this man, he admitted that the local police were *struggling,* I tell him that they were fucking useless."

"Jorge, I don't think…"

"I know, *mi amor,* I know you worry," Jorge replied as he sniffed, pulling his chair forward. "But you do not understand why he came to me. He comes to me because he knows what a fucking mess the police are, and he thinks that I can help them."

"It sounds like a trick."

"And, *mi amor*, it could be," Jorge agreed. "But they cannot trick me. I am watching them closely. I have Marco on it."

He referred to his company's head IT specialist, who was most valued for his hacking abilities. The Filipino-Canadian had saved the day on more than one occasion.

"So how did he try to explain this exactly?" Paige continued to be suspicious. After spending many years in the criminal world, her instincts were sharp. "I can't imagine a situation where the head of the police sits down with Jorge Hernandez to discuss potential tactics to improve his department."

"Ah! But *mi amor*, he did," Jorge clarified as he raised an eyebrow. "Of course, he did not come right out and say it that way, you know. He made it sound like he thought I might have some *insight* on how to improve things. I say yes, *senor*, if you want help, then you must work with me."

"Are you sure he…"

"Chase, he checked him before our meeting," Jorge insisted, referring to one of his youngest associates who had been loyally by his side for years. "I assure you, he did not even have a phone on him, let alone any listening devices, nothing. Marco hacked him. This was not part of a plan, and this man, he comes to me on his own. I had it checked out."

"I wish you had told me about this before," Paige shook her head. "I feel like I'm not in the loop…"

"Once I knew everything was ok, I tell you," Jorge grew serious and leaned forward in his chair. "*Mi amor,* you were *shot* last year, for the *second* time. I would rather not get your involved unless…"

"You can't lock me in a cage just because…"

"Paige, I am not locking you in a cage," Jorge corrected her, speaking abruptly. "You are my wife, and it is my job to protect you. To protect this here whole family. I will do whatever it takes to do so."

"But you can't cut me out of what is going on," Paige insisted. "I'm still part of this world."

"I know," Jorge said and looked away, not wanting to argue. "The irony of all of this is that I do it to protect you, to keep you safe, so you do not have to worry, not to hurt you."

"I know," Paige seemed to calm as their eyes met, and they both fell silent. "But you can't protect me from everything. I need to know what is going on."

He looked away and didn't reply.

"Don't shut down on me," Paige spoke emotionally.

"Paige," Jorge looked back and saw her eyes watering. "I do not shut down on you. It is...it is a difficult memory."

There was so much blood.

"I understand," Paige sniffed. "I do, I do. I just...I feel like I'm locked out of the group."

He thought she was going to die.

"But I'm ok," Her voice lifting. "Everything is ok."

Jorge didn't reply.

"Can you please tell me the rest of the story," Paige seemed apprehensive. "What happened today?"

"Well, this man," Jorge slowly regained his train of thought. "He wanted to talk to me about helping him out. His police, there are so many issues. So many unsolved cases..."

"Racial profiling, cops beating up and killing innocent people..."

"Yes, well, there is all of that too," Jorge nodded. "He cannot control his people, so this here is why he talk to me. He sees that I have a very well-organized and loyal group of people surrounding me. He wanted to learn how he can do the same."

"What did you tell him?" Paige coaxed.

"I tell him that it goes both ways," Jorge replied. "you cannot expect loyalty if you do not show the same. It runs much deeper than I think this department is capable of doing."

"So, that was it?" Paige appeared suspicious.

"He wanted to pick my brain," Jorge replied. "And this here is all he got."

"You aren't holding back from me?"

"No, *mi amor*," He let his guard down. "I promise you this; I am not holding back. The meeting was very uninteresting however, it was humorous that he admitted to me that his police department is terrible. Fortunately for me, that this is the case."

The two shared a smile.

"So, that's it?" Paige asked. "That's all?"

"He would like to work with me," Jorge replied. "He feels that perhaps it is easier for us to do so than against one another. But of course, this is because he has no hope of working *against* me."

"And how does this look exactly? Should you trust him?" Paige continued to be suspicious.

"There is nothing to trust," Jorge shook his head. "It is not like we had a teenage sleepover and discuss our deepest, darkest secrets. We merely had a short discussion where he wanted my help. I told him that I was unsure how I could help him, and he, in turn, suggested that this could be a mutual thing. He said that from time to time, he may call on me, and from time to time, I could call on him. I asked what he was willing to do for me."

"And?"

"He said he has the resources when needed."

"I can't imagine what those resources could be that makes it worth the risk."

"Well, let us just tuck away this card and see what happens," Jorge spoke thoughtfully. "In Mexico, I had a very strong….working relationship with the *policia* so who knows, maybe this is also possible here?"

"I'd be cautious. This *isn't* Mexico."

"I know, *mi amor,* as I said, we are looking into it some more," Jorge leaned back into his chair. "You must relax. I am always careful."

She looked away. He stared at her for a long moment.

"Paige, I know that I have been doing wrong," He spoke evenly, and she looked slightly startled by his words. "I know that I try to protect you when you do not wish to be protected but, I cannot tell you how scared I was when you were shot. I know I keep saying it, but I do not think you understand."

"But, I'm…"

"I know you are fine," Jorge quickly cut her off. "But this is the thing, *mi amor,* my job, as your husband, is to make sure you continue to be fine. And this is something I take very seriously. Maybe this here makes me a chauvinist or sexist or whatever. I do not care. Miguel, Maria, they need you. You cannot take these chances anymore."

"Neither can you," Paige quietly reminded him. "We both can't. We came close to…he meant to kill you, not me."

"I know, Paige, I know," Jorge nodded in understanding. "You are right, but what do we do?"

She didn't have an answer.

And neither did he.

CHAPTER

2

"The *policia?*" Diego Silva jumped into the conversation, dramatically swinging his arms in the air in protest. "Are you out of your fucking *mind?*"

Jorge merely grinned at his longtime *amigo,* noting that everyone else in his office was doing the same. Known to exaggerate, the middle-aged Colombian never missed an opportunity to get caught up in the drama.

"I assure you," Jorge calmly put his hand up in the air. "I know what I am doing."

"They are...how you say, crook?" Jolene Silva loudly jumped in, glancing toward her brother and back at Jorge. "You know, doing things wrong?"

"Crooked," Paige spoke evenly. "Although, crooks probably isn't far off either."

Jolene scrunched her face up in confusion as if unsure but remained silent while beside her, Chase Jacobs, the youngest member of the group, spoke up.

"I don't know," He said with a shrug. "I don't trust the police even if that guy didn't have anything on him that day. There could still be some investigation, and he could be trying to win your trust."

"Oh, I have thought of that," Jorge nodded toward the young, indigenous man. As time moved forward, his native instincts were growing stronger, overpowering his caucasian side. "Of course, but I also know that Marco, he is on it."

"Of course, sir," Marco Rodel Cruz looked up from his laptop. "I have looked into their files, emails, everything, and I am not finding anything that is suspicious."

"I suspect you won't either," Jorge assured him. "This man, the one I speak with, he comes to me because he is in fear for his job. Those who are below him are restless, stupid, and out of control. This puts him in a vulnerable situation."

"I do not understand," Jolene spoke up, shaking her head as she sat back in her chair, pushing her breasts out. "He is their boss, no?"

"He is," Jorge nodded and looked away. "But imagine if all of you were like his department, where would that put me? I may be at the top of the pile, but this is not much good if the whole motherfucking thing crumbles, and he knows this too. His department is a reflection on him."

"So, he wants you to take care of the loose cannons?" Chase guessed. "Get rid of the ones that might drag him down too?"

"I believe so although, nothing was confirmed as of yet," Jorge nodded. "You see, this here meeting, it was merely an introduction. He wanted to test the waters. He will be back, and when he is, I will learn more, however, from what he has said and what I have seen in the news and heard, his department is a shitshow, and he's swimming in it. He wants me to pull him out, clean him off, and let the others burn."

"But why the fuck should we do this?" Diego jumped back into the conversation, his dark eyes narrowing. "Why should we even get involved?"

"Isn't it obvious?" Jorge shrugged. "I control the media. I own the government. What is next?"

No one replied.

"It is important I keep these people in my control," Jorge continued. "Previously, I did not bother with the police because it hardly seemed worth the effort. It was not as if the department was strong enough for me to be concerned, and yet, in their inefficiency, it was hardly worth my time to take them over. But now that this man has introduced a vulnerability to me, well, this is a whole other story."

"I think," Paige finally spoke, having remained quiet throughout the meeting. "I think this man must be very desperate if he is willing to take the chance coming to you. I'm sure he's aware of your reputation."

"That, *mi amor*, is *exactly* why he is coming to me," Jorge confirmed. "He knows that it is much better to be my friend than my enemy."

No one replied.

"And, of course, he will do whatever I say," Jorge continued. "I am not helping him out of the generosity of my heart. But he must be careful. If he is seen with me, people will talk. So, if anything, he is in a much more difficult position. I can easily expose him, I can easily ruin him, and I can easily kill him."

"Knowing that's an option," Paige calmly replied. "You have the upper hand."

"I would still be careful," Diego continued to be suspicious while Chase nodded at this comment. "I don't fucking trust the police. I don't care where they are, what country, or what they say."

"Yet, it is *us* that gets a bad reputation," Jorge smirked and winked at his wife. "But at the end of the day, we're *all* criminals. I do not care if these people carry a badge and have taken some fucking pledge. They are out for number one, and they are out to push their weight around. The only problem is that they do not have the weight that they think. It's an illusion. And when reality sets in, it will not be pretty."

"Diego, you would think," Jolene spoke up, turning toward her brother. "You would know all of this because you had a relationship with Michael? He was the police…"

Jolene referred to a dark chapter in Diego's past, something she did so naively even though, from across the desk, Jorge could sense the sorrow weigh down on his friend.

"Jolene, this here, we do not need to revisit," He quickly remarked, giving her a look that caused the Colombian to pull back and nod. "The point is that we do have the upper hand. It may not seem like that at face value, but it is true. And at the end of this, my goal is to be the power behind this force."

"To make them corrupt?" Diego returned to his usual vigor.

"They are already corrupt," Jorge reminded him. "But the only difference is that now, they will be corrupt for me."

"So, what do we do?" Chase spoke up. "What's the plan?"

"Plan? There is no plan," Jorge confirmed. "I will sit back and wait. This man, he will get back to me when necessary, and I will be waiting."

"I don't get it," Diego jumped in again. "So, he met with you, introduced himself, and said, what? 'You run your crime organization so well, would you be willing to give me some tips to run mine'?"

Laughter surrounded him after making this comment.

Jorge thought for a moment and finally nodded.

"More or less."

Everyone laughed again.

"He put it, of course, in a much different way," Jorge continued. "He mentioned that he was having personnel issues, and he thought maybe I would have some insights that would be helpful."

"And you say?" Jolene raised an eyebrow.

"I say that I might be able to help," Jorge replied. "I did not get into any details. I just allowed the man to talk. That is all he wanted at this time, to talk, to be heard. I heard him. And I listened to what he was and wasn't saying. It was pretty clear to me that he is a desperate man and these here are my favorite kind of people to do business with."

"So, we wait...." Chase commented.

"We wait."

"Meanwhile," Paige jumped in. "I'm getting back into everything. I know I've been *encouraged* to stay away for the past few months..."

The group shared looks as she spoke.

"But I want back," She continued to speak. "I need to be a part of this."

"Paige, it was not that we did not want you involved," Jorge reminded her. "You know this. It took some time to recover, then the holidays, you were busy with the children...."

"And now, we're into a new year," Paige reminded him. "Spring is around the corner. I think it's time for me to get back into it."

Jorge nodded.

"Paige," Jolene hesitantly spoke up. "It was not just Jorge who want you to be away for a while...it was all of us. We worry for you."

"I'm fine," She calmly replied. "I've been fine for months. I mean, it took some time because I lost a lot of blood...."

A silence followed, which she quickly filled.

"But it's ok," She assured them. "*I'm* ok."

"Paige, you do not see yourself that day," Jolene spoke with caution while Jorge looked away. "You do not understand how bad it was when you were shot."

"I know," She shrugged. "There was a lot of blood, but..."

"Paige, it scared us!" Jolene spoke with emotion in her voice.

"It...it didn't seem good," Chase spoke hesitantly. "When I found you...I..."

"We thought you were dead," Jolene cut him off. "Paige, it scare us all. I know you feel fine and you wake up, look around, that day, you feel ok, but you were unconscious when this happen. We, *we* were there, and it was scary!"

An uncomfortable silence followed. It seemed to hit Paige much harder than in the past. Sensing the emotion in the room, she turned pale and looked down.

"Paige, we are not trying to make you feel bad," Jorge gently added while Diego leaned in to look into her face. "It was, you must understand that it was…. traumatic for us at the time, and we all agreed that it would be better if you take some time off to recuperate. To spend time with the children over the holidays, to make sure you were ok. This is why…."

"I understand," Paige nodded. "I didn't mean to scare everyone."

"No! No!" Jolene automatically jumped in and turned toward Paige. "It was not that….you cannot help. You save my life when you stop that man. So, I felt responsible that you were ok too."

"We all did," Diego added. "We're family, and we look out for one another. That's what we do."

"He is right," Jorge added. "We *are* family. Together, we look out for each other. Together, we take on the world."

CHAPTER

3

"Why not? You run the rest of the puppet show. It only makes sense that the police would be next," Prime Minister Athas replied from a secure phone line, his voice echoing through Jorge's office. "Me, the media…."

"Well, diversity, it is always nice," Jorge cut him off as he glanced at the nearby clock. "The point is that the police are shit. I think this is something we must talk about in greater detail in the future."

"I would think you'd benefit from them being shit," Athas quipped back, his comments much harsher than they had been in the past. Working as the prime minister had hardened him, to a point, the Greek-Canadian was proving again and again to be one of Jorge's most useful people. "Isn't that what you want?"

Jorge considered his question for a moment and suddenly began to laugh.

"Well, they hardly give me a challenge," He spoke with humor in his voice. "It is, you know, kind of a joke how lazy they are, but I will not deny that this here, it is good for me."

"So, Chief Maxwell is having staff issues?"

"It would seem to be so, *si*."

"And you're going to help him out with this?"

Jorge thought for a moment.

"We will see what happens."

"I suspect you'll get a handle on this quickly," Athas confirmed. "There have been rumors for many years, a lot of stuff kept quiet, people shuffled around…"

"Insecurities, vulnerabilities…"

"You could say that," Alec Athas agreed. "I was aware of it long before I was the prime minister, back when I was in social work. Let's just say that the police weren't often my client's friend, and in fact, made most situations worse. They certainly weren't there to help the victims when they needed them. I could tell you stories."

"We must hold back on the stories for today because I have somewhere to be," Jorge glanced at the clock again. "However, this here is good to know. We will talk again."

With that, Jorge ended the conversation with the Canadian prime minister and glanced around his office. Collecting his thoughts for a moment, he eventually rose from the chair and headed for the door. He was barely out of the room when he heard the sound of his daughter arguing with Paige in the kitchen.

"It's not too much!" Maria Hernandez stood with both hands on her hips, her large backpack in the middle of the kitchen floor while Paige struggled with their two-year-old son, who didn't want to put on his coat. "I'm 13, almost 14, it's normal for me to wear makeup to school, and I…"

"Maria!" Jorge automatically barked at his daughter, who jumped at the sound of his sharp voice. Turning around, he could see Paige was right to be concerned. "Get upstairs and remove some of that makeup! It is too much."

"It's not!" She argued at the same time that Miguel laid on the floor and began to cry. "*Papa,* I…"

"Maria, I can barely see your eyes. You have so much black stuff around them," Jorge remarked while Paige attempted to lift the screaming toddler from the floor. "You're 13 years old, not 30. Get upstairs and take it off, *now,* or you will not be leaving this house on the weekend."

"Why do you keep treating me like a child?" Maria spoke dramatically as tears formed in her eyes. "You won't let me do anything! You want me to be a kid forever, and I'm almost 14…"

"Fourteen, it is still a child," Jorge argued back, his voice growing louder over his son's screaming.

"*That,*" Maria pointed toward her younger brother, who cried hysterically. "*That's* a child. I'm a teenager."

"You are already crying," Jorge abruptly pointed out. "The only difference is that you are not rolling on the floor like he is….now, go upstairs and remove some of that makeup."

"Maria, you can wear *some*…." Paige attempted to negotiate.

"*Some!*" Jorge repeated. "This here is not the circus. Take some of it off."

Glaring at them both, Maria swung on her heels and stomped upstairs. On the floor, Miguel stopped crying, closed his eyes, and appeared to fall asleep. Just then, the family's nanny walked upstairs from her basement apartment.

"Ah! Juliana," Jorge shook his head. "I do not know how you deal with these two, sometimes, they are impossible."

The Mexican woman was silent but merely smiled as she approached the toddler on the floor and picked him up, causing the little boy's eyes to spring open and he started to laugh.

"Mi amor, maybe it is just us," Jorge pointed out. "They do not want to listen."

"I think it's a full moon," Paige muttered as she headed back to the kitchen, while Juliana smoothly slid Miguel's arms into his coat.

"I think we have a lot of full moons in this house," Jorge said just as Maria stomped back down the stairs. "*Chica,* I better turn around and see less makeup."

"She's fine," Paige muttered as she glanced over his shoulder.

"I look so…mediocre and boring now," Maria complained. "I might blend in with the curtains."

"Maria, there are days I wish I blended in with the curtains," Jorge turned around, nodding in approval. "You look beautiful."

His daughter smiled in spite of herself but quickly tried to conceal it.

"Maria, you're a very pretty young woman," Paige seemed to pick her words carefully. "You don't need all that makeup."

"This is true," Jorge jumped in. "The girls who need all that makeup, they are perhaps ugly or….like, *putas.*"

"Jorge," Paige gave him a warning look.

"What?" Jorge replied as his daughter giggled. "it is true."

"Some women," Paige attempted to correct him. "Wear a lot of makeup because they have a lot of insecurities, maybe don't like themselves much."

"Yes, well, that too," Jorge shrugged. "I guess."

After Juliana left with the children, Jorge and Paige sat at the kitchen table with their coffee.

"It is not even 8 am, and I'm exhausted," Paige complained.

"This is why you must take it easy," Jorge insisted. "I know it's been a few months since you were shot, but…"

"It was in the fall. It's almost April."

"It does not matter," Jorge shook his head just as his phone beeped. "It takes time. Plus, you had two very active children in the house, so it is not as if you had enough rest."

"You helped a lot," Paige reminded him. "So did Juliana."

"I know, but the children, they are relentless."

"They're…energetic."

Jorge rolled his eyes.

"I know but, I want to move on," Paige spoke calmly, her eyes on his phone. "So, what's going on for today?"

"You should come to my meeting with Tony and Andrew about the next season for the docuseries," Jorge referred to the popular series called *Eat the Rich before the Rich Eat You* that he co-produced for a streaming site. The first season examined the pharmaceutical industry's role in the opiate crisis while highlighting how Jorge's cannabis company was the saint among sinners. "Big Pharma never fully recovered from the first season. Imagine what we can do next."

"We have to be cautious," Paige reminded him. "They came out swinging last time. You know they're probably filling their arsenals as we speak."

"Let them fucking fill them," Jorge said as he narrowed his eyes. "I got no fears."

"I've noticed," Paige purred, causing Jorge to relax.

"You know me, Paige," Jorge spoke in a more seductive tone as he fixed his tie. "There is nothing that scares me. Not Big Pharma, not the police, not the politicians because I am stronger than them all. I can take on anyone."

"And you have,"

"And I always win," Jorge reminded her.

"So," Paige continued to speak gently. "What's the plan this time for Big Pharma?"

"I have some ideas," Jorge replied. "We are going to review last season, talk about what happened as a result, and see what would be good this time around."

"The public demanded that they be more transparent."

"But you know, these companies, even when they are transparent," Jorge replied. "They are not. It is orchestrated to seem that way. We must look at their weaknesses and move in on that."

"After the series, there were a lot of weaknesses exposed," Paige reminded him and paused. "I just don't think we should push them too far."

There was an awkward silence, and Jorge looked away. As much as he thrived on warfare, he hated when innocent casualties were the result.

"I....sometimes, think, we need to back away from all this…"

"I know *mi amor,* we have talked about this before, but even when we say this," Jorge reminded her. "We never really do. Maybe this time, I will not attack with the same ferocity as before."

"We both know that's not true," Paige spoke smoothly. "It's not in your nature to take things down a notch, but at a certain point, you might have to. If Big Pharma gets desperate, then we could all be in danger."

Jorge considered her words before speaking.

"They killed Tony's mother," He remembered. "You were shot by a bullet that was for me. And Big Pharma held the puppet strings. This time, *mi amor,* it is not about poking a lion. It is about slaying a dragon. You do not hurt my family and think there will be no repercussions."

Paige reminded silent, a nervous expression on her face.

"Someone," Jorge paused for a moment. "Someone is going to pay for this. I promise you that."

CHAPTER

4

"What do you *mean* you do not think we should have a second season?" Jorge barked at the two men who sat at the desk. Both Tony Allman and Andrew Collin showed signs of nervousness with the Latino's sudden outrage. Surrounded by computer monitors, stacks of papers, and various video equipment in the cramped section of Tony Allman's apartment, they both seemed pathetic under Jorge's eyes. "Look at what we have done! The series was a hit! Why would we not do a second season?"

Neither replied but glanced at one another. It was finally Jorge's wife that attempted to explain.

"Jorge, it was powerful," She calmly reminded him. "Maybe we don't need a second season. Maybe we should look at something else."

"Or," Tony nervously jumped in. "We take it from a different angle. I don't feel we should focus on Big Pharma anymore. I think we accomplished what we set out to do, and I'm not sure we should push them too hard."

"Dude, your wife was shot," Andrew bravely spoke up, having dealt with Jorge's anger in the past. "Isn't that enough reason to leave it alone?"

"I never really was clear," Tony asked. "Were the two connected? There was so much confusion at the time…"

"The man," Jorge spoke with apprehension in his voice. "The man behind it, he also had his reasons for wanting me dead, but…"

"Why did he shoot Paige?" Andrew pushed. "And not you?"

"We suspect that this here was more of an impulse decision," Jorge reluctantly answered. "But regarding Big Pharma, they were financing a hit on me."

"It's complicated," His wife added. "Regardless, it doesn't matter. The point is that if we get in their crosshairs, they will attack. Especially now that we ended the season with a class-action lawsuit against them from the many opiate users that became addicted to their pills."

"See, this here," Jorge turned toward his wife. "This is why we cannot back down now. They will come at us full force because of that there..."

"But do they even care?" Tony shrugged. "They'll drag it out in court for years so that people forget, then sweep it under the rug and move on."

"That's another problem," Jorge replied. "At first, it was breaking news and quickly, people forget. That is why we must do another season to make sure they don't forget."

"I don't know," Paige shook her head. "It might put us all in danger, but at the same time, I see your point."

"I can handle danger," Jorge reminded her. "I always do."

"But it was a little too much this time," Paige rationalized.

"See, this here is why I wanted you to not get back into everything," Jorge reminded her. "You need to be safe and out of the line of fire."

"I understand," She assured him. "But why are we attacking Big Pharma again? Why can't we do a second season but have it about some other evil empire? Why not, Big Food? Big Oil?"

"Big Food and Big Pharma are connected," Tony reminded her as he shuffled awkwardly in his chair. "All these super-rich oligarchs own everything. It ends up a lot are connected. That's why I was apprehensive about the second season. It would be like trying to break into someone's house a second time, except a different door."

"But this here," Jorge countered. "It might be a good thing. We can show how they are connected."

The room was solemn.

"Let us, maybe," Jorge thought for a moment and took a deep breath. "Maybe, we should review what we have already done. We had one of the most popular shows on a streaming service last fall. It was all over the world. People were talking about it, including the news. These companies felt the pressure and had to make some changes. We had Athas change laws. This was big."

"Then, Tony's mother was killed and Paige was shot," Andrew sharply remind him again, quickly retreating when Jorge shot a look at him.

"But in the end," Jorge reminded him. "We got the man who killed her and shot Paige. We also reached all our goals with Big Pharma. Their shares dropped. People are less trustful of them. We created insecurity in their world."

His own company also rose in sales by a significant amount, but he didn't think it was the time to bring it up.

"They want us to be scared," Jorge reminded them, recognizing that he had to pick his words carefully to get what he wanted. "They want us to have second thoughts on another season. They want us to be intimidated. They want us to back down. Do you not see this? If we do not do a second season, they win. They get what they want. We are now their worst nightmare. They have already taken a hit but, they cannot afford to take another."

"But if they feel desperate…" Paige began.

"*Mi amor,* I do not think that they will be taking chances," Jorge insisted. "They are too busy trying to lift themselves out of a shithole. It is not that easy because people do not trust them. The court system is breathing down their necks. People are talking on social media about how they have ruined their lives."

"Look, maybe we can do a second season of *Eat the Rich Before the Rich Eat You* but maybe…a little less controversial?" Tony attempted to reason. "Maybe slightly toned down?"

"What do you got in mind?" Jorge asked with some apprehension. "This here, it cannot be a fairy tale."

"No, what I mean is maybe not go for the jugular like last season," He suggested. "We had the class action suit, but we also had the proof that they helped in creating deadly viruses and selling it to the highest bidder…"

"Not everyone believed it was true," Paige reminded him. "A lot of people questioned if the interviewees were telling the truth despite the proof they had."

"No one trusts anything anymore," Andrew nodded. "Everything can be faked."

"We showed their victims," Tony spoke up. "We talked about the strain on our social programs, to our communities at large. We showed how they fuck us, essentially."

Jorge nodded.

"Why not this time, instead of showing how they fuck us," Tony wondered. "Instead, we show who they are and how they operate their business."

"Isn't this here kind of the same?" Jorge asked. "The two?"

"Not really," Tony shook his head. "Last time, we focused more on the victims, but this time, I think we need to focus on what animals *they* are. Maybe that is perfect revenge. Instead of attacking Big Pharma as a whole, we'll be attacking individuals and picking them off, one by one."

"Yeah, the top guys in these companies are often assholes," Andrew added as he nodded. "Just total gutter trash in nice suits."

"Terrible human beings," Tony agreed.

"If you want to call them humans," Andrew shrugged. "Shit, the stuff we found last year…."

"How they treat their staff, customers with complaints…."

"Oh yeah, and the way they get doctors," Andrew laughed. "Hookers and blow, strippers, you name it. They don't care. They will get their pills out there any way they can."

"I did see something about a possible cancer cure found, and they blocked it," Tony added.

"Now this here," Jorge jumped in. "*This* is *perfecto*. And that cancer angle, that is what we should end the season with."

"Well," Tony appeared hesitant. "See, that might be similar to what we did before. Maybe that's one of those things that pushes things too far."

"How about," Paige jumped in. "We cross that bridge when we come to it? For now, maybe we need to explore what angle we're taking and map out the potential shows. I mean, I know last time different things came up along the way to change the original structure, but I like the idea of focusing on the sinister characters within the company rather than attacking specific companies."

"They will protect their company's name," Jorge spoke thoughtfully. "But their people, that is another story. These companies do not have loyalty to employees. They mean nothing. They use them up and toss them away. So if there is too much heat on one person, they will get rid of them. One person, he does not hold the same power as a big company."

"We can *take* one person," Paige nodded.

"As if, *mi amor,* one person alone would not even try to come back at us," Jorge reminded her. "They need an army to back them, but the company will not comply. They will do the cheapest angle, and that is to fire them and move on with someone else."

"Another soulless piece of shit," Andrew predicted.

"Leave this with me," Tony glanced at each of them. "Me and Andrew will do some more investigating and brainstorming, but this might just work."

Later as Jorge and Paige climbed back in the SUV, they exchanged looks.

"What?" He asked once they were on the road. "You do not think this is a good idea?"

"I do, actually," Paige nodded. "But, a part of me still feels like we need to get away from this. Do we have to be as involved in the second season? Can't we back away gracefully and start making a plan to…."

"To what?" Jorge grinned. "Earlier today, you were asking to get back in, but then you also talk about getting out."

"I talk about *us* getting out," She reminded him. "Together, but as for me alone, I won't do it until you do."

"Paige, I do see your point," Jorge reasoned as they drove through traffic. "But it is not that easy for a man like me to….disappear, you know?"

"It's not that I want you to disappear," She shook her head. "I think you need to retire as CEO, for real this time. Let Diego take care of things. And us, we can back away…"

"And what?" Jorge asked. "Move to some redneck town, drag the kids away from everything? Hide? Even when I tried to back away from everything, Diego still relied on me for help. For advice, so I will always be a part of this."

"But I feel like we keep upping the ante, and now that you're talking to the police…"

"I am careful, *mi amor,* you know this," Jorge reminded her. "My point is that we will never escape this life."

"But now that *he* is dead…"

She referred to the man who Jorge Hernandez had once seen as a father figure, the crime boss that had groomed him only to plan his protege's murder. It was a shocking twist, the biggest deception he had ever experienced.

"That does not mean that it is over," He quietly reminded her.

They exchanged looks.

CHAPTER

5

"But for me, it was never about the money," Jorge assured Tom Makerson, the young editor for *Toronto AM,* as they sat at the back corner of a coffee shop close to the newspaper's office. "It was about power. It was about revenge. But it was never about money. Me? I have lots of money. This is irrelevant."

"You're one of the few that would say that," Makerson assured him as he looked into his coffee cup, then back up at Jorge. "Most will admit, if anything, it's about the money."

"But those men, they are idiots," Jorge shook his head. "You can only buy so much. You can only have so much. It does not bring happiness, and it does not bring respect. Power is the only thing that makes people sit up and take notice. That has been my experience."

"And you would know," Makerson spoke playfully, and the two men laughed.

"It is true," Jorge nodded humbly. "In very little time in Canada, I have gained a bit of a...how you say? Reputation?"

"I think that's exactly how you would say it," Makerson grinned and nodded. "But hey, I'm here because of you. Newspapers are fucking burning to the ground now, but we're flying."

"That there it is because of you," Jorge reminded him. "You are not afraid of doing the work. So many now, they do not want to do anything, let alone their jobs. You, you are accommodating to work with, and this here, it is what makes people get ahead. At least, in my world."

Makerson didn't reply. They both knew what kind of world Jorge Hernandez lived in.

"But even with my work," Makerson spoke sincerely. "It wouldn't have mattered. There are lots of other reporters out there, losing their jobs now. Papers are closing, laying off staff. We're *hiring*. You make sure I get the stories first, and sometimes access to information others can't get."

"Well, you know how I say it," Jorge spoke calmly before lifting the cup of coffee to his mouth. "If you work for me, I will work for you. This here, it makes sense."

"That's always been the case, but after the controversy with your docuseries…"

His words drifted off, but they both knew that Jorge gave him access to information that people craved and only available with *Toronto AM*. It caused a massive increase in traffic to their website, allowing them to charge more for advertising. One of the ads found near articles about the scandalous ways of Big Pharma was often for Our House of Pot, which in turn caused the Canadian cannabis industry to boom. People no longer trusted the pharmaceutical industry, which is what Jorge wanted.

"Well, it was always there," Jorge reassured him. "We just, you know, broke it up into small, digestible pieces that were easy to understand."

"That you did…"

"And from there, things took off," Jorge grinned. "In the news, social media, everyone was talking about their corruption so much that it was an automatic association. See, there are only three places you can get human beings. You get in their head, you get in their heart, or you get in their pants."

Makerson began to laugh.

"Hey, it is true," Jorge insisted. "If you cannot make them emotional, and you cannot influence their thoughts, you make them horny. Of course, this here, it wouldn't have worked because there is nothing sexually appealing about Big Pharma, so we had to work with the other two, you know."

"That's a good point," Makerson nodded with a smirk still planted on his face. "But your company is a different story…"

"My company's products, it quiets your thoughts. That is what people want."

"True."

"And it does not work with your heart, it quiets your emotions. That is something people need."

Makerson nodded, his expression thoughtful.

"But it *does* work with your hormones," Jorge said and raised an eyebrow. "And this here, people like."

Makerson's face turned pink, and he laughed again.

"My point," Jorge continued. "Is that we, my company, it is the polar opposite of Big Pharma, in every way. Just as your paper, it is the opposite of the others. They are dinosaurs. You are progressive. You have your online content, live streams, and this here is what people need. It is easily digestible for busy lifestyles. Once a habit is formed, it is hard to break. We created a habit with people in this country going to *Toronto AM* for the most scandalous news. Now, we just got to keep their attention."

"Why do I have a feeling you have something specific in mind?" Makerson asked, tilting his head slightly.

"I may have a few things up my sleeve."

"Do tell."

"I may be working on season two of the docuseries."

"And?"

"And we are taking a slightly different approach," Jorge replied as he leaned back in his seat and glanced around the room. "Maybe this time, we focus on specific players rather than the game as a whole."

"Intriguing."

"As it turns out, there are a lot of predators that make up this industry."

"This is true."

"If I learned anything from my last season, it is that it's sometimes better to take on one rat at a time, rather than burn the whole building down to kill them all."

"Wouldn't it be more productive to take care of them all at once?"

At first, Jorge didn't answer but seemed lost in thought.

"That is what I originally thought too," Jorge finally replied. "And although it has advantages, sometimes the firetrucks arrive too fast, and some of the rats survive. My job, this time, is to make sure they do not."

Makerson nodded in understanding.

"This here, it is complicated," Jorge considered. "But, at the same time, it is not. There are people, I believe, that makes this world a better place, and there are savages that do not."

Makerson remained expressionless.

"And although, at times, some would say that *I* was the rat," Jorge spoke thoughtfully. "I would argue that it is not the same thing, but then again, maybe it is. Maybe what we look for in our enemy are the qualities in our old selves we hate the most."

"I suddenly had this thought," Makerson spoke gently as if in a moment of intimacy. "That someday, I'm going to be writing your biography. I don't know when or why, but I can see it clear as day, but quotes like that, are pure gold."

Jorge considered the idea for a moment.

"You know, that might happen," Jorge admitted. "But you can only publish it when I am dead."

Makerson laughed.

"Hey, do not laugh," Jorge quickly joined him. "With my lifestyle, that could be any day."

"Would you seriously be interested in doing something like that?"

"I never considered it before now."

"I think you'd have a lot to say."

"I think I may say too much."

"The beauty of you being involved in a project like this is you can... tell things how you *remember* them."

"This here is true."

"It's something you can consider," Makerson said and looked down. "But to get back on track..."

"To get back on track," Jorge nodded. "I believe that the enemies I seek may remind me of who I used to be....or maybe, who I am. Maybe my attack on them is, I don't know, in a way, signifying what I want to destroy in myself. It has been something I have been thinking about a great deal lately."

"Maybe this is the case with us all," Makerson said and shook his head. "That's what I mean, about a book, you have so much to say. So much insight."

"I am flattered," Jorge said as he touched his chest. "Humbled, but right now, I need to focus on other things."

"Other than exterminating rats..."

"Well," Jorge began to laugh as he moved his coffee cup aside. "A different kind of rat. I had a conversation with Phillip Maxwell recently..."

"The head of the police, Phillip Maxwell?" Makerson leaned in his voice low. "Are you serious?"

"I am quite serious," Jorge nodded as he started to rise from his seat. "He wishes for us to work together."

Makerson's eyes widened as he stood up and turned on his phone.

"We shall see what happens," Jorge spoke with some hesitation.

"I sense some big stories in the future...."

"Regardless, there always are," Jorge reminded him. "You just need to know where to look for them."

"True, but with you..."

Makerson's phone beeped multiple times, and he halted their conversation to read something.

"Holy fuck!" Makerson sat back down.

"Language!" Jorge teased as he did the same. "What is it you see?"

"We were just talking about the police," Makerson leaned in, phone in hand. "Check this out..."

CHAPTER

6

"It's all over the news," Paige referred to the story that broke on Twitter earlier that day and quickly made its way to mainstream media. "It's getting international attention now."

"I bet it is," Jorge replied as he glanced at the laptop on the table before sitting beside his wife. "My new friend, Phillip Maxwell, I am guessing, is not happy right now."

"He can't control his police department," Paige muttered as she watched an independent journalist discussing the very public act of police brutality that was used against a 10-year-old indigenous child that morning. "What kind of *sane* adult physically attacks a disabled *child* then tries to say he was a danger?"

"What he think?" Jorge shook his head. "The child, he had a knife or gun hidden in his wheelchair."

"He *ripped* the kid out of the chair," Paige's eyes began to tear up as she spoke, causing her to stop, merely shaking her head. Her reaction was reflective of many who watched the same video on social media and the news.

Recognizing his insensitivities, Jorge glanced again at the replaying video of the 10-year-old being aggressively pulled from his wheelchair and felt his body slump forward. It was pretty horrific, but up until that point, he had focused more on the scandal and disgrace it put on the police rather than the traumatic experience it was for the child.

"*Mi amor,* you are right," Jorge reached out to touch her shoulder. He leaned forward to kiss the top of her head. "But you know, if that were a white child, it would not have happened."

"We don't know that for a fact," Paige attempted to be fair but then dropped her head as tears ran down her face.

"Oh, Paige, it is ok," Jorge pulled her into a hug. It was rare that his wife showed this much emotion. He knew why. They had talked about it before.

"Our kids, they…"

"Paige, if this here were to happen to either of our kids," Jorge spoke abruptly, feeling his whole body tighten with each word. "That motherfucker right there, he would be going through my crematorium right *now,* and that is after I put him through the most fucking painful torture of his life!"

"I know," She muttered as his hug grew stronger. "But still…."

"Paige, it is ok," He spoke gently, as she pulled away and wiped the tears from her face. "This here, it would not happen to our kids because they know the consequences, and if they did not, they soon would."

"But what if…"

"No, Paige, we are not doing this," Jorge reminded her as they stared into each other's eyes for a long, silent moment. "Our children, they will always be protected. This, I promise you."

"But…" Paige looked away. "I'm not just talking about here. Racism is everywhere and…."

"And we have two brown children,' Jorge nodded. "Paige, I know this. I have lived my entire life as a brown man. Do you not think that when I was working in the US as a young man, I was not talked to like a piece of shit? That I did not have to be extra vigilant, especially with the police? Do you think I do not deal with racist assholes here in Canada too? Even with my money. Even with my power. Remember when I was going to get into politics? This, you do not have to tell me."

"I hate it." She spoke evenly.

"I do too," Jorge nodded as he reached for her blonde hair, his fingers running through it for a moment. "But my children, they must know that many people are racist, and yes, I worry about it. And having a daughter, I worry about that alone, without the color of her skin."

"I know," Paige spoke in a quiet voice.

"But all we can do is make our kids strong," Jorge reminded her. "And as for other kids out there, we can try to find a way to make this stop."

"We can't change the world," Paige spoke hopelessly.

"Like fuck we can't!" Jorge insisted, causing Paige to laugh. "I can do anything Paige, and the first thing I want to do is to get my hands on that piece of shit who hurt that kid."

"But they are talking charges…"

"Paige, it will get pushed away, forgotten about, and he will end up slinking away," Jorge insisted. "Perhaps, he will get some paid time off to sit home and jerk off to porn while that poor kid, he is traumatized. No, we will find a way to make sure his life comes to a sudden end."

"I think your phone is beeping," Paige pointed toward the counter where he had left his iPhone.

"My focus, Paige, it is you, not the phone."

"I'm fine," She nodded. "I just…"

"I know, *mi amor,* I know."

"Go get your phone," Paige said and took a deep breath, and started to stand. "I think I need to go clear my head."

"Get that meditation pillow out," He said as they shared a smile as she headed for the stairs.

Glancing toward his phone, he stood up to get it.

Did you see this shit online?

That was Diego.

Yup. I think we need to do something as a company to show our support for diversity. Talk to PR.

Will do.

The next message was from Chase. Jorge felt his heart sink before he even opened it.

Fucking police. Of course, they hurt an indigenous kid. We're subhuman to them.

It was personal for Chase. Being half-indigenous, the youngest member of the group became increasingly aware of the prejudice he received after leaving the safety net of the small town where he grew up.

Chase, our company, we are thinking of doing something to show our support for diversity. If you have any ideas, can you let Diego know?

A few seconds later.

My thoughts? My thoughts are on that POS cop.

Chase, we will discuss this more later. Trust me.

They couldn't say much in a text. Although Marco went above and beyond to make sure their phones and text messages were protected, one could never be too careful.

Jorge's eyes returned to the screen him and Paige had been watching moments earlier. Moving closer, he turned on the video again. The police officer was hovering over the child, who appeared to be explaining something, shaking his head. It was clear the cop was getting more confrontational as he moved closer to the child. The person recording the video suddenly let out a gasp when the policeman abruptly reached forward, pulling the kid out of his wheelchair.

"Oh my God! I can't believe….oh my God!"

The woman recording the video was upset as the video began to shake, indicating that she was moving closer. A crowd of people rushed forward, including what appeared to be the child's mother. She was attempting to reason with the cop while he pushed the child to the ground and began to pat him down while yelling at the people to back off. When he found nothing on the boy, he began to frantically search his wheelchair. He pulled out what was an obvious toy gun. It was orange and blue.

"Dumb fuck," Jorge muttered just as the door opened, and Maria walked in, followed by Juliana and Miguel.

"Papa! Did you see that kid, Oh my God!" Maria rushed over and pointed toward the laptop. "We were watching it at school. The teacher started to cry in class and then we discussed it this afternoon and oh my God, why are the police allowed to do that? What is wrong with them?"

"Maria, please, you must relax," Jorge spoke evenly, attempting to calm his anxious child, even though he was equally frustrated. "I know, yes, I agree with you. It was completely unacceptable for him to act this way, but the police, Maria, you cannot trust them."

"The teacher at school said there was probably a misunderstanding."

"Yeah, and what's your teacher, a white lady?"

Maria hesitated before nodding.

"Then this lady, she does *not* know."

"I know, white privilege," Maria shrugged. "But she's a nice lady. It wasn't like she didn't care."

"That is not what it means, *chica,"* Jorge corrected her. "It means that she does not understand because she never had to worry about being targeted by the police because of the color of her skin. I did not say she was a bad person."

"But why did she make excuses for the cop?" Maria asked. "That was so obviously a toy gun. Miguel has the same one."

"Maria," Jorge let out a sigh as his phone beeped again. "I do not know. I guess because she has to make kids believe that the police are better people, but *chica,* they are not."

Maria stood up a little straighter.

"People are people," Jorge spoke sternly. "You do not trust someone more because they have a fancy uniform or because they have a fancy title. You trust yourself."

"I will," Maria spoke dismissively as she moved on to another thought. "A guy in my class told us that the police stop his older brother all the time for stupid things. Like they might say he fits the description of someone they are looking for, something stupid like that. He never *ever* looks like the guy they are looking for other than the fact that he's black too."

"Yes, this here happens."

"My teacher said it was probably a misunderstanding too."

"Your teacher, she is a moron," Jorge grew impatient, and Maria began to laugh.

"That's what most people in class think too," Maria continued to giggle. "Even the white kids were arguing with her, and she looked like she was going to cry again."

"Maria," Jorge started as he heard his phone beep again. "You know the truth. Think for yourself."

"I always do."

Jorge nodded in approval as he reached for his phone and glanced at it. A huge grin crossed his lips. He knew this text was coming.

CHAPTER

7

He arrived in an unmarked car, wearing civilian clothes. Jorge was giddy as the older man approached the door but was able to keep it together until Phillip Maxwell entered the house. The muffled sound of music could be heard from upstairs, but it took the cop a minute before recognizing the mocking familiarity of 'Fuck the Police', and that's when Jorge burst into laughter.

"My daughter," Jorge said with a casual, unapologetic shrug as he closed the door. "What can I say? She follows what is popular, and this song is trending on Twitter for some reason. I wonder why?"

Maxwell appeared slightly deflated by the comment but merely nodded as Jorge pointed toward a dark corner of the house.

"Come to my office but first, turn off your phone and leave it there," Jorge nodded toward a hall table.

Following his instructions, Phillip Maxwell didn't say a word until they were behind closed doors.

"See the news?" Maxwell automatically jumped in as he sat down. "I knew a shitstorm was about to erupt, but this is even worse than I could've imagined."

Jorge sat behind his desk and listened to the defeated head of the Toronto police rant. This would be too easy.

"Yes, it *is* a shitstorm," Jorge agreed as he leaned back in his chair. "Not that this here is a surprise to me either. Your police are hardly known for your cool, calm approach, especially when it is not a white person."

"Hey, that's not me," Maxwell pointed toward himself, indicating the fact he was Caucasian. "Not all white people are racists."

"This I know," Jorge decided to back off slightly. "I work with white people and have white people work for me. I assure you, none of these people disrespect me."

Maxwell nodded.

"But this isn't about me," Jorge continued and pulled his chair forward. "I do understand your position. You must keep the public happy but still, your force, they assume you will defend them to the public."

"I got to do a press conference later today," Maxwell spoke anxiously. "What the fuck am I supposed to say? I have pressure from both sides, but how can I possibly smooth this over?"

"You fire the motherfucker."

"But they're all coming at me saying he has PTSD," Maxwell explained. "We're short on people and can't lose another officer..."

"I see," Jorge nodded as he began to get the picture. "But you must keep the public happy, or there will be an uproar."

"There already is," Maxwell pointed toward the window. "There's a protest in front of city hall, and if we don't calm things down, it'll get worse. But try to tell anyone that. I got politicians breathing down my neck, indigenous leaders, everyone."

Jorge thought for a moment.

"All this, and you sit in my office?"

"Look, I know I wasn't clear the other day," Maxwell leaned forward. "But I knew something like this was coming. We've had a lot of...similar incidents that went under the radar. I don't know what the fuck I'm supposed to do. I just want to finish this job, collect my pension, and go see my grandchildren. Right now, I'm probably gonna have a heart attack or get fired before I can retire."

"When is this?"

"Next spring."

Jorge didn't respond.

"It's out of control," He shook his head. "You got to be sensitive to everyone even when it's an asshole like that guy today."

"That guy today," Jorge pointed out. "If that was my child...."

"Hey, you don't need to tell me," Maxwell was already shaking his head. "As I say, I have grandchildren. If *anyone* were to do something like that to one of them, I would beat the living shit out of the fucker."

"That there," Jorge said as he pointed toward Maxwell. "Is nice compared to what I would do."

There was a slight pause.

"That's why I'm here," Maxwell spoke humbly. "I know you're the only person who can help. I know you know how to…"

"Put the fear of God in people?" Jorge asked.

"Yes," The older man replied. "I don't know what to do. I know you take care of problems. I'm limited because of HR and other bullshit. Like anyone gave a fuck about that kind of thing when I started out. Now, it's all red tape and politically correctness."

"Oh yes, these times! Now people have a problem when you throw a disabled kid to the ground, imagine that?" Jorge spoke abruptly, allowing the sarcasm to ring through.

"You know that's not what I mean," Maxwell said as he put a hand in the air. "I have always been more than fair to everyone. Race never affected anything."

"But your officers, they are another story."

"I'm not saying there's no prejudice in the department," Maxwell spoke clearly. "I know how I always did my job. I can't speak for anyone else."

"Ok, so," Jorge took a deep breath. "I got other places to be today. Just tell me, what you want."

"I want help," Maxwell spoke honestly. "I want that son of a whore from today out of my department, one way or another."

"So you can't fire him?"

"PTSD," Maxwell shook his head. "The union is coming down on me because it's a *health condition.* That's the political correctness I was talking about."

"Are you fucking kidding me right now?"

"Nope," Maxwell shook his head. "And this guy, he's a fucking asshole. He's a psychopath. We get calls because he beats the piss out of his wife, and you know what happens? Nothing. PTSD. We have unions who wanted him in therapy for anger management. You see how much that shit helped."

"So you want him out of the way."

"I want him dead," Maxwell spoke with some apprehension.

"What makes you so sure I can help you?" Jorge asked and raised an eyebrow.

The two men exchanged looks.

"Is this a serious question?"

Jorge's head fell back as laughter filled the room. Although the outburst originally caused Maxwell to tense up, he began to relax after recognizing that Jorge was enjoying the moment.

"Well, I do," Jorge started to calm down. "I do appreciate your directness and this, it should not be a problem."

"How soon can it be done?"

"I must talk to my people but I'm sure it won't take long. What was his name again?"

"Dan Alwood."

"And this here, is the problem we originally discussed?"

"He is...*one* of my problems."

"Well, I will tell you this," Jorge said as he leaned back in his chair. "Sometimes when one problem is removed, it can send a message to the others."

Maxwell didn't reply but nodded.

"But tell me this," Jorge continued. "Why do I trust you?"

"I can give you something in return."

"What would you have that I would want?"

"I know about your series," Maxwell pointed toward the closed laptop on the desk. "There's talk on the news you're doing another season. I got something on someone at Big Pharma."

"Is that so?"

"It won't go anywhere because there's money and power behind him, but it's big."

Jorge felt his ears perk up.

"And let's face it," Maxwell spoke evenly. "I know who you are and I know what you're capable of...I take a chance even being here today. If the police arrest you today, you'll be out before tomorrow and meanwhile, my entire family would be...gone."

Jorge didn't respond, but the two men shared a look that said everything.

"But," Maxwell continued as he looked down briefly before returning his attention to Jorge. "I also know you are a reasonable man. I know you get things done and I know you keep it under the radar. I wouldn't be here if I wasn't desperate."

"So, I am curious, why not do it yourselves?" Jorge wondered. "I get that there is paperwork and investigations, but if it was an accidental shooting in the line of duty…"

"The problem with that is there are too many things to align," Maxwell shook his head. "It's too tricky and puts other people in danger. I can't take that chance."

Jorge nodded.

"This way, no one will think anything of it," Maxwell pointed out. "Alwood pissed off a lot of people so if he shows up dead, no one will be surprised and tell you the truth, no one will care either."

Jorge nodded.

"That's why I had to see you right away."

"Well, I will talk to my people," Jorge said and paused for a moment. "You have a press conference today?"

"Yes."

"Do me a favor," Jorge said as he pulled open a drawer in his desk and reached for a business card. "This guy here, Makerson, give him an exclusive interview after your conference and make sure he gets more information than the others. Give him something to run with."

Maxwell took the card and nodded.

"I can do that."

"Good," Jorge said as he stood up. "Then we should have no problem working together."

After Maxwell left, Jorge messaged the others to meet him at his bar. It was still early and the *Princesa Maria* wouldn't be opening for a few hours, allowing them time to discuss a plan.

Just as he was about the head out, his secure line rang. It was Athas.

"Jorge, I got a problem…"

"I know," He replied. "I saw the news."

"This officer…"

"I know about him and his past," Jorge replied. "I have the information. It will be taken care of."

There was a slight pause before Athas replied.

"That's what I was hoping."

8

"I'm doing it," Chase automatically chimed in from behind his desk. The conversation that started on a calm note quickly got out of control. "I'm going to kill the fucker with my own bare hands..."

"Nah Nah," Diego cut in, shaking his head dramatically "We don't get involved. It's the fucking police. I don't care *what* he says, we can't trust them. Maxwell's got something on us, I know it!"

"Sir," Marco, the company's IT specialist quickly jumped in. "His phone, I am tracking him, and I will find out if there is anything about this man we cannot trust. So far, I see nothing to be suspicious of."

"What?" Jolene shook her head, confused. "I do not understand. What tracking? Who is this man? Is this the man from the video you show me earlier, Diego?"

"Nah," Her brother shook his head, his face scrunching up. "Nah, this guy Jorge is talking about is the head of the police. He's that lunatic's boss or something."

"If I could get a word in edgewise," Jorge spoke loudly, as he glanced at his wife beside him, who merely shrugged and looked away. "I understand what you all are saying, but could you hear me out."

"I don't trust him," Diego repeated. "Never trust the fucking police."

"Yes, I agree with Diego," Jolene nodded. "This is not a country where the police work with criminals like in Mexico."

To this, Jorge gave her an amused look before glancing away and regrouping.

"Ok," He paused for a moment until everyone finally fell silent. "As Marco said, we are tracking his phone."

"Like he's not going to notice that…" Diego mocked him.

"Sir, he will not know," Marco insisted, directing his comment at Jorge. "I hid it carefully. He will see nothing new."

"How did you hack his phone so fast?" Diego asked. "I know you're good but, didn't you say it was a short meeting Jorge?"

"It does not take long," Marco shook his head. "He left his phone outside Jorge's office. Paige let me in the house, and I took care of it."

"I told him I never allow phones in the office."

"Last time, I broke the code to get in," Marco continued. "So this time, I just had to install the software."

"And snoop around?" Jorge asked.

"Yes, sir, there was not much there," Marco replied. "But I have greater access now so I can learn more but so far, I have no reason to believe he is a concern."

"And you can listen in on him…"

"As long as the phone is on him," Marco replied. "I can listen anytime and see through the camera. It is all covered."

"*Perfecto.*"

"Wow," Diego spoke loudly. "You amaze me, Marco."

To this, the Filipino man giggled and looked away.

"Do not say too much or Jolene," Jorge pointed toward the Colombian. "She will have you track all her boyfriends."

"I do like that idea," She muttered, causing Paige to laugh and Diego to roll his eyes.

"You shouldn't have put that idea in her head," Diego said as he purposely looked away from his sister.

"Men, if they were trustworthy, I wouldn't have to," Jolene defended herself. "They lie."

"Ok, no soap opera today," Jorge cut things off before they got out of hand. "When we are certain he can be trusted we got to figure out what to do with this piece of shit from the park."

"Sir," Marco automatically replied. "I am dividing my time between watching Maxwell but also, I want to look more into this Dan Alwood man. So far, I see a lot of complaints made about him on record, but he is never disciplined. I even see that he has been abusive to several women…"

"*Several?*" Paige cut him off.

"Yes, his wife," Marco replied. "And it seems like other women, maybe that he was arresting. He can be quite….rough with them if they are not cooperative."

"But he got PTSD," Jorge reminded them. "This here is an excuse to get away with anything. Who knew? Maybe I got PTSD."

With this, Jorge's head fell back in laughter despite how inappropriate it was at that moment. The others joined in.

"Can we be serious here?" Diego complained. "You mean to tell me that if you have PTSD, you're suddenly allowed to do *anything,* and no one gives a fuck? So this asshole pulls a disabled kid out of a wheelchair, and that's ok because he has PTSD? Is that what you're telling me?"

Jorge shrugged. "I am not saying any such thing. I am just saying that this cop will have it tied up with his union. They argue that it's not his fault because he was traumatized on the job, and he should be treated as a victim because he cannot help himself."

"For fuck sake," Chase snapped, his face growing red. "Do you mean to tell me that he will get away with it because of this PTSD bullshit?"

"What I am saying is that he will never be charged," Jorge corrected him. "They won't allow any black marks on his record since it is supposedly a medical condition."

"That's crazy," Paige jumped in. "I had PTSD, but I would never do what he did to that child."

"Ah, but *mi amor,* you did become violent," Jorge teased her. "So, you know…"

"Hey now," Diego cut in. "Paige would never do what that piece of shit did."

"But she does have a violent streak," Jorge winked at his wife. "So, perhaps, this here is an issue."

"She could use it as a defense too," Jolene began to laugh. "Maybe we all have PTMD…ah….wait, what it is?"

"PTSD," Chase answered. "Post-traumatic stress disorder."

"Ah, but we all have this, no?" Jolene spoke innocently. "Stress, no?"

"It's a little more extreme than regular stress," Chase attempted to explain.

"Ok, this here is enough," Jorge cut in again. "My point is that he will get away with it, and he will not be charged because of his union, they believe he has this here medical condition, and it is unfair. He will go on leave, *with* pay, and the department will investigate it and hope everyone forgets."

"Fuck," Chase shook his head. "So he'll get away with it, that's what you're saying?"

"Well, on their terms, maybe," Jorge agreed. "But on our terms, he will not."

No one replied.

"We must find enough information on this Dan Alwood man, then make some decisions from there," Jorge replied. "Meanwhile, Maxwell will have to try to appease the media today by saying they are 'still looking at the facts surrounding the case', then try to ease out of the press conference without answering any hard questions. Then he'll talk to Makerson, for a real interview and….we will do our own thing."

"I want to do it," Chase once again insisted. "This is my people. I'm doing it."

Impressed with the young man who once cowered away from violence, Jorge didn't say anything. He had seen Chase Jacobs grow over time to become a fierce foot soldier and was confident of his ability.

"I see no problems with this here," Jorge replied. "Once we learn more about who this man is, his lifestyle, all the information needed, we can come up with a plan."

"But you're a little too close to things," Paige reminded Chase. "So we'll work together on this one."

"*Mi amor,*" Jorge cut her off. "No, you must stay back."

"I am not staying back," She spoke forcefully.

"Paige, since you were shot," Jorge automatically glanced at the arm that still carried a scar, now covered by the vibrant red material.

"I'm fine," She reminded him. "We'll see when the time comes, but I'm gonna help him figure out the best course of action. He's going to need someone calm to help him work out the details."

"And that ain't you," Diego pointed toward Jorge.

"This here, I can do," Jorge shook his head. "Paige, after…"

"I'm fine," She spoke more forcefully this time, and an awkward silence followed. Jorge felt something churning inside him when he saw the passion in her eyes but didn't reply. "I want back in. I don't want to be on the sidelines."

Jorge nodded and looked away.

"Ok," Chase took a deep breath and broke the tension. "So, we'll get updates on this."

"We will meet as soon as Marco has something," Jorge said as he glanced back at his wife, his eyes glancing over her body and he quickly looked away. "Until that time, we must keep our ears to the ground."

"Marco will keep his ear to that phone," Diego pointed toward the Filipino man. "Our ears won't find anything near the ground."

"As soon as I know something, sir," Marco spoke up. "I will let you know. This is my priority."

"He needs an assistant," Diego insisted. "He got a lot going on."

"I'll help," Chase replied. "Since I got that new night manager at the bar, my schedule's free."

"Me too," Jolene insisted. "Crematorium, it is depressing."

"You," Jorge pointed. "I need you to be free in case something else comes up. Plus, who knows when we will need your help with a special project at the crematorium."

Without further explanation, she merely nodded. Jorge felt she was a good foot soldier when needed, but she also tended to get off track easily.

"Now, I need to talk to my wife," He sternly gestured toward Paige while dismissing the others. "If you do not mind."

"Sure," Chase seemed to reply for the others as he stood up from behind the desk. "We can go."

"I would appreciate it."

There was an awkwardness as the others followed his lead, slowly leaving the small office, closing the door behind them.

"You're not going to give me a hard time about this, are you?" Paige bluntly asked as she stood, clearly frustrated.

Jorge didn't reply but stood up and crossed the room. Glancing around, he located some black tape on a shelf behind Chase's desk and broke off a piece, placing it over the camera pointed at the desk. Then he locked the door before turning to see the defenses drop from his wife's eyes.

"I am going to give you a hard time all right," Jorge spoke in a seductive tone as he approached his wife, glancing down at her body. "But *mi amor,* I think this here, you will like."

CHAPTER

9

"….no soul," Diego was saying when Jorge and Paige finally rejoined the rest of the group in the main bar after their own, private meeting in the office. If there were any suspicions about what occurred behind the closed doors, no one was showing any signs. This was confirmed when Diego turned toward them with a look of concern on his face. "Is everything ok?"

"Of course, Diego," Jorge insisted, recognizing that their encounter went unsuspected. "We just….you know, had to talk about if Paige should be involved in these matters now. It is a disagreement we sometimes have."

"You need to be careful," Diego directed his comment at Paige.

"What were you saying about no soul?" She immediately changed the topic.

"I said that this piece of shit that grabbed the kid," Diego pointed toward Chase's open laptop on the bar. A reporter was speaking about the incident. It was non-stop on the news channels. "He got no soul."

"Diego, to some," Jorge shook his head. "A soul, it takes up too much real estate. Trust me, I have been there."

"*You*, you're another story," Diego quipped, and Marco started to laugh from the other end of the bar. The hacker tapped furiously on his laptop, with an earbud in one ear.

"So, did Maxwell have his press conference?"

"Yeah yeah," Chase answered this question, his face full of exasperation. "Same old bullshit. They are *investigating* and can't give further details at this time."

"That's it?" Jorge shook his head as he reached for his phone and turned it back on. "Nothing else?"

"He's stonewalling the reporters," Diego added as Paige walked over to the bar and sat beside him.

"Well, this here is what they always do," Jorge reminded him as he glanced at his phone. Jolene took over the conversation.

"There is an interview with Makerson," She pointed toward the screen. "He will say more now."

"I gotta make a call," Jorge commented as he noted a message from his daughter. "I'll be right back."

Returning to the office, he closed the door and hit a button.

"Hello," Maria's voice sounded shaky on the other end.

"Maria, is everything ok?" He felt his heart race. "Your message, it sounded urgent."

"I'm fine," She spoke lazily, causing Jorge's blood to boil.

"Maria, this here better not be you being overly dramatic about something stupid like makeup again."

"*Papa,* you know I don't do that," She whined on the phone. "It is important."

"And?" He coaxed.

"We were talking about the crazy police officer at school again today," She started. "They said he had a disorder so that he couldn't help himself, he overreacts. *Papa,* I think I have this PSTD."

"PTSD," He corrected her and felt his heartbreak. "Maria, this is possible. You have had some…terrible experiences. Things that you should never have had, not in a lifetime."

His daughter was once held at gunpoint by her biological mother. At the time, he would've gladly given his own life to save his daughter, but the experience had left them both shaken. It was the most terrifying day of his life, but his concern was more for Maria, who was merely a child, traumatized by her mother.

"I was thinking that maybe I could use some counseling…"

"Of course, Maria, whatever you need."

"But then I thought, that wasn't going to help me," She continued, stalling for a moment. "*Papa,* I want to learn how to shoot a gun."

"Maria!"

"*Papa,* you all know how and I think I should too," She continued, speaking more quickly this time, her voice full of energy. "The cops are racist. Like Cameron said, I have to be able to protect myself because they don't care about minorities like me, and they don't care about the gays, like him."

Jorge took a deep breath and closed his eyes. He had to calm himself before speaking, otherwise, everything would come out wrong.

"Maria, I am not saying no forever," Jorge spoke evenly. "But right now, you are too young."

"Lots of kids my age know how to shoot a gun," She insisted. "I think given who I…"

"Ok, Maria," Jorge cut her off. "This is a discussion we will have at home, not on the phone."

She fell silent.

"Now, this here, we will talk about later."

"Ok," She agreed with some exasperation in her voice. "But you have to stop treating me like a kid. I turn 14 this year and…"

"Yes, Maria, like I said," Jorge cut her off. "We will talk about this at home."

Jorge ended the call and closed his eyes. His heart raced erratically as he leaned against the wall. For a man who once lived on adrenaline and cocaine, it was as if he could no longer cope with the simplest things. However, the safety of his family was a grave concern to him. He would do anything to ensure that none of them were ever in danger, but what was the answer?

Taking a deep breath, he opened his eyes and attempted to regain his usual confidence before returning to the bar. If he seemed out of sorts, no one noticed when Jorge entered the room. They were all too busy gathering around Chase's laptop.

"….at live footage from downtown Toronto, where people are protesting local police…" Makerson's voice could be heard, while images of crowds gathered with signs as they walked through the streets.

"What is this?" Jorge was confused as he watched people angrily screaming, a sense of unrest was apparent. "I thought there were just protesters in front of the city hall or something?"

"It's moved on," Diego pointed toward the screen. "They got streets shut down. We might never get the fuck home tonight."

"I thought Makerson was interviewing…"

"He is," Paige cut him off and shook her head. "But after Maxwell's press conference, people took over the streets. They essentially used the PTSD excuses and, well…"

"People lost their fucking minds," Diego jumped in. "They're all over the fucking place, and there's talk of riots. We'll be lucky if our businesses aren't burnt to the ground by morning."

"I don't think it's going to get that bad," Paige interjected. "At least, not yet."

"They need to burn the police station to the ground," Chase muttered. "With a few of these cops in it."

"Ok, we gotta calm down here," Jorge said as he attempted to collect his thoughts. "What's Maxwell saying?"

"Not much," Chase replied. "Just the usual bullshit."

"Anything more than the press conference?"

"He's talking again!" Paige pointed toward the screen, and they all fell silent.

"…understand their frustration," Maxwell spoke in a calm voice. "Nobody is saying that Constable Alwood's conduct was right. And personally, as a father, watching that video makes me cringe, but we also have to consider the other side. This is a man who has PTSD and…."

"Oh, fuck off!" Chase suddenly erupted in anger. "I want to kill *this* guy too!"

"Calm down," Jorge instructed. "He's playing the game. Trust me, he's helping us."

Chase appeared skeptical.

"Trust me," Jorge repeated and watched as Chase's defenses lowered. "We are working on this here situation together."

"He did say," Jolene cut in. "He did say that they are still investigating. They have to make like, you know, they are listening to him too."

"I think that's the only person they plan to listen to," Chase said just as the screen jumped over to a video of the same child who had been ripped out of his wheelchair by Dan Alwood. It was a prerecorded video that Makerson managed to get exclusively.

"He…he just grabbed me and…I didn't understand why," The indigenous child appeared small in his wheelchair as he stuttered through his sentence. "I…I wasn't hurting anyone. I…I…I didn't do anything. I swear."

The innocence in his voice was undeniable. Paige looked away, clearly upset, while Jolene shook her head in sorrow. The room felt heavy. There was a dramatic pause on the screen before Makerson began to speak again.

"Has Constable Alwood explained why he reacted so...*brutally* to this *child?*" Makerson spoke with hesitation in his voice, as if he wasn't sure how or if to go on. "Is there something that we aren't aware of? I think I speak for everyone when I say that the PTSD defense falls short when we watch, first the video of the incident, followed by the one we just viewed together."

Phillip Maxwell's original strength began to crumble, and for a moment, Jorge thought he was going to fall apart on camera.

"Again, there are many things we can't comment on at this time because the investigation is still ongoing," He finally replied with a touch of emotion in his voice. "The Special Investigation Unit will look into this matter, of course, and will come back to us with a full report. It would be unethical to get ahead of ourselves until we know all the facts."

"But wouldn't you say," Makerson paused for a moment, "Wouldn't you say that there's an unfair power advantage between Constable Alwood, a police officer, who carries a gun, who's in a position of authority, and a 10-year-old child with disabilities?"

When Maxwell didn't reply, Makerson continued.

"The indigenous community is speaking out," He spoke gently. "Black lives Matter are speaking out. There are protests in downtown Toronto at this time. Many people say that they are tired of the obvious racism and unnecessary brutality within the Police department, and you're the one in charge. We're looking to you for reassurance that Constable Alwood will be accountable for his actions. What do you have to say to this?"

Maxwell looked like a deer in headlights, and for a long moment, Jorge thought he wasn't going to answer.

"*If* he's found at fault," Maxwell said, and Jorge was already cringing. "He will be made accountable."

That's when everything took a turn for the worse.

CHAPTER

10

"You gave him *nothing!*" Jorge yelled at Maxwell through the phone. "That interview, it was a fucking waste of everyone's time."

"My hands are tied, I…"

"Don't give me this bullshit," Jorge snapped back as he walked through his kitchen, searching through the cupboards for Miguel's favorite crackers. "The way you left it. If he is at fault! What did you fucking expect? I barely got home because of the traffic backed up near the club. Now, I got one of my best people handing out fucking bottles of water to protesters, so they do not start to riot and burn my fucking bar down."

Jorge didn't realize he was yelling until he turned to see an alarmed Maria holding the baby. Miguel appeared intrigued by the box of crackers as he struggled to get out of his sister's arms. Jorge continued to talk as he walked across the floor and handed them to Maria.

"I understand and, I…"

"No, I do *not* think you *do* understand, *señor,*" Jorge spoke in a condescending tone as he headed for his office. "We got a big fucking problem right now, and you made it worse."

Just as he ended his call, the phone rang again. Closing his office door, he took it as he headed for his desk.

"*Hola,*" He snapped into the phone without even looking to see who was calling. It was Makerson.

"I got something," He spoke reassuringly.

"Ah! If only all these people were like you," Jorge commented as he calmed slightly. "These here are the words I want to hear. Not more problems."

"Well, it's thanks to one of *your* people," Makerson began to laugh. "I plan to live stream shortly and post the article."

"Ah, yes," Jorge nodded as he sat down. Marco had dropped by the newspaper to visit Makerson. He had everything needed to break the real story about Dan Alwood. "This here, it does make me feel better because Maxwell, what the fuck was he thinking?"

"He added fuel to the fire," Makerson confirmed. "I'm looking out my window here at the office, and I see a lot of protesters. It's a shitshow."

"What did Maxwell expect when he seemed to side with the enemy."

"I don't think he had a choice," Makerson commented. "His balls are on the line."

"They may be on the line with me too if he keeps it up," Jorge confirmed. "And I don't play this here game like the others."

There was laughter on the line.

"I'm posting the article and going live in five," Makerson commented. "Just wanted to let you know."

"I will text everyone."

Jorge ended the call and sent off a message to the others, including Paige, who was upstairs. He quickly found the link where the live stream was to take place. It already had thousands of viewers popping on, awaiting Makerson's big reveal. The bait he used was impossible to ignore.

A knock at the door interrupted his thoughts.

"Come in, *mi amor.*"

The door opened, and Maria stuck her head in.

"It's not Paige, *Papa,*" She spoke in a little voice. "It's me."

"Where's Miguel?"

"I took him upstairs with Paige," She replied as she walked in. "I want to talk to you about what we were talking about on the phone…"

Just then, Makerson's face appeared on the screen, and Jorge's phone lit up with a text message.

"Maria, I have to watch something important right now," Jorge replied and pointed toward a seat across the desk from him. "Come, sit with me. I think you should see this too. Then we will talk."

She didn't reply but slowly walked toward the chairs. Jorge turned the laptop around so she could see the video while quickly glancing at his phone; he would have to take care of that later. First, he had to see the live stream, then talk to his daughter about her idiotic idea to learn how to use a gun.

Makerson began to speak. After introducing himself and giving some background on the story, he immediately jumped into the news.

"At this time, protests continue to take place in downtown Toronto," Makerson reminded his viewers. "This has only grown in size throughout the day, bringing attention to the fact that people are united and are frustrated by this latest, in a series of unacceptable actions by the Police."

Jorge noted that his daughter leaned in and was carefully studying Makerson on the screen as he went on to discuss some previous situations that had made the local police seem incapable of doing their job. He reminded the audience of racist and homophobic incidences that had taken place weeks and months earlier.

"*Papa,* that is what I was talking about today," Maria reminded him. "The police don't care about minorities like us, and like Cameron said, they aren't going to protect a gay man like him…"

"Maria, he is 16 years old. He is not a man," Jorge reminded her. "He is still a child, like you, which is why I do not wish…"

Makerson started to talk about the information brought to him today about Alwood, and both Jorge and his daughter fell silent.

"…an abusive past in both his work *and* personal life," Makerson made a dramatic pause. "One of these attacks was on his wife last year. *Toronto AM* has learned that the department kept this information under wraps. Alwood got a short, *paid* suspension then put back to work because the department was short-staffed. This was even though he had shown abusive behavior toward those he arrested and even one of his colleagues."

"Wow! Look at the comments," Maria's eyes grew in size as she pointed toward the screen. "They're going so fast. I can't even read them!"

"Maria, these people, they are very passionate about this topic," Jorge reminded her. "This affects many in this city."

"Look, this one woman says the police are *always* bullying her son," Maria spoke as she leaned forward on the desk. "That they grabbed him by the arm once and called him the N-word! Wow!"

"Maria, when you are the police, you can get away with anything," Jorge reminded her as Makerson reviewed people's comments and questions as the number of viewers continued to grow. "This is how it is."

"That's why I want to learn how to shoot," Maria quickly jumped in. "I can't rely on these people to help *me*."

Jorge didn't reply but bit his lip and looked away.

His secure line rang. It was Athas.

"Maria, I must take this," Jorge said as he picked up the phone.

She shrugged and continued to read the screen.

"What the fuck is going on?" Athas started immediately. "I thought you had a grip on this situation."

"Talk to Maxwell," Jorge corrected him. "He is the one who blew this all to hell."

"Fuck!" Athas was complaining. "What the fuck are we supposed to do about this mess?"

"Get Makerson to interview you," Jorge suggested. "Say that you do not think Alwood's behavior was acceptable regardless of the situation. Say that you plan to..I don't know, have an inquiry on the whole department. Something. Anything that says that you are proactive. Say you are doing an overhaul of the department."

"People like that word," Athas confirmed. "Overhaul."

"If you sound like you're angry, that you care," Jorge reminded him. "People will not think you are merely pissing in their ear."

There was a pause.

"I will see what I can do."

"Well, do something," Jorge insisted. "I got Chase passing out bottles of water to protesters, so if riots start, they won't tear my fucking bar apart, so if I were you, I'd do something and do it *now*."

He ended the call. Maria watched him with interest.

"*Papa,* it's my bar, remember?" She reminded him.

"Ah! But not yet, *chica,*" He laughed. "I said when you are older, it was your bar to do what you wish. However, my concern is that it will still be standing by that time. We must make sure riots don't break out because people, they will go *loco,* and we can't have that."

"Yeah, that's scary," Maria said and took a deep breath. "About me learning how to shoot..."

"Maria," Jorge cut her off and took a deep breath, glancing at his phone again.

"How about you give me time to think about it? I cannot decide how I feel right now. There is too much going on."

"But you do admit that I need to learn, eventually..."

"I do think, yes, you should," Jorge replied. "But maybe not right now."

"But *Papa,* back in Mexico…"

"Mexico, it is a whole other thing," Jorge reminded her. "It is not like here. Although I see there is also corruption in this police department, but it is not as bad.

"I don't trust the police, *Papa.*"

Jorge watched her with interest and smiled.

"Maria, if I have taught you anything," He nodded. "This is it."

CHAPTER

11

"Athas, your hair, it is getting grey," Jorge spoke condescendingly toward the Canadian prime minister as he took a seat in his office a few days later. "We are, what? The same age, you and I, and yet, I barely have any grey at all."

"If you were running this country," Athas said as he sat down and gestured toward the window. "Your hair would be grey too."

"I *am* running this country," Jorge countered with a smirk on his face. "And me, I am doing pretty good, no?"

"I gotta give you credit where it is due," Athas agreed as he crossed his legs and nodded. "You kept us out of a full-blown riot."

"Well, I do thank you for acknowledging this," Jorge said as he relaxed back in his chair. "I knew that once this other information got out about Alwood, the police would have to suspend him indefinitely, however, with pay? Really?"

"They had no choice," Athas confirmed. "Anyway, he's not returning. Once the SIU investigates…"

Jorge laughed.

"Oh yes, Athas, because the Special Investigations Unit is *so* known for doing the right thing," Jorge spoke sarcastically. "They will wait till the heat is off and slip him back in the department. They always side with the police and never with the people."

"But with all this attention…"

"It does not matter," Jorge shook his head. "Please, I am a new Canadian, and even I see this. I would think that of all people, you would too."

Athas took a deep breath as he ran a hand over his face.

"At any rate," Jorge continued. "He will no longer be a problem."

Exhausted and beaten down, Athas shook his head.

"Do I want to know?"

"I do not know, Athas," Jorge mocked him. "Do you?"

"Let's leave this one here," Athas suggested. "I assume you already have plans to feed him to the lions."

"Ah! If only I had lions, this would give me great pleasure," Jorge grinned. "Unfortunately, the best I can do is a crematorium."

"You are truly the *worst* person to own a crematorium," Athas commented in a low voice.

"Some would argue that I'm the *best* person to own a crematorium," Jorge countered. "No body, no crime. It's nice and clean in these here times when suddenly people are paying attention again."

"Tell me the truth, Jorge, how much do the police in this city miss?" Athas asked as he waved his hand around.

"Let's see how long have I lived here?" Jorge reminded him. "Believe me, Athas, you cannot grasp the number of things that the police miss. I assure you, there's a lot."

"Fuck!" Athas shook his head. "When I was in social work, I thought they were inept, but now, it's much worse than I suspected."

"Well, for me, this here is nothing," Jorge reminded him. "I am, after all, from Mexico, so police corruption and incompetence are normal. We did not trust the police to be of help when needed. This here was just the way it was."

"So," Athas paused for a moment. "Alwood was suspended, so people are happy, but we have an even bigger problem. As you said, the entire department is a dumpster fire, and we have to sort it out. The problem is that we don't have enough people."

"But why is that?" Jorge asked. "Maybe there is a reason that people do not wish to work for the police. Poor working conditions? Management? Pay? There is always a reason. To me, find out from the people who work there and give them what they want."

"But wouldn't that work against you?" Athas asked suspiciously. "If the department is more efficient, wouldn't that put you at a disadvantage."

"Athas, I assure you that like you, Maxwell knows better than to cross me, especially when you've both come to me for help."

Athas didn't reply.

"I would suggest," He paused for a moment. "No, I misspoke. I *insist* that like Alwood and his aggressive ways, you also keep *me* under the radar. If I fall, everyone else that I am holding up falls with me. And none of us benefit from this, *si?*"

"I understand."

"Now, we have resolved this to the public's satisfaction," Jorge reminded him. "Alwood is taken care of. You announced the overhaul and *swift* investigation of the department, and now, the protests have stopped. There are no riots. This here is good. Just do as I have suggested, and I think you will have this situation completely resolved over time. But for now, unless there is anything else?"

"I think that covers it," Athas uncrossed his legs and moved to the edge of his chair. "I will get working on this immediately and maybe talk in more detail with Makerson?"

"See, this here, it would be perfect," Jorge nodded. "Meanwhile, let me deal with Maxwell. He and I are about to become very good friends."

Athas appeared skeptical as he stood up and headed for the door.

"Oh, and suggest to Makerson that you are considering making it mandatory to have body cams on officers at all times," Jorge suggested as he slowly stood up.

Athas thought for a moment.

"But wouldn't that also work to your disadvantage…."

"But the thing with body cams," Jorge reminded him as he followed him to the door. "Is that they can be turned off."

Athas left shortly after, and Jorge returned to his office. Turning on his phone, he found a series of messages. The first one was from Tony.

Would you be free to meet soon?

Today should be ok.

The next was from Chase.

We gotta make plans.

Jorge thought for a moment.

This sounds good. Were you talking to Marco and Paige?

Yes, I have an idea.

Perfecto. I will head to the bar shortly.

It was time Alwood was taken care of once and for all. It did concern Jorge that perhaps Chase was too close to the situation to look after things. Then again, sometimes, that was better.

The final message was from Jolene.

You never give me anything to do. Give me something to do.

Jorge rolled his eyes and shook his head. As much as he held Jolene in high esteem after she saved his wife's life, she was still unruly at times, which concerned him. However, if she had a project, Jolene tended to keep more in line.

I might have something for you. I will talk to you later.

He wasn't sure exactly what that was yet, but he would figure it out as the day went on. Perhaps she could help Chase.

Just as he stood up to leave the office, Paige entered the room with a skeptical look on her face.

"Was Alec here earlier?"

"Yes, *mi amor,* we had to have a short meeting regarding the police and that nonsense. It was fast."

"Oh, I didn't hear him come in," She mused. "Usually, there's so much fanfare when he arrives."

"We are doing our best to keep it low profile," Jorge reminded her. "The last thing he needs is some busybody reporter noticing that he's at my house."

"So, it's sorted out?"

"*Si*, we got it."

"What's up now?"

"I'm going to see Chase at the bar," Jorge replied as he walked around the desk and put his arm around her. "He is anxious to take care of Alwood and has a plan in mind. Do you think, *mi amor,* this is a good idea?"

"I'm not sure of the exact plan," She admitted as they walked toward the door. "But I know he's prepared for anything. It shouldn't be too difficult since Alwood lives alone now."

"You mean since he beat the shit out of his wife?"

"Well, she stayed around until it became public," Paige confirmed. "Turns out, some women can live with the secret abuse, but they can't live with the public humiliation."

"So, he lives alone?"

"He lives alone."

"This might be easy for Chase."

"I assume so."

Jorge stopped outside the office.

"Are you coming with me, Paige?" He noted that she didn't seem like herself. "To the bar, then to meet with Tony."

"Not unless you want a baby in on the meeting," Paige pointed upstairs. "Juliana had an appointment this afternoon, so I'm looking after Miguel."

Jorge paused for a moment.

"Well, I suppose it…

"I think it might be better to keep Miguel out of this," Paige let out a laugh. "Besides, I have to pick up Maria later."

"Call Jolene." Jorge immediately thought of a way to solve both problems.

"Jolene?"

"She's bored," Jorge replied with a shrug. "Tell her I got more for her later, but for now, get her to babysit Miguel so you can meet Chase and me at the bar. I'll let him know we will be a bit late. I gotta go see Tony. I may as well go there first because we need your help with the plan for Chase."

"Ok," Paige said and perked up. "Sounds good to me."

"I will meet you there."

CHAPTER

12

"So what you got for me? Jorge asked as he walked into Tony Allman's apartment. He noted that Andrew Collin was lounging about on the couch, staring at his phone. "The last few days have been a bit insane, you know?"

"Yeah, saw that fucking thing downtown," Andrew called out without even looking up from his phone, his scrawny body stretching out as if he was about to stand up. "Did you like, start the riot, or end it?"

"There were no riots," Jorge quickly corrected him. "We just had some protests. Now, whether or not it was about to turn into riots, is another thing."

"The cops, that fucking department, man, they are *tainted*," Andrew dragged out the final word as he slowly rose from the couch and glanced at Jorge. "In my circles, you keep the fuck away from anyone wearing a blue uniform."

"Preaching to the choir," Jorge reminded him as the three men headed to the small office area of the apartment.

"Yeah, but here, they are useless twats," Andrew continued to rant. "My aunt had to call them once because the jerkoff she was dating was beating her. You know what they did?"

"Helped *him*?" Jorge offered as the three men sat at a desk containing monitors and a mess of other equipment, papers, and empty coffee cups. "That Alwood guy was beating his wife and getting away with it."

Tony made a face but didn't say anything.

"Yeah, well, they might as well have," Andrew complained. "Fuck, they came in, asked her a lot of invasive questions, and did nothing! Like, left the guy there and told him to 'cool off'. Like, what the fuck is that?"

"Wow," Tony finally spoke. "That's terrible."

"*They're* terrible," Andrew shook his head. "And that guy who ripped the kid out of the wheelchair? What an incredible shitstain he is. Like seriously, there's got to be something wrong in his head."

"He's a bully," Tony reminded him as he turned on his laptop. "Which appears to be acceptable if you're a cop."

"Well, as I have said before, he wouldn't want to do that to my kid," Jorge bluntly commented while shaking his head. "It would not end well."

Andrew pretended to slit his own throat with an invisible knife.

"And that there," Jorge pointed out. "Would be pretty compared to what I would do to him."

"Can't say I'd blame you," Tony muttered and started to nod his head. "Ok, I got something I wanted to show you here."

"What's that?" Jorge was intrigued.

"Now, we have an idea," Tony started with some hesitation as he hit a few buttons on a laptop. "And you might say no, but hear us out."

"It's a good one," Andrew threw in. "Trust him."

"I'm thinking rather than go down the whole Big Pharma road again....we step back and think about it....eat the rich, what does that mean?" Tony continued

"I feel like you are doing a Powerpoint presentation," Jorge shook his head. "What you getting at?"

"Maybe we let go of Big Pharma," Andrew blurted out. "We can't beat a dead horse."

"I started to do some interviews and stuff," Tony shook his head. "It's not going anywhere, and it's repeating the same information we did the first time around. But, what if we were to do a series about the police."

"It don't got to be just the local police," Andrew jumped in. "It can be RCMP, other places in the country...."

"Really dissect them..."

"Show what douchebags they are...."

"Ok, ok," Jorge put his hand up in the air, indicating they stop. "I hear you, but I do not know if this...fits, I don't understand."

"Well, with Big Pharma, we wanted to demonstrate that they were corrupt," Tony reminded him. "That they weren't honest with people.

That they created addiction issues, but people still saw them as the holy saviors."

"See the connection now?" Andrew butted in. "Really?"

"He's right," Tony added. "We think the police are above us, but many events, especially recently, have demonstrated that this is not necessarily the case. There seems to be a lot of corruption, even in this Alwood story alone."

"We could start the series with that," Andrew suggested. "Then go back, see what else we can uncover, what makes these departments tick."

"In essence, they may not be 'the rich' like Big Pharma," Tony said as he seemed to grow more comfortable. "But they do hold the same amount of power. And when you give someone too much power...."

Jorge nodded as his brain scurried in different directions.

"Then again," Andrew shrunk back a bit. "Do we want to poke the lion?"

Jorge didn't answer at first, as he contemplated everything involved.

"There's definite corruption, but where does it come from?" Tony continued. "Who signs the paycheques?"

"That is a good point," Jorge considered.

"And it does kinda play in with Big Pharma," Andrew added. "Remember how the fentanyl got on the streets? What did the fucking cops do about it? Turn a blind eye? Come on."

Jorge nodded and continued to think. Could he help the department on one side while bringing them down on the other?

"Let me think about this," Jorge finally replied. "But meanwhile, do some research and get back to me. Try to keep the local stuff to a minimum."

"We could start with the first episode about Alwood," Tony reminded him. "Then, say we wanted to see if it was the same across the country and take the attention away from the local police."

"That would be good," Jorge nodded. "I have to think about this more, but I am leaning toward a yes. I would do more research though, see if this here has legs."

"From what I've found," Tony said as he turned his laptop around to show some notes. "It does."

"No doubt, man," Andrew spoke up. "They are greasy motherfuckers, the police."

"We will talk," Jorge commented and stood up to leave. "But I'm liking this idea."

He quietly considered what they said after leaving the apartment and heading for his SUV. Once there, he turned on his phone and saw he had a message from Paige. She was on the way to the bar to meet him and the others.

As he drove along, Jorge weighed the idea the boys had presented him with, and a smile slid on his face. He saw an angle, and it would work. But he would wait to share it with the others.

The usual suspects were waiting at the *Princesa Maria* when he walked through the door. Diego was telling Paige another decorating story regarding his home renovations, while Chase appeared preoccupied as he stood behind the bar, his arms crossed over his chest. At the end of the bar, Marco tapped on his laptop while occasionally grinning at a comment made by Diego. All was well with his *familia*.

Chase was the first person who spotted him.

"Do you know Maria wants to learn how to shoot a gun?" He looked slightly concerned. "You're not going to show her, are you?"

"Not now," Jorge confirmed as Diego and Paige turned their attention to him. "But eventually, I feel like I must."

Paige looked mournful.

"It concerns me that she doesn't feel safe."

"It concerns me too," Jorge agreed as he sat beside his wife. "However, these kids, they live in the real world and this world, sometimes things, they can be dangerous. We all know this."

"She doesn't believe the police would ever help her," Chase commented in a soft voice.

"She is probably right, you know?" Jorge replied, and everyone around him agreed. "And that is fine, I want her to be able to protect herself, but at this time, she does not have to know how to use a gun. I...I do not want to think about it just yet."

"Family business," Diego nodded. "It's coming..."

"Well, like her dating, this is something that I would rather not consider quite yet," Jorge confirmed. "So you guys figure out a plan or what? Is Alwood a dead man walking?"

"He is planning a vacation, sir," Marco spoke up from the end of the bar. "I have hacked his emails."

"We gotta get to him before he leaves," Paige commented.

"When does he take off?" Jorge wondered.

"Tomorrow night, sir."

Jorge nodded and turned his attention to Chase.

"I've been thinking," Jorge commented. "This might be a little too close to home for you."

"That's exactly why I need to do it," Chase confirmed. "That kid was indigenous, and what we saw was the tip of the iceberg. This is how the police have treated my people for years. If that man is going down, I'm the one taking him."

He spoke with such strength that Jorge sometimes didn't recognize the same young man who had started to work for him years earlier, back when he wasn't much more than a wide-eyed teenager.

"Well, if it is in you to do," Jorge confirmed. "I have no problem with that."

"He lives alone," Paige repeated her earlier comment. "It doesn't sound like he's very popular socially…especially now."

"His family is embarrassed by him," Marco confirmed. "I see it on his Facebook messages, and also, in some text messages, I was able to hack."

"Hmm…." Jorge nodded.

"Chase and I are gonna do it," Diego confirmed, which made Jorge feel a little better; first of all, because his wife wouldn't be in the line of fire, and also because he didn't want Chase going alone. "We got this."

"Do I need to know anything else?" Jorge asked but recognized that the plan had already been hatched, long before his arrival.

"Nope," Diego replied. "We're going tonight, but we're gonna need Andrew to do us a little favor."

Jorge nodded. Andrew worked at the crematorium and helped them when a body turned up.

"This fucker has it coming," Diego insisted.

"Well, Diego," Jorge replied. "It has been my experience that when you seek an opportunity to die, you generally find it."

CHAPTER

13

"I'm glad we sorted out the details," Paige commented later that night as the couple relaxed in the living room, each with a glass of wine. The house was quiet since Miguel was in bed and Maria was in her room doing homework. "It feels strange that we're not there with them and..."

"I know, *mi amor,* I know but, we must leave this to them," Jorge insisted as he put his hand in the air and shook his head. "It is, as you have said before, time for us to move away from this lifestyle. We must trust our foot soldiers. They will do well without us hovering over them."

"I don't think they exactly thought we were *hovering* over them," Paige appeared amused as she lifted the glass to her lips and took a sip. "But usually we're in the midst of everything."

"And now we are not," Jorge shrugged. "To be honest, I do not miss it. I have enjoyed the last few months of quiet."

"Is that because you want to keep me out of things?" Paige gently asked.

"*Mi amor,* it is hardly a secret that I do not want to see you in danger again," Jorge reminded her. "But, it is as you said, time for us to step back. Everything is in line for tonight. Chase, he has his plan. Diego, he is not a new kid on the block. The two of them, they will take care of this."

"Marco will have the cameras turned off," Paige continued as if going through a checklist in her head. "We're sure he'll be alone?"

"I am thinking that he is alone more than he is not these days," Jorge insisted. "Do not worry, Paige, they will take care of this, and we, we can spend a relaxing evening for a change."

Taking a deep breath, she looked into her husband's eyes and silently communicated.

"It seems a little too quiet," She finally mused. "Which makes me nervous."

"Do not invent problems."

"I'm not," She insisted. "It's just...I don't know. I never trust the silence."

"I thought you meditators, you loved the silence." Jorge teased.

"But this," Paige shook her head. "This is a different kind of silence."

He didn't respond.

"So," She shifted gears. "Tell me about your meeting with Tony. You mentioned something about doing season two on the police?"

"Yes, but I am not sure," Jorge replied as he leaned in closer. "How can I help Maxwell while shooting down the police in my series?"

"You said that local police would only be the first episode," She reminded him. "Make him come out smelling like roses. That's all he cares about in the end, himself."

Jorge didn't respond but thought about her words.

"Remember how the first season created so much distrust for Big Pharma?" Paige reminded him. "We can do the same here. It's a way to undermine them, put them on shaky ground, and if they're busy trying to regain their public image, they won't be in our way."

Jorge raised an eyebrow but didn't respond. The sound of feet hitting the stairs halted the conversation.

"*Papa,*" Maria sang out as she entered the room. Glancing at the wine bottle, she hesitated. "Are you drunk?"

"Maria, we had one drink," Jorge pointed toward the bottle of wine that was almost full. "Does it look like we are drunk?"

Ignoring his question, Maria bounced to another topic.

"I was thinking," She began slowly, her eyes glancing between Paige and her father. "I know you don't want me to learn how to use a gun right now, *but* what if I played a video game that allowed me to learn how to shoot? I saw online that they teach you to be pretty accurate."

"You read this online?" Jorge asked skeptically. "That playing a game is going to make you a good shooter?"

"I have heard that," Paige nodded, causing Jorge to wonder if it was true or if she was looking for a way to get Maria off track. "Hey, it can't hurt."

Tired, defeated, Jorge merely shrugged.

"If that is what you wish, Maria," He finally replied. "Then, you can do this, but Maria, you must remember, it is *just* a game. In the real world, things are often much different."

"I know, *Papa*," She rolled her eyes dramatically. "I'm not a moron."

"I know, Maria, but what I am saying is that real–life circumstances, they are not always as….cut and dry as what you see on a screen."

"I know that *too*," She insisted with some attitude in her voice.

"Well, if you know everything," Jorge countered. "I guess there is nothing more for me to say here."

Giving him a skeptical look, Maria turned on her heels and headed for the stairs.

"I'm gonna research the best games," She called out as she headed back up the stairs. "Cameron wants to play too."

"Isn't that the religious guy?" Jorge muttered after she was gone. "They let him play games where he's shooting people?"

"His family is," She replied. "He's sixteen. I'm sure he does a lot of things they don't know about."

Jorge raised his eyebrows and glanced back toward the stairs before returning his attention to her.

"I hope she isn't too."

Paige didn't respond but reached for her phone. She turned it on.

"Anything yet?"

"Not unless you got a message?"

Jorge reached in his pocket. Pulling out his phone, he turned it on and winced at the first message.

"Jolene, she is driving me crazy," He complained and shook his head. "She is the only person in the world that complains of having nothing to do."

"What if…." Paige thought for a moment. "You have her help Tony and Andrew? I mean, you even said Andrew is pretty busy at the crematorium so she could fill in. There must be something she can do to help?"

Jorge thought for a moment.

"Doing research or helping them with little odds and ends they don't have time to do, I'm sure there has to be something?"

Jorge began to nod as he considered her words.

"That also allows you to just oversee things."

"I do like that idea."

"She might drive them crazy, though," Paige grinned.

"If it keeps her out of *my* hair, I do not care."

"And the police aspect," Paige continued. "The more I think about it, the more I like it."

"I am thinking, *mi amor,* they take instructions from the top, that is who signs their paycheque," Jorge thought of a conversation he had with Tony earlier that day. "I must admit, this is power I would like to have myself."

"You can," Paige quietly reassured him. "If you shake their foundation, they won't get in your crosshairs."

"That is true," Jorge considered. "I like to think I control the government and the media. The police, is this not the next step?"

Paige raised her eyebrows.

"The more we control, *mi amor,* the better it is for my organization," Jorge continued to think. "I could do many things with this power. Many beautiful things."

"It's a power you want to have," Paige agreed. "We have to be cautious about how we do it."

"I will meet with Jolene separately and tell her what my goals are," Jorge nodded. "That way, she can oversee things and make sure the series continues to go in a way that would please me."

"You know, something else to consider," Paige added. "Maria's always talking about how you should get involved in movies and television. What if you sent the same kind of messages through fictitious characters as well? Maybe not now, but in the future?"

"This here, I like…."

"People don't always watch documentary type shows, but they do like to be entertained. We can say a lot through that entertainment. We can influence how people think."

This caught Jorge's attention.

"And the general narrative," Paige continued. "You have no idea how much the entertainment industry has affected how people see the world. The media feeds us ideas every day, and we don't live in a world where people think for themselves anymore. It wouldn't be that hard."

"As usual, *mi amor,* you have many great ideas."

His phone beeped.

Glancing at it, a grin swept over his lips.

"It looks like the task, it was completed."

"Are they headed to the crematorium?"

"It appears they are already on the way."

"And they don't need help?"

"It does not appear so, *mi amor.*"

"Oh."

There was something in her voice that aroused him. Jorge ran his hand over her thigh as the two shared a look.

"Tonight, it is for us," He pointed toward the bottle of wine. "So drink up, *mi amor,* you are in for a busy night."

CHAPTER

14

"...leading police to believe that Dan Alwood had plans to go on a vacation while on paid leave..."

Jorge heartily laughed as he clapped his hands together, while Paige, Diego, and Chase showed signs of amusement as the group sat around the bar at *Princesa Maria*. It was only a couple of days after the victim disappeared that family and friends grew concerned, however, their original fears that the officer had hurt himself, were dismissed.

"...together with no sign of foul play, indicates that Dan Alwood may have left the city..."

"*May* have left the city?" Diego quipped as he reached for his drink. "The guy had a ticket out of the country booked after the shit hit the fan, and they think he *might* have left the *city?*"

"But he didn't use those tickets," Paige gently reminded him.

"It don't matter," Diego shook his head. "Everything still adds up. No body, no sign of foul play, and he had been planning to run away. All arrows point to the center of the dartboard."

"Even if it looks suspicious," Jorge jumped in. "They got nothing. No case. He disappeared. He's a cop. They know how to do it."

"Having his gun missing was a nice touch," Paige appeared impressed. Chase didn't respond but grinned.

"Hey, we can never have too many guns around," Diego jumped in.

"We might need it sometime in the future," Paige mused. "The police don't tend to investigate shootings that happen with one of *their* guns...."

"Of course not, *mi amor,* they cannot let the world see what incompetent fuckups they are."

"It's only to our advantage they are," She reminded him.

"True," Jorge agreed and turned his attention to Chase, who had remained silent throughout Makerson's live stream that broke the news that the police were attempting to hide. "But I must say, I am impressed with how everything turned out."

Chase didn't reply but gave an appreciative smile before looking away.

"It is," Jorge continued as he glanced at Diego. "It is quite impressive. The two of you, you did well."

"All in a day's work," Diego said as he sat up a bit straighter and fixed his tie. "We get shit done."

"Did he put up much of a fight?" Paige was curious. "They said there were no signs of a struggle in his house."

"That's cause we got him out of his house," Diego said as he swung his hand around dramatically. "Hook, line, and sinker. It was the easiest fucking thing I ever did."

Chase began to laugh.

"Perhaps, you need to tell us more," Jorge insisted. "No one saw anything?"

"No, Marco found out he was on some dating site," Diego proudly told the story. "We created a fake profile, lured him in right away, and he thought he was meeting some *fan* who saw him on the news and thought he was being unfairly portrayed..."

"And she thought he was a hero," Chase added.

"Who was it?" Jorge was confused.

"Not real," Diego shook his head, pursing his lips together.

"Something Marco whipped up for us...fake picture, we created a profile," Chase began to speak with enthusiasm. "We got him. He came to meet us...."

"I assume you erased the history?" Paige calmly asked.

"Marco did...all of it," Diego nodded. "It's taken care of."

"There's no trace of their conversation."

"Didn't he drive to meet you?" Jorge asked.

"Nope, he took the subway," Chase explained. "He hated taking his car to certain areas of town because he thought someone would vandalize or steal it, so we made sure that's where we met him."

"Yeah, we met him all right," Diego nodded. "With a baseball bat to his fucking head, we met him."

Jorge once again laughed heartily, knowing Diego's intrigue with baseball bats.

"We got him in seconds, took care of him at the crematorium, and that was that..."

"And all is cleaned up?" Jorge confirmed, feeling much like a concerned parent rather than a mob boss. "No traces, no signs, cameras...."

"Nothing, we got it covered," Chase insisted. "As far as the police will see, he left the house and didn't come back."

"I wonder how long till Maxwell is calling," Paige said with a raised eyebrow.

"He probably already has," Jorge said as he pulled out his phone. "Let me turn it on to see."

Sure enough, he had. Maxwell insisted that he and Jorge meet right away.

"I enjoy how he seems to feel comfortable enough to give me orders," Jorge said with a nasty grin. "This here, it will be changing. I do not work that way."

No one responded, but there was a shared look around the bar.

"I will tell him, if he wants to meet me," Jorge squinted his eyes as he started to tap a reply. "He can do so here, *now*. I do not have time for this bullshit today."

"Have him come in the back door," Chase suggested. "If he doesn't want to be seen."

"Good idea," Jorge nodded. "That makes two of us who do not want to be seen talking to the other."

"So what's this about the docuseries taking on the police," Diego spoke up. "You want to put a target on our backs?"

"Diego, it will not be like this," Jorge shook his head and shut off his phone, placing it on the bar. "We will point out the truth that they are incapable of doing their jobs. That will make the public wary, and it just takes one shaky leg to make people not trust the entire table. That is our goal here."

"But aren't you helping that Maxwell guy..." Chase appeared confused.

"I'm helping *him,* not his whole fucking department," Jorge nodded. "He came to me with a problem, and we took care of it. I do not think he's in any position to complain."

Jorge was wrong. When Phillip Maxwell arrived, he was full of accusations and panic.

"You wanted my fucking help!" Jorge roared through the VIP room, where the two met. "You got my fucking help. What do you want?"

"I don't care if he's dead," Maxwell was quick to point out, speaking in a calmer voice this time. "But it looks like he just took off. Couldn't you leave a body?"

"I could have," Jorge nodded. "But that would've opened a whole new can of worms. As it is, he *was* planning to leave town which, to me, suggests that having him leave *permanently* seemed like the most logical step."

Maxwell didn't reply but appeared to be in thought.

"You can thank me later," Jorge spoke condescendingly. "After all, a body makes a case. No body, no case."

"But now it looks like he left town, and we have to look for him..."

"Good luck finding him," Jorge started to laugh. "You will not."

Maxwell didn't reply. The two men attempted to stare the other down, with the police chief looking away.

"Now, what I tell you is that he is gone, history," Jorge said as he waved his hand in the air. "You say, the police nationally, internationally, whatever, they are aware we are looking for him. It is out of your hands."

"But it still makes us look like incompetent fucks."

"You *are* incompetent fucks," Jorge snapped back. "But this way, there is no case to solve, no work to do. You tell the people that he clearly planned an escape because he had no way out. After a while, everyone forgets him."

Maxwell didn't reply.

"In fact," Jorge shrugged. "I've *already* have forgotten him."

Maxwell finally gave up and shook his head.

"I guess...you're right."

"I'm always right," Jorge corrected him. "Now, what else you got for me?"

"I might have another major issue in the department," He started but paused. "I need a few days."

"I got time," Jorge replied. "But that is not what I mean. I mean, what you got for *me*? I am not doing all this out of my generous heart."

"What you want? The info on Big Pharma I have?"

"I want…" Jorge sat back and thought for a moment. "I want reassurance that your fucking people don't come sniffing around me or any of my people or businesses."

"Have we before?"

"You do not ask the questions here."

Maxwell obediently nodded.

"I want you to cooperate with me with my next season in the docuseries, which will feature the fuckedness of the police."

"What?" Maxwell shot back. "I thought you…"

"The first episode," Jorge cut him off. "It will focus on the local police, but it will have you come out smelling like roses. I promise. The rest, they will focus on other places but I need you to cooperate with the first one, and any helpful information for other places, the RCMP, anything you got."

"Oh fuck," Maxwell ran a hand over his face. "You know I can't do that."

"You can and you will," Jorge insisted. "As I said, you will come out smelling like roses. The rest, not so much. Isn't that what you want? To be the hero in your own story? Even if, in the end, it is just an illusion?"

His final comment seemed to hit Maxwell hard as he sunk in his seat.

"I would think that this here…it would suit you."

"Why are you doing this?" Maxwell appeared curious. "I don't understand."

"Why not?" Jorge replied. "You, you do not need to worry about my motives. Just worry about you. And considering that you know what I am capable of, I would think you would find reassurance that I'm on your side and not against you, *amigo.*"

Maxwell sat up straighter but didn't reply.

"Trust me, it is a better place to be," Jorge shook his head. "Because the other side, you don't want to know…"

CHAPTER

15

"I'm starting to miss the days she was obsessed with acting," Jorge quipped as he reached for his coffee cup and headed for the kitchen table. "I get up in the middle of the night because I think I hear something. It was Maria, still up, playing her fucking shooting game. She got a little too much into it and forgot that even though she had the ear things in, we can still hear her yelling at the screen."

"Oh God, Jorge, at the time, I thought this would distract her, but she gets obsessed," Paige shook her head and took another drink of her coffee. "I don't know what to do. I feel like everything she becomes interested in becomes an obsession. It's not healthy."

"*Mi amor,* all I know is that from what I saw last night," Jorge glanced over his shoulder as if he expected her to sneak in the room. "I would not want to put a real gun in her hand then piss her off. She was quite fierce."

"It's a game," Paige reminded him. "Not real life."

"I know, but it shows her passion for shooting," Jorge reminded her. "It reminds me of….well, me. I believe that this might not necessarily be a bad thing, but yes, you are right, it is a bit of an obsession."

"I guess it's still new though," Paige considered. "So, maybe it's just because it's something new."

"Well, you must remember," Jorge reminded her. "That Maria, she has had many interests in the last few years so by next week, who knows? Maybe she will want to be a doctor?"

"You wish…" Paige grinned.

"I do, actually."

"I somehow think she will fall on the other end of the spectrum," Paige quietly suggested. "Creating the patients, not fixing them."

"Again, just like her *Papa.*"

Paige didn't respond but shook her head, a smile on her lips.

Turning on his phone, Jorge glanced at the screen.

"The first episode of the series is coming out in May," Jorge commented as he glanced at the April page on the calendar nearby. "I forgot to tell you this. But instead of being out exactly one week from one another, they will be out...when they're out. No set schedule."

"You can do that?"

"Paige, I can do anything," He reminded her and she laughed. "This here, it is a very popular series. *We* make our own rules. It creates suspense."

"There's a lot of anticipation."

"That is because of Makerson," Jorge reminded her. "He is talking about it in his articles, especially in light of the situation with the police."

Paige grimaced. Since the death of Alwood, there had been a lot of speculation that the police had let him escape since a body wasn't found and, there was no evidence of foul play. They were home free. Only his family were worried about him but, even they were starting to assume he had blown out of town with no intention of returning. They blamed the media for shaming him rather than appreciating that he was doing his job. It became a public debate, and yet, Jorge Hernandez walked away from it and was on to the next thing.

"And Jolene," Paige continued. "She's helpful?"

"More so than I thought," Jorge admitted. "Turns out, she is doing a lot of the leg work for them."

"She's a smart woman," Paige reminded him. "She catches on fast. Look at all the jobs you've had her do over the years..."

"This here is true," Jorge considered. "I've had her running several businesses..."

"All different," Paige reminded him.

"Yes, all very different."

"And some of your dirty work."

"Oh, Paige, there is always dirty work in my line of business."

She laughed, and he joined her.

"So what's up for today?" She finally asked.

"Today, *mi amor,*" Jorge replied. "I must meet with Chase then Maxwell, he has more information for me regarding the police somewhere in western Canada. I am curious what this is about."

"He's good at finding the dirt," Paige mused. "Who knew he would be so cooperative?"

"He had no choice."

"Things have been going..."

"Do not say it," Jorge automatically cut her off. "We do not want to jinx our luck. All has been quiet since Alwood *disappeared.*"

"Well, all winter, actually," Paige conmented. "Maybe things are finally..."

"Again, *mi amor,* I am not superstitious, but it is better to enjoy the calm waters than it is to talk about them."

"True," She nodded.

"Maybe this is where everything comes together, and we happily ride off into the sunset. You know, it was bound to happen eventually."

Paige appeared skeptical. Neither said a word but shared a look.

"At any rate, I must go..." Jorge rose from his chair and leaned forward to kiss Paige before grabbing his phone. The two shared a look before he headed toward the door. "*Mi amor,* you worry too much."

"I usually have reason to worry."

"Not this time," he attempted to reassure her as he turned before reaching for the doorknob. "Sometimes, a beautiful silence is just a beautiful silence."

He didn't believe it either. He wanted to so much, but something was amiss.

Outside, he got into his SUV and glanced around. It was good to make sure nothing stood out in the neighborhood. Everything was quiet. He gave an extra glance around before pulling out of the driveway.

In truth, he didn't want to alarm Paige, but he felt unsettled. In the past few weeks, Jorge's *familia* had been busy. Diego had officially taken over the company as CEO, his daughter got caught up in a world of video game obsession, Chase had become caught up in indigenous issues that distracted his focus from work, and Jolene was attempting to take over the entire docuseries. The fires were small, but all had the potential to grow until they caused a massive explosion.

His first visit was with Chase.

"Good morning," Jorge said as soon as he entered the club, locking the door behind him. He noted that Chase was behind the bar. "I see the coffee is on."

"Always."

"We gotta talk."

Chase didn't reply but instead headed for the office. Jorge followed him and shut the door.

"I know what you're thinking, Jorge, and I…"

"No," He automatically cut him off. "You do not know what I am thinking."

Pointing toward the chair, he indicated that they both sit down.

"Now," Jorge took his place on the other side of the desk from Chase. "I understand why you got involved with this group. They are your people. Missing and murdered indigenous women is a problem in this country. I respect that you want to take part in this issue, but you must know that this is an extremist group. They are being closely watched. I can help protect you in my organization, but I cannot promise anything when you are with them."

"I know, but…"

"I can pull some strings," Jorge cut him off. "But I cannot do more than that."

Chase didn't reply.

"I know, your heart, it is in the right place," Jorge continued. "But if you are going to get involved, it cannot be with this group. You can take care of anyone who needs to be taken care of with my full support, but only if you do it carefully, and not with this group."

"It's….it's not just about what they do," Chase attempted to explain. "It's because they're my people…"

"*We're* your people," Jorge pointed to himself. "We're your family. Chase, you know that me, I support you, as I have said, but you cannot have it both ways in this situation. I have had Marco check them out. This group, they are being monitored by the RCMP. He has assured me there are no traces to you, but you must disconnect immediately."

Chase appeared stunned, finally looking away, he nodded.

"Again, I do support whatever it is you must do," Jorge reminded him. "But it cannot be with this group."

"No, I do…I understand. I can be a lone wolf."

"You are never alone," Jorge reminded him as he slid to the edge of his seat. "You have us."

Chase nodded and smiled.

"I have something for you," Jorge reached in his pocket and pulled out a box, and handed it to Chase.

"I got this for you."

Chase appeared surprised as he reached for the box. He opened it to find a finely crafted knife.

"This here, it is one of a kind, made by the best in the world. It is for you. It is a gift, a way to tell you that you have moved ahead in this organization. You are one of my top people who has proven himself again and again."

Chase picked up the knife and ran his thumb over the symbol etched into the side. The careful details suggested it was expensive, beautifully made with great consideration for the final product.

"That is the symbol of family," Jorge continued. "*Our* family and the connection we all have."

"This is...amazing..." Chase finally said in a quiet voice. "I don't know what to say."

"It is one of kind, a specialty order," Jorge spoke calmly. "it is the best knife you can get. Now, please, think about what I said here today."

He left Chase with his thoughts and messaged Maxwell to meet him.

He didn't reply.

CHAPTER

16

We often drift a long way from where we started. It was a lesson that Chase Jacobs learned again and again from his merciless teacher, Jorge Hernandez, who was in many ways like a father figure to him. His own father died many years earlier, but even when still alive, he had done little to teach Chase about facing the obstacles in life. He was weak and had Chase stayed in small-town Alberta, he would've been weak too.

But the world had different plans for him. It only took a drop of curiosity to lure him in another direction, while a tidal wave of loyalty, trust, and family had help support an entirely different life. However, hadn't it always been in him to do? Hadn't he tended to drift to the dark side?

Jorge Hernandez had given Chase an opportunity. He had given him more than his blood family was ever able to provide. It wasn't that they withheld love and affection; it was that they didn't have it to give. He saw that now. As time marched forward, he recognized the reality of his former life. However, there had always been a part of him that was curious about his heritage, about the indigenous side his blood family never talked about when he was growing up.

"So, it was some *woman* that dragged you into this?" Diego spoke spitefully as the two sat at the *Princessa Maria*. Holding a drink in his hand, Diego attempted to hide his emotions. "So she shows you her tits, and you decide to become part of this stupid group?"

Chase opened his mouth to reply, but nothing came out. At the other end of the bar, Marco let out a laugh then suddenly grew serious.

"Sir, it is important that you stay away from this group," He reminded Chase. "They are being watched closely by the RCMP because they're extremists. They want to blow up stuff and riot."

"Amateurs!" Diego rolled his eyes toward the heavens. "It's almost like they want to get caught."

"Some do," Marco injected. "It brings attention to their cause."

Diego rolled his eyes again.

Chase felt naive and looked away. How could he have missed that?

"Women," Diego replied, almost as if he heard the question in his mind. "You straight men, they bat their eyelashes, and you turn into fucking idiots, that's what happened here. And *that* girl, she knew it."

"Does she know where you live?" Marco cut in, a nervous look in his eyes.

Chase shook his head, hoping this somehow gained him some ground.

"Of course not," He finally affirmed. "We went to her place."

She had been incredibly sexy. She spoke with such passion. It reminded Chase of a girl from his past, someone he would probably never see again. Seductive, aggressive, a woman who knew what she wanted and took it. He could give up the group, but even his arousal when thinking about their encounters made him unsure of how he'd forget her.

Diego raised an eyebrow, and Chase looked away.

"Don't fuck her *again*," He pointed his finger at Chase. "Find someone else, anyone else. For fuck sakes, you work at a *bar*."

"Yes, he is right," Marco nodded enthusiastically. "You need to keep away from this lady. Does she know where you work?"

"No," Chase said and took a deep breath. "She doesn't know who I am, where I work....I'd find her at the meetings, and we'd hook up afterward."

"Do not do that again," Marco advised, and Chase nodded.

Diego shot a dirty look in his direction, and Chase felt his original desires deflate. They were right.

"Jorge will fucking kill you if he thinks you're not listening," Diego put the final nail in his coffin. "You know how he is about trust."

"I know, I know, Diego," Chase nodded.

"You're moving up in our organization," Diego reminded him. "He's trusting you to do a lot. Don't fuck that up."

"I don't plan on it," Chase assured him. "I promise."

"Find another girl," Diego insisted.

"I will.."

"*Fuck* another girl," Diego emphasized. "I don't care who, just someone else."

Marco laughed at the end of the bar.

"I understand," Chase nodded as his cheeks started to burn. "But I still believe in the cause. Missing and murdered indigenous women, the police don't care."

"May I suggest," Marco spoke up. "That you find another way to help them?"

"You could find out who's getting away with this shit and…"

"Sir," Marco shook his head and cut off Diego. "What if you teach these women self-defense? You are a boxer, correct? Teach them ways to protect themselves? Maybe there is someone you can find to help you do that?"

"You know who to ask," Diego nodded rapidly. "Athas, he was a social worker. He got all kinds of connections."

"Mr. Hernandez, he will help you too," Marco suggested. "Maybe as part of his company…"

"Good fucking PR," Diego nodded rapidly. "Talk to Athas, see what he's got to say."

Chase felt a fire light within him. He liked the idea, but this quickly disappeared.

"But will it help?"

"It will help some, sir," Marco insisted.

"And the rest, the ones it doesn't help," Diego jumped in. "We find who is dropping the ball or who did this shit, and…we do our justice, but *not* as part of that group."

"I know, I know, Diego….:

"Jorge, he ain't gonna fuck around if he thinks you aren't listening."

Chase gave Diego a warning look.

"I'm just saying," Diego shrugged. "You did good work the other day. You're a man who can kill with one hand tied behind your back. You don't even need a gun, like the rest of us…"

"None of you do," Chase reminded him.

"Yeah, but we don't have your…*power!*" Diego turned to Marco. "You should've seen him with this Alwood character after I hit him with a bat…"

Diego demonstrated twisting a neck while he made a face.

"It was fucking ruthless."

"Sir," Marco suddenly looked concerned. "Was Clara in…"

"Yeah yeah," Chase nodded to the reference to the woman who regularly checked their homes and businesses for listening devices. "She was in and checked the place out; there's nothing here."

"We've been good," Diego insisted as he finished his drink. "Nothing in a long time, but you can never be too careful."

"Mr. Hernandez, he was saying that things, they have been too quiet lately," Marco commented and bit his bottom lip. "I hope it stays that way. I mean, when Mrs. Hernandez was shot…"

"Yea, that makes all of us," Diego cut in. "But nothing stays quiet here for long. You never know what will happen or when…."

The door swung opened, and Jorge walked in. He was alone.

"What the fuck, you guys got a meeting going on here?" Jorge spoke in his usual, broken English, his dark eyes inspecting each of their faces. "You already look into something."

"We were talking about the girl Chase was fucking from that extremist group," Diego spoke dramatically, swinging his arms in the air. Marco laughed. Chase grimaced.

"Oh, is that right?" Jorge looked amused, and Chase felt his face burning. "So this here, is it the real reason behind you joining or what?"

"No, it was part, but…."

"You gotta keep away from her," Jorge shook his head. "If you're looking to get laid, you're young, and you got money, it shouldn't be a problem in this town."

"Well, that's what I said," Diego attempted to suck up. "And he works in a *bar*."

"Ok, can we not talk about this," Chase felt embarrassed as he turned to Diego. "I wish I never told you anything."

Diego shrugged with a mischievous grin on his face.

"Sir, we are talking about getting Chase into being more proactive," Marco jumped in as if to alleviate some of the tension in the room. "Maybe teach indigenous women self-defense…."

"Yeah, Athas, he probably got people," Diego grew serious, twisting his lips in a self-satisfied expression as if it was his idea. "You know, help them out."

"This here, it is ok," Jorge nodded. "But we can still break balls if necessary…"

His phone rang, and he reached in his pocket.

"That better be Maxwell," Jorge complained. "That fucker is avoiding my calls…."

Glancing at his phone, he squinted.

"You need *glasses*…"

"Fuck off, Diego," Jorge replied as he walked away and answered.

"He's getting old and *blind*," Diego insisted to the others.

"Most people, they cannot see as well up close at his age," Marco calmly reminded him. "I will remind you that you…"

"Holy fuck!" Jorge suddenly spoke abruptly, pulling the attention back at him. "Unbelievable."

"What?" Diego asked. "What happened?"

"It's Maxwell," Jorge pointed toward his phone. "The fucker was found dead."

CHAPTER

17

"Oh, you got to be fucking kidding me," Jorge abruptly spoke when he opened the door to find a police officer on the other side. "What the fuck do you want?"

The young officer looked stunned by Jorge's reaction but quickly got back on track.

"Mr. Hernandez?" He asked and without waiting for a reply. "My name is Constable Mark Hail, and I'm here to talk to you about the death of Chief Phillip Maxwell. Can I come in?"

"I don't got time for this, so make it fast," Jorge snapped as he moved aside to reveal his wife, who was calmly standing aside with Miguel in her arms. The child immediately started to cry when the young man walked into the room.

"It's the gun," Paige calmly spoke as she glared toward the exposed weapon on the constable's belt and attempted to shield the child's eyes. "It's scaring him."

The constable looked slightly dumbfound as Paige glared at him, finally scurrying off with the toddler, while Jorge shut the door behind them.

"You happy now? You got my kid crying?" Jorge complained as the child continued to scream all the way upstairs. "You know how long it takes to get him settled once he starts? He's going to be upset all fucking morning now!"

"Sir, I…"

"It's fucking 7 a.m.," Jorge continued. "What the hell are you doing here so early?"

"I have to talk to you about Chief Maxwell…"

"We will go to my office," Jorge snapped and pointed him in the right direction. "Before my daughter, she comes downstairs, and you upset her too."

Unprepared for his intimidating introduction to Jorge Hernandez, the young officer obediently followed the Latino into his office.

"Sit down," Jorge continued to speak with abruptness in his voice, pointing across the room. Closing the door behind them, tension filled the room as the powerful figure headed behind his desk and sat down. It was only then that he took a good look at the officer.

"Well, at least they did not send me a white boy," Jorge spoke curtly, as he inspected Mark Hail. "You act so *white* that I almost did not notice you weren't."

"I'm mixed….anyway, this isn't important," Mark Hail seemed to catch himself and shook his head. "Mr. Hernandez, I'm here because, as you probably heard, Chief Maxwell was murdered and…"

"And you think I did it?" Jorge let out a laugh.

"No one is accusing you of anything," Constable Hail spoke calmly as his eyes focused in on Jorge. "But there's a record of you calling him on the day he was killed. It's the only record of you speaking, so it stood out."

This was because Marco was a superior hacker. There had been a lot of text messages and calls. He had managed to make them all go away, except for the last one.

"Look, I do not know what kind of nonsense you have made up in your head," Jorge spoke abruptly, pointing toward his forehead. "But the man was about to bring me information about your fucked up department for my docuseries. That is why I call."

"It seems a bit unlikely that he would speak of such matters," Constable Hail spoke assertively as if he finally found his backbone. "Why would he do this?"

"I do not know," Jorge said with a shrug. "I mentioned that I was working on a series and joked that he might have some good stories he would like to tell me. I said that we do not reveal our sources, and it would be a good way to expose those who cannot or do not want to do their job. As a police chief, I am sure this here is the kind of thing that must have frustrated him. He said he would have something for me, and we were to meet the other day, but then, this man, he died."

Jorge stopped speaking and shrugged.

"And that was the last time you talked to him?"

"Obviously."

"I mean, you didn't meet in person?"

"We were supposed to, *but he died first.*"

"I see."

"You know," Jorge said as he leaned forward on his desk. "it would seem to me that if anyone wanted Maxwell dead, it would most likely be one of your own. Maybe he was about to say a little too much, and you know…."

Jorge used his fingers to symbolize a gun being shot.

"How did you know he was shot?" Constable Hail countered.

"It was in the motherfucking news," Jorge snapped as his eyes narrowed in on the constable. "Do you have a real reason to be here, or is this just your dog and pony show, to make it look like your department is doing something."

At first, the constable didn't respond. His eyes widening, he looked stunned by the remark.

"Look, I do not know or care what you think," Jorge spoke abruptly. "The man was about to bring me information about the corruption and stupidity of the police for my docuseries. So, why would I *murder* the fucker? No wonder you police, you never get anything solved."

"Well, we also have to consider that he may have been coerced," Constable Hail spoke in an even tone. "We have to look at all possibilities."

"Does that include your *own* department?" Jorge turned the tables on him. "Who knows what kind of dark secrets he was about to spill. Maybe he was going to walk on the wrong toes."

"Again, I can't see the same man who worked for the police for years and moved up the ranks to become police chief as someone dissatisfied with his job," Constable Hail reminded him. "We aren't even suggesting anything regarding your call. We just wanted to piece together the last hours of his life."

"Oh, is that so?" Jorge asked condescendingly. "So, you want to know when he took his last piss and whether or not he fucked his wife that morning? How lovely."

Constable Hail glared at him.

"We aren't that exact."

Jorge shrugged as he continued to glare at the constable.

"You got anything else?" Jorge asked as he fixed his tie. "Cause unlike you, I have work to do today."

Constable Hail didn't say anything but shook his head.

"Great," Jorge spoke sarcastically as he rose from his chair. "Then we can both get on with our day."

"Thank you for your cooperation," Constable Hail attempted to make peace with the sinister Mexican but to no avail. Jorge gave him a cold look as the two men headed toward the door in awkward silence.

Once back in the living room, as Jorge escorted Constable Hail to the exit, he heard a gasp and turned around. Maria stood on the stairway with a shocked look on her face.

"See, I tell you, you scare my children," Jorge pointed toward his daughter. "She is not used to seeing someone with a gun in this house."

Constable Hail shot him a skeptical look before turning his attention toward Maria.

"I'm sorry, I didn't mean to scare you," He spoke in a relaxed tone. "I was just here to ask your father a few questions."

Maria didn't reply but continued to stare at him.

"Well, you got her to stop talking," Jorge said as he opened the door to show the constable out. "So, there is that, I suppose. You make one of my children scream in fear, and the other, she is too scared to talk. Terrific."

"Again, I'm sorry," Constable Hail muttered as he shrunk in size as he walked out the door. "Have a good day."

"I will now," Jorge muttered as he closed the door behind him and glanced out the window to see Constable Hail return to his car.

"*Papa!*" Maria rushed downstairs with a pained expression on her face. "What was *he* doing here? Are we in trouble?"

"Maria, no, this is fine," He reached out and hugged his frazzled daughter. "He was just asking about a phone call I made to Chief Maxwell since he was killed…"

He heard something and glanced toward the stairs. Paige was walking down with a worried expression on her face.

"…he was trying to retrace his final moments or something like this," Jorge said as he let his daughter go, still looking at his wife. "it is nothing."

"What did you say?" Maria asked as her large eyes filled with anxiety.

"Maria, you have nothing to worry about," Jorge assured her. "They are nervous because Maxwell, he was going to cooperate with me for the docuseries. I would assume the wrong person found this out and wanted to keep him quiet."

"So they killed him?" Maria asked while beside her, Paige looked uncomfortable.

"We…we don't know that," Paige jumped in. "He was a cop, so it could've been anyone…"

"This is true," Jorge insisted. "But Maria, you do not have to worry about such things. It is ok. I am not in trouble. As I pointed out to him, maybe he should look at his own people because they had something to lose if Maxwell talked. Me? I am the one losing in his death."

"He's not going to try to frame you, is he?" Maria stumbled through her words.

"Maria," He let out a laugh. "You watch too many detective shows. If I do not teach you anything, let me tell you that much of what happens on television isn't realistic. And the police, Maria, they are lazy. They just are going through their procedure, and you do not have to worry. It will be fine."

She didn't look convinced. And neither did Paige.

18

"All this killing is going on, and for once, my hands are clean," Jorge announced as he joined the others in the VIP room while Paige closed the door behind them. "I do nothing, and *this* is the time the police, they show up at my door?"

"They're trying to frame you for something the fuckers did themselves," Diego ranted and turned his attention toward Jorge as he sat beside him. "I knew we shouldn't have poked the lion. Now that they got a taste for blood, they're never going to leave us alone."

"They heard about the series, sir," Marco interjected as he pointed toward his laptop, now turned off. "That is why they are angry."

"And I suspect," Jorge said as he glanced at his wife. "That is why they show up at my door *now*. Maxwell probably had a lot of info to share with me about the local police, and also, I believe some others. Someone wanted him to keep his mouth shut."

"You'd think he'd be smart enough to keep it quiet," Chase wondered out loud. "It obviously wasn't going to go over well."

"We should not have done this," Jolene jumped in, her voice loud. "I tell you, we should have focused on something else for this series."

"So what?" Chase shrugged, jumping to Jorge's defense. "It's not like the police haven't been attacked in the media before."

"But they see what Jorge did to Big Pharma," Jolene reminded him. "He destroyed them."

"And I will destroy these fuckers too especially now that they send someone to my door," Jorge sternly insisted. "Now, everyone must calm down and listen to me."

The room fell silent as all eyes turned to him.

"We do not need to worry," He gestured toward Marco. "We had the history of our conversations removed, *but* the problem was that I call him just after he was killed because he was late for our meeting. He wasn't getting back to me."

"Did you leave a message?" Diego asked suspiciously.

"Of course not," Jorge shook his head. "This here is not my first day on the job, Diego."

Marco laughed.

"At any rate," Jorge continued. "The police, this little shit stain that shows up at my door, he wanted to know why I would be calling Maxwell. I tell him the truth. I pointed out that it was probably one of their own that killed him."

Chase laughed this time.

"You *told* him we were doing a series on the police," Diego asked as his eyes widened.

"Diego, pay attention. It is already known," Jorge reminded him. "I do not care and in fact, everyone should know about this. I will be talking to Makerson about it later today, just to add another nail to their coffin."

"Ok, so, we need to focus," Paige jumped in and got everyone's attention. "We're all over the place."

"It is simple," Jorge added as he leaned back in his chair. "Maxwell was murdered because he knew too much. He was about to sing to me, and I, in turn, was about to expose them. They send a policeman to the door as a way to supposedly intimidate me….but I tell you, I was not the one intimidated."

Marco started to laugh, and the others followed.

"You're gonna have to give us a little more detail than that," Diego insisted as he twisted his lips. "So he shows up *just* to ask why you called Maxwell?"

"There were insinuations that it was suspicious we talk," Jorge shrugged. "But it does not matter because I have an alibi. I was at the office the morning it happened."

Diego leaned in as if in confidence. "Were you *really* at the office this morning?"

"Yes, Diego, I was," Jorge said with humor in his voice. "You were still at home. Something about your fucking dog."

"Priscilla had a little tummy trouble this morning," Diego attempted to explain. "I got to the office late."

"It does not matter," Jorge shook his head. "Everyone saw me, I was on cameras, I scanned my badge to get in….they got nothing."

"They might think you got someone else to do it?" Paige countered.

"Who? They got nothing because there is nothing," Jorge insisted. "I do not worry about such things, and neither should you."

Everyone fell silent.

"What now?" Jorge shook his head. "The police, they will not be around again, and if they are, they will not get further ahead."

"What if they come after us after this?" Jolene countered.

"You, you're making a docuseries," Jorge pointed out. "It would look bad on them to interrupt this and put more suspicion on them. Chase runs a nightclub. Diego is a CEO. Marco is the IT guy. Paige, she is a stay at home mom, who pretended to the police that we never had guns in our house, and it upset Miguel."

Everyone started to laugh.

"I pinched him," Paige spoke quietly. "I wanted him to cry because I saw him looking toward the gun."

"Because he knows what they look like," Diego spoke abruptly. "That's for sure."

"But Paige, she tells the cop that it scared him."

Everyone laughed again.

"It's important to affect him emotionally, if possible…"

"It takes down his defenses," Chase said as he loosened his tie.

"Yup," Paige nodded.

"Maria, though, she *was* upset," Jorge spoke with emotion in his voice. "This here, it concerns me."

"She said something about that," Chase admitted with a sympathetic smile. Jorge's daughter had always been close to the youngest member of the group, often confiding things to him before her family. "She thought he was there to arrest you."

"Well, if any cop ever arrests me in front of my child," Jorge spoke abruptly and put his finger up to his temple as if it were a gun he was about to shoot. "You don't fuck with my children. My Maria, she is already very emotional, I cannot have anything else upset her. She's seen enough in her childhood."

"He can't arrest you, can he?" Diego suddenly jumped in. "This is the police. They can make shit up to cover their own asses."

"If he does, he already knows that I have lawyers," Jorge spoke confidently. "But meanwhile, Marco, can you do some research?"

"Of course, sir, what did you say the policeman's name was again."

"Constable Mark Hail."

"Sounds like a white supremacist name..." Diego muttered.

"He is not white."

"Really?" Diego was surprised.

"It does not matter though," Jorge insisted. "This here only means that he is trying to impress the white men, that is how it goes."

"So, we are safe?" Jolene appeared skeptical. "I do not like police poking around. Maybe we should look at another topic for the series."

"No," Jorge automatically shook his head. "Nope. If anything, I want to do this even more now."

"Like you said, that's what this was probably about," Paige spoke up. "They can't connect Jorge with this, and they know it. This was their way of warning him that if he goes forward with the series, to expect a lot of visits from the police."

"I do not think I made this man today feel welcomed," Jorge said and threw his head back in laughter. "I was very....rude."

"You were very *yourself* in other words," Diego smugly replied. "But that might not keep them away."

"I think it won't encourage them to make a lot of social calls," Jorge considered. "It is too soon to say. If this here becomes a habit, I can shake things up."

"You can't start killing them off one by one..." Chase started but his words drifted away.

"I can," Jorge insisted. "But that's not what I have in mind here. As my lovely Paige would say, there is more than one way to skin a cat."

His wife grinned but didn't respond.

"We can shake things up again," Chase suggested.

"Exactly, and later today, I plan to do just that," Jorge insisted. "Makerson and I will do a live stream. And in it, I will discuss how my focus for the series is not only police but specific topics like racial profiling, police harassment, and of course, missing and murdered indigenous women."

The last comment caught Chase's attention, and hope sprung in his eyes.

"We will talk about how the police," Jorge seemed to direct his comment at the youngest member of the group. "they never seem to be able to resolve those crimes, and we will investigate if there's a reason why..."

"Cover-up," Diego snuffed. "Because they don't give a fuck."

"Well, we will certainly find out," Jorge grinned.

"I like this here idea...." Jolene started to speak.

"And Jolene, you," Jorge cut her off. "You are working *with* Andrew and Tony. They are not working *for* you."

"I just..."

"You just want to take over everything," Jorge cut her off again. "No more, Jolene. You're there to help them, not piss them off. They are the pros. They know what they're doing. You, you are the student."

"I can help too," Chase jumped in. "You know, if you need anything..."

"I will keep this in mind," Jorge said as he pushed his chair out. "Now, Paige and I, we must go meet with Makerson. We are going to have an interview that will tell the fucking police that *I* rule this town and to stay the fuck out of my way."

CHAPTER

19

"And this happened this morning?" Makerson chatted with Jorge as he prepared for their live stream that was scheduled to start within minutes. Paige sat across the room, gauging the response to the upcoming event on her laptop. "The cop showing up at your door?"

"At 7 fucking o'clock he shows up," Jorge replied and watched Makerson raise an eyebrow. "Exactly what I want to see first thing in the morning."

"You know, they do that on purpose," Makerson said as he tapped a few buttons and stared at the screen. "It's to catch you off guard."

"It is difficult to catch me off guard, *amigo*," Jorge spoke firmly. "Not with the life I have had. I am always prepared for anything."

"That's a good way to be," Makerson finally looked away from his computer and back at Jorge. "I wish I had that skill."

He didn't respond to the young editor but merely grinned.

"I think we're all set to go."

"Tread carefully," Paige warned from across the room. "I don't want a different cop at my door every morning."

"It scared the hell out of the children," Jorge said as he looked at Makerson. "Especially my Maria."

"Maybe this is something we should bring up in the interview," Makerson wondered.

"Tread lightly," Paige repeated.

"We'll see how it goes," Makerson suggested. "Shall we begin?"

The two men sat in their usual positions, and the live stream started. As usual, Makerson introduced Jorge as the founder of Our House of Pot, the chain that swept over the country and became Canada's source for cannabis products. After some friendly chitchat, the real interview got started.

"Of course, the first season of the docuseries *Eat the Rich Before the Rich Eat You* was a huge international success," Makerson jumped right into the topic at hand. "I'm curious what your part is in the production and why you got involved? It seems like your schedule is already pretty busy, so what drew you to this project?"

"Hey, I like being busy," Jorge replied with his usual, charismatic smile. "My wife, she says it keeps me out of trouble, you know?"

Makerson laughed.

"But to be honest," Jorge grew more serious. "I was introduced to Tony Allman, who, of course, is the lifeblood behind this entire project. I recognized a man with a vision, who was willing to put in the hard work to create a successful series. It seemed like a great investment, so I was excited to become involved."

"There's been a lot of comments in the media that perhaps you had a more, personal reason for backing this project, is this true?"

Jorge laughed.

"Well, my friend, I will not lie," Jorge spoke gleefully, his handsome face looking directly at the camera. "Big Pharma, it is often my competitor, but you know, I also wanted to allow the people who have suffered to have a voice. The amount of people who die each year from opiate addiction is quite astonishing. It is sad."

"But now you're moving on with another season…"

"Yes, we are currently working on a new season of *Eat the Rich*. We are hoping to drop the first episode in late May, early June," Jorge hesitated and thought for a moment. "However, this will depend on when Tony and his crew are ready. I do not want them to rush. I know it is a lot of work."

"And season two, it's going to focus on corruption within the police?"

"It will look at various ways the police have sometimes let the public down," Jorge spoke solemnly. "Of course, we recently saw a situation where a young, indigenous boy was attacked by one of the local police, and this is not the only situation where we have seen the police reacting inappropriately. As a father, I was appalled by his actions. This is what made us consider this topic for season two."

"Does that follow the original narrative?" Makerson questioned. "Eat the rich implies big corporations, doesn't it?"

"Sometimes," Jorge nodded his head. "However, you must also think of the powerful in our country. The police hold a powerful position in our society, and who gives them the orders? More powerful people."

"Isn't it the taxpayers?" Makerson acted as if he were surprised by Jorge's comment. "Aren't we, the people the ones in charge of the police? After all, it's a public service."

"It is a nice fantasy," Jorge replied to his question with a shrug. "But is it true? We have to look at who gives the police their orders. What is that person's motivation? Why are certain cases given more attention than others? Why is there racial discrimination?"

"*Do* you think some cases get more attention than others?" Makerson countered.

"Absolutely!" Jorge paused for a moment. "For example, why are there so many murdered and missing indigenous women? They are also someone's wife, someone's daughter. If that were your wife, your daughter, would you not want the police to make a serious effort to find out what happened? These are Canada's first people, and yet, why are they treated like second-class citizens? To me, that is the definition of racial discrimination."

"Will racism be a central theme in the second season?"

"We are not certain, but it will definitely be involved," Jorge nodded. "There are so many questions that we are looking forward to exploring in this series. Questions that *need* to be answered."

The interview wrapped up shortly after this final bomb was dropped.

"Wow," Paige commented as soon as the live stream ended. "People are going nuts in the comment section."

"Good or bad nuts?" Jorge asked as he rushed across the room.

"A little bit of both," Paige replied. "But the point is that they are showing up fast and furious, which means people are passionate about this subject."

"I see a lot of personal stories," Makerson commented as he glanced at his tablet. "That might come in handy for your series."

"I will bring this to Tony's attention."

"He's already been on here," Paige replied. "He put up a comment that he was in charge of the series and would welcome any information that people felt would be helpful."

"*Perfecto*," Jorge grinned and glanced at his wife, suddenly feeling aroused. "This here is perfect."

"Not everyone is happy," Makerson reminded him. "They see this as an attack on the police and suggest that there are some bad apples. That not all are the same. The usual thing."

"I never said they were all bad," Jorge replied with a shrug. "They are often useless fucks, but I did not say this, did I?"

Paige laughed.

"No, you did not," Makerson replied with a grin. "But the fact that you're putting this kind of attention on the police is making *some* people unhappy."

"Not all," Paige added. "Some say it's about time."

Jorge nodded, a smooth grin crossing his lips.

"We'll definitely follow up," Makerson suggested. "I'm sure you'll have more to say before the season launches."

"You know me," Jorge replied. "I always got lots to say."

Paige turned her phone back on, and Jorge did the same. She sat hers aside while Jorge's lit up with messages from everyone, most of which was commenting on the interview.

"Marco, he's got something for me," Jorge said and bit his lower lip. "He must mean on this Hail man that showed up at the door."

"It could be about anything," Paige reminded him. "He's always got lots of irons in the fire."

"That's because *I* always have lots of irons in the fire."

Across the room, Makerson started to laugh.

"What's up?" Jorge asked.

"Oh, some nutcase in the comment section," Makerson replied. "Claims she's a psychic and that she senses an 'evil presence' from you."

"You need to be a psychic to see this?" Jorge asked before laughing. "Are the others responding?"

"Some, most are telling her she's crazy and how you've done a lot for the community," Makerson said as he scanned through the comments. "A couple who agree, but that's the same with everyone. You always got lots of opinions on these things."

"I see who you mean," Paige was clicking through a bunch of pages. "She looks like she's pretty established. Maybe Jolene and I should go for a reading sometime soon."

Jorge laughed out loud.

"A lot of people believe that shit," Makerson reminded them. "I'm not saying to take her or her comments too seriously, but it's nice to be aware in case she starts to stir up anything."

Jorge rolled his eyes.

"What? You don't believe in any of this?" Paige asked. "Some people do have the ability."

"It is called common sense," Jorge countered. "It is called being perceptive or a good guesser. But for me, I do not believe in psychics. *Psychos*, now that is another matter."

Paige grinned and shook her head.

"I got a million messages I must follow up on," Jorge said as he tapped on his phone. "I must see Marco first. Everything else, it can wait."

"So, to the office?" Paige asked as she closed her laptop.

"I believe so," Jorge replied and looked back at Makerson. "We good here?"

"Your interview got a ton of attention, and you broke a story," Makerson nodded. "It's a good day."

"For you, maybe," Jorge insisted. "For the police? Not so much."

CHAPTER

20

"Lady, up until recently, I was the CEO of this here company," Jorge ranted to the new receptionist at the Our House of Pot office. Paige stood behind him grinning, as she watched her husband attempt to explain who he was to the older woman. "Diego, he took over, but this is *still* very much my company."

"But you aren't listed as someone who is allowed in the office," She reaffirmed, standing her ground. "I don't understand why you even have a pass to get in and…

Before she had time to finish her sentence, Diego flew out of his office and down the hallway. His eyes blazing, he glared at the new receptionist.

"What the hell is going on here?" He snapped at the older lady while Jorge watched with an amused expression on his face. "This is the founder of the company you work for, so you might want to learn his name!"

"But you said that only people…"

"I know what I said," Diego cut her off as he dramatically swung his arms in the air. "But I figured you'd at least know the company founder. It's not like he's *not* in the news all the time."

"In fairness," Jorge smoothly added. "Not all the time, but I was today."

Diego appeared to calm down, twisting his lips together as if in thought.

"I will add him to the list," The receptionist attempted to calm Diego. "But really, you should've told me this in the first place. How was I supposed to know that he didn't leave the company on bad terms? Maybe there's a reason why he wasn't on the list. I don't know."

Diego glared at her, swung on his heels, and headed toward the empty boardroom. Jorge gave the receptionist a shrug before following his *hermano,* while Paige silently followed them both. Once behind closed doors, Diego erupted again.

"I can't believe I even had to add you to the list," He ranted. "How the fuck does she not know…"

"Diego, this here, leave it," Jorge suggested as he found his way to his usual seat. "It does not bother me."

"Really?" Paige quietly asked as she sat beside him. "It sure seemed that way."

"At first, but now, it is ok," Jorge shrugged. "Plus, we have other things to discuss."

"Chase should be here soon," Diego glanced toward the door just as Marco entered the room. "Jolene is too busy torturing the film crew. You know, they're gonna quit on you if she's on their ass all the time."

"I already spoke to her about it."

"Like that fucking matters," Diego shook his head and glanced at Marco, who sat across the table from Paige and Jorge.

"She must listen, or I will remove her from the project," Jorge replied with a shrug just as Chase rushed in the room and sat down. "This here, it will be fine."

Diego looked unconvinced.

"So, the interview today," Jorge jumped right in. "It was good. The results they are…mixed but mainly good."

"What's with that psychic?" Chase asked as he pulled his chair in. "I keep seeing she's warning of your 'dark energy', whatever the fuck that means."

Marco rolled his eyes as he tapped on his laptop.

"I do not worry about such things," Jorge shrugged.

"A lot of people listen to psychics," Diego reminded him. "They trust them."

"What does that say about these people?" Jorge countered. "She is another crazy."

"We'll keep an eye on her," Paige gently added. "I don't see it being much of an issue if any."

"Superstitious nonsense," Jorge shrugged. "Now, as I said, the interview, it went well. The police, they must watch their step, or they may end up in this series too."

"This man, sir," Marco jumped in. "Mark Hail, he is new to the department, sir."

"Is that so?" Jorge showed some interest. "Fresh off the lot?"

"He's fresh, sir," Marco nodded. "And from what I managed to find, he is not liked by the others. They tend to ostracize him."

"What the fuck?" Chase asked as he turned toward Marco. "This sounds like high school."

"And they," Jorge pointed toward Marco's laptop. "Are a bunch of teenaged girls."

Marco grinned and nodded.

"Sir, for the police," He closed his eyes for a second and shook his head. "There are a lot of nonsense texts and emails between them. It would seem that they like to bully this man. It is a power game, I believe."

"Is that so?"

"I do not know why," Marco continued. "But he has reported numerous incidents where they have....performed cruel jokes on him, put him in bad situations..."

"Like sending him to the door of the most dangerous man in the city?" Diego added as he glanced at Jorge.

"At 7 a.m," Paige added. "They wanted to taunt you, but not get in your crosshairs."

"So they sent him," Chase suggested as he pushed up his shirt sleeves. "Because they want you to make his life hell."

"Very interesting," Jorge nodded. "But it seems like a valuable piece of information because, of course, they will send him to my door again, and *of course,* now that I know what I'm working with, I can perhaps reel him in."

"I always enjoy a good underdog story," Paige calmly threw in. "This sounds like it might get interesting."

"He maybe won't mind fucking over these guys," Chase suggested. "Depending on what they did."

"Oh, they did plenty!" Marco's eyes widen as he tapped on his keyboard, suddenly stopping. "They put things in his locker...shit, used condoms..."

"What the fuck?" Diego cut in. "Is this a college fraternity or a police department?"

"Contrary to what people think, Diego," Jorge turned toward his friend. "They are *not* the city's finest and brightest."

"It seems," Marco added. "It is just for this man, this Mark Hail because I do not see any other issues with bullying...now, the RCMP is another story."

"Oh, yeah, there's been huge complaints with them," Paige nodded. "Especially by women."

"It seems that Mark Hail is the local police's version of a woman," Jorge suggested. "This here, it is valuable, thank you, Marco."

"I have more sir," He looked up from his laptop. "The police, they hardly have anything on file for the Maxwell case."

"An inside job?" Paige asked.

"I do not know," Marco shook his head. "But the information I was able to locate, it was very vague. It does not seem like they are putting much effort into the case."

"Gee, I wonder why," Diego rolled his eyes.

"They have to have something," Chase reminded them. "Or it looks suspicious."

"I think they are trying to suggest that it was random," Marco wrinkled his forehead. "The notes on the case are strange, not clear. Just details on how they found him, that kind of thing."

"Where did it happen again?" Paige asked.

"At his house," Marco replied. "I think they are trying to make it seem like it was a random break-in."

"No wife, family?" Chase asked.

"Not home at the time," Marco shook his head. "Just him, dead."

"It is what it is," Jorge replied. "Anything else?"

"Not for me, sir," Marco shook his head. "I am continuing to look into everything, but so far, that is all."

"I'm still not crazy on the idea of attacking the police," Diego jumped in. "We don't need these fucks at the door. I don't want them at *mine.*"

"That makes two of us," Chase replied.

"I'm just the IT guy," Marco put both his hands in the air, causing them to laugh.

"They don't want any of you. They want me," Jorge insisted. "They got nothing anyway."

"They're the police," Diego complained. "Who knows what they will *find* if they take the notion."

"Let us not make new problems," Jorge reminded them. "So far, they have only directed their attention at me. We have no reason to think this will change."

"Let's hope it stays that way," Diego sniffed.

"Do not worry," Jorge insisted. "I am told, however, that many leads are coming in for the series. We are not sure all are valid, but this here, it will make the police even more jittery."

"And you think that's a good thing?" Diego asked. "They're going to get pissed and come after us."

"Or they will see that coming after us," Jorge shook his head. "Is never a good idea. You must understand the long-term goal. This here, it is exactly like Big Pharma, and now, they know their place. Soon, the police will too."

"They never bothered us before," Diego reminded him.

"This will reassure that they never do again," Jorge added. "Trust me. This is important as we move into the future."

"Sir," Marco cut in as he glanced down at his screen. "There is one more thing. I forgot to mention about the police. Sir, they see the Maxwell situation as a way to remove attention from the Alwood case. People are distracted and also, one policeman, he suggested that maybe they..... 'will think he was Maxwell's murderer since there was a lot of bad blood between them'."

Marco looked up just as Jorge exchanged looks with the others.

"We don't gotta eat the rich before the rich eat us," Jorge said with laughter in his voice. "Because in the end, they're too busy eating each other."

CHAPTER

21

Jorge's final words at the meeting continued to flow through Chase's mind long into the day. Something was fascinating about a group of people of the same status fighting amongst themselves, attacking one another, that intrigued him. You didn't have to get your hands dirty if the animals were sinking their teeth into each other, but sit back and watch. It was a card worth playing.

Jorge Hernandez already knew this. He knew the many ways to create a war and win. Chase was merely a student, always rushing to catch up to the others.

Alone at the bar, he enjoyed the peacefulness. Long before his employees arrived, Chase was able to do his work without distraction. Except for the occasional text.

Can I come to see you?

Making a face, Chase wasn't sure if he should answer this message. He finally did.

Maria, aren't you supposed to be in school?

Yeah, I'm here but I can leave.

Stay in school.

But it's important. I can't ask you about this over the phone.

Chase tossed his phone on the desk and ran a hand over his face. As much as he wanted to help Maria if she was in trouble, he also wouldn't hide anything from her father. She often put him in a difficult position. Thinking for a moment, he picked up the phone.

Maria, if it is important, come here after school. Who's picking you up?

Juliana.

Have her bring you here before you go home.

See you then.

Satisfied that he had handled this well, Chase attempted to go back to work, but his phone beeped again.

We will meet at the usual place tonight. Same time.

Chase didn't answer. He sat the phone aside.

Jorge had given him a strict warning to avoid the group he had joined in good faith, assuming that they were out to help a cause close to his heart. Instead, he had naively got involved with an extremist group that was attempting to groom him into becoming one of their fall guys. At least, that's what he discovered after the fact. Jorge had warned him, but Marco had filled him in on the details. He had immediately cut all ties, but they still had his number.

He would block them.

But for some reason, something held him back.

His body became aroused as he thought back to the encounters with the young woman who was passionately involved in the group. She insisted they not share names even though they had a physical relationship that followed each meeting, fast and furious sex, in his car, in a bathroom, one time at her dumpy little apartment. She was an animal, full of lust, wanting more and more until it seemed like an addiction more than for pleasure.

He thought of the last time they were together. Just when he was on the edge when she whispered in his ear...

"Fuck!" He said out loud, bringing his hand down hard on the desk. Embarrassed by his naivety, once again, he realized that this had been part of the game. This was the way to pull him in to do their dirty work. How had he been so fucking stupid?

Grabbing the phone again, he abruptly blocked the number and tossed it aside.

Had Jorge recognized his stupidity? Did the entire group? Even years later, he was still the dumb, small-town country boy, unable to recognize when he was being manipulated. It was as if he had learned nothing since living in Hennessey, married to Audrey, and controlled by his mother. Even with everything that had happened since it was as if nothing changed at all.

His phone beeped again.

I'm here.

It was Maria.

Here?? Now? You're supposed to be in school.

Rather than wait for her answer, he jumped out of his chair and headed for the main door, where he found Maria waiting on the other side. Glancing over her shoulder, he noted that Juliana was in her car. She gave him a quick wave, which Chase self-consciously returned. He would have to make sure Jorge knew about this visit from her because he was sure the nanny reported everything back.

"I said after school…" Chase calmly reminded her as she walked into the bar.

"School ended early today," She insisted as she headed toward his office.

Locking the door behind her, he was skeptical but didn't reply.

"You don't believe me, do you?" Maria said as he followed her. "But we had a short day, so I asked if I could come here on the way home to discuss my project. Remember, for when I someday own *this* place?"

Dramatically waving her hand in the air to indicate the bar, she entered Chase's office and plunked down in the chair on the other side of the desk. He sat in his usual spot.

"So you told Juliana that's why you're here?" Chase asked, and she nodded. "Is that the *real* reason?"

"Of course not," Maria shook her head and sat up straighter. She crossed her legs and carefully fixed her uniform skirt as if attempting to present herself in a more mature light. "I'm not going to tell *her* the truth."

"Which is?"

"I want to learn how to shoot a gun?"

"And so you come to *me*?"

"No one else will teach me," Maria attempted to explain. "I've asked *Papa* but he says no. Paige said no. Diego said no. Juliana said no…"

"You asked all these people to teach you how to use a gun?" Chase was slightly stunned. "Maria, you're only.."

"I know," She waved a hand in the air as if he was speaking foolishly. "But I'm *Mexican*. There are kids back in Mexico that can shoot a gun long before my age, and let's face it, I'm part of a crime family."

Chase sat back in stunned disbelief. She knew too much.

"So it only makes sense," Maria continued. "What if someone broke in our house or something happened that…"

"Maria, someone is always around," Chase reminded her. "Your parents or..."

"But not always," She countered. "And we can't count on them always being there. What if something happened? I need to protect myself. It's not like I'd take a gun to school and shoot my enemies. I need this to protect my family."

"Maria, you're 13."

"*Almost* 14," She reminded him. "If I'm old enough to work here this summer, I'm old enough to learn how to use a gun."

He was starting to dread that already. Not that he didn't adore Maria, but he envisioned many similar conversations to what they were having now. It was a hard tightrope to walk.

"Ok, look," Chase attempted to get a grip on things. "Even if I wanted to teach you how to shoot, which I would *never* do without your father's permission, I wouldn't be the best person. I'm not good at it either."

"Is that because of your son," Maria asked gently. "That was shot?"

Chase took a deep breath. It was still like a knife in his chest, regardless of how many years passed. He glanced at a framed photo of his three sons on his desk briefly before meeting Maria's eyes.

"It's complicated."

"But if anything," She insisted. "That should make you want to know how to use a gun *more*. What if you ever needed to protect people you care about?"

Chase had a quick memory flash of him strangling Alwood after Diego hit him with a baseball bat only a few weeks earlier. Looking into Maria's innocent eyes, he merely shook his head.

"There are always other ways."

"I want to learn them too."

"Maria," Chase shook his head. "You got to let this go for now. You're too young. This isn't my decision to make. It's your father's."

"You're scared to go against him?" Maria asked and tilted his head.

"I respect his decision," Chase spoke curtly this time. "And you should too. He's a smart man. He hasn't got where he is by being dumb."

"As the leader of a crime family..."

"Maria, he owns a company," Chase attempted to divert her line of thinking.

"Chase, I *know* what my father is," Maria corrected him. "I'm not dumb."

"You're smarter than me, Maria," Chase insisted. "Because if I were your age, I probably wouldn't see that."

"I've seen a *lot.*"

Chase looked away. She saw much more than he'd ever want his children to see. For that reason, he was glad they were back in Alberta. Although he missed them, they were safer.

"You have," Chase agreed. "I will give you that, but that doesn't mean you have to learn how to shoot a gun. What about your self-defense?"

"I'm not good at it," She referred to the Brazilian jiu-jitsu that she had started but never really fell in love with like everyone had hoped. "I think I need to learn something else."

"I promise you," Chase leaned forward on the desk. "That every line of defense you can get is important. A gun won't solve all your problems and it won't always be what saves you. Do you understand?"

She took his words in and her face grew serious.

"Maria, if I've learned anything, it's that being smart is the most important defense you can have," Chase attempted to explain. "Guns, weapons, they're great if you know how to use them properly, but it's going to be your brain that keeps you safe and protects you...much more than any weapon."

Maria didn't respond.

CHAPTER

22

"When did this here become *news*?" Jorge abruptly gestured toward his laptop while Paige attempted to feed Miguel at the end of the table. The child was throwing pieces of cereal on the floor and laughing each time she had to pick it up. "A fucking *psychic* says something, and now it is *trending* on Twitter. Are you fucking kidding me right now!"

"Jorge!" Paige cut him off as she finally gave up picking the cereal off the floor and gave Miguel a warning look. "Please, I don't want the baby walking around the house *swearing*. He's at an impressionable age."

"Paige, he is not paying attention," Jorge shook his head and gestured at the laptop again. "This here is unbelievable to me."

Footsteps could be heard on the stairs just as Jorge's phone beeped.

It was Diego.

Did you see Twitter today?

Jorge was too irritated to answer.

"*Papa*," Maria spoke with excitement in her voice as she entered the room. "Did you see you were trending on Twitter? Like, this is so crazy! Who is this psychic? Like, why does she hate you?"

"Maria, I do not know who *Madame Anika* is or why she makes these comments here about me," Jorge attempted to calm himself. "But she is, of course, wrong."

Maria took out her phone as she dropped her book bag in the middle of the kitchen floor. Her fingers tapped on the screen as she made her way to the coffee pot. Paige and Jorge exchanged looks.

"Maria," Paige began. "Sometimes, people will make up stuff *just* to get attention."

"Yes, because her business, it is probably a failure," Jorge joined in. "But for me? I think it is nonsense. I cannot believe the people believe in this psychic bullshit."

"*Papa,*" Maria began as if she weren't listening at all. "She says you're a very 'dark' person and that the world should fear you. That she thinks you're dangerous and a psychopath…."

"I should sue the bitch."

"Jorge," Paige muttered and glanced down at Miguel, who was listening to his father with fascination.

"This here is crazy," Jorge insisted. "The fact that anyone believes this, it does say something about them as well."

His phone rang. It was Diego.

"Yes, Diego, I know all about it," Jorge immediately snapped into the phone. "I see the comments."

"I'm coming over."

Jorge slid the phone into his pocket and sighed loudly.

"This here, I do not have time for," He rose from his chair and headed toward the door, opening it before his neighbor had a chance to knock.

Without saying a word, Jorge pointed toward his office, and the two men made their way there. Neither spoke until they were inside the room, the door closed, phones turned off.

"We gotta take care of her," Diego insisted as they both made their way toward the desk. "This stuff freaks me the fuck out."

"I know, Diego, but…"

"She's trouble, and I *knew* it as soon as…."

"Yes, Diego, we agree here," Jorge insisted as he raised his hand in the air before sitting behind the desk. "This is too much."

"Do you think it's for real….you know, the psychic thing?" Diego lowered his voice as if it were a secret. "Because if that's the case…"

"If that is the case," Jorge insisted. "Then, she'd also know to keep her fucking mouth shut."

Satisfied, Diego nodded.

"Now, the question isn't *if* we are doing it, but how," Jorge continued. "We could attempt to make it seem like she's crazy, but we both know that this won't stop her from talking and from other, equally stupid people from listening."

"I know. Did you see some of the comments on here," Diego pointed toward his lifeless phone. "People are agreeing, and it's building up steam. What if someone is behind this, telling her to say this shit?"

Jorge considered the idea.

"This here, it is possible."

"I will get Marco on it. See if someone is paying her to say this shit."

"That you should do," Jorge nodded. "I do not have time to deal with this today because I have too many other things."

"Maybe we get Marco to pop up in the fake accounts opposing her," Diego suggested. "See where it takes us."

"In the end, Diego, this woman must die," Jorge confirmed. "I am not playing around with any of this here. It is important to take care of matters before they get out of hand. In this case, we might get Paige and Jolene to go for a reading....then again, perhaps I will visit her myself. We shall see. Either way, she is finished."

Diego nodded and didn't reply.

"Now, we have other matters to deal with," Jorge continued. "First of all, as *I* predicted, they are trying to say that Alwood murdered Maxwell. Which means that one of their own took care of him....this here, Marco came to me with last night, so we plan to find a place nearby to leave Alwood's gun."

"Yeah, but why you helping them?" Diego was confused. "Why not let them squirm."

"Because Diego, I do not wish them to come after me for this one," Jorge replied. "Me, I can handle them, but I don't got the time. Now, if this case is tied up neatly for them, they assume Alwood is still alive and go on a very public, wild goose chase for him. It will only make it easier to make fools out of them in my series."

Diego grinned.

"Which reminds me, I must meet with Tony to discuss everything," Jorge continued. "The first episode, it is almost finished. He wants me to see some of the clips and get my approval, my thoughts."

"You know, if the police start being a pain in the ass," Diego sat up straighter and leaned forward. "We can always have Andrew address how they're putting all their resources in one direction on his channel."

Diego referred to the YouTube channel where Andrew supposedly worked on topics independent of the series but usually instead helped to gain momentum from potential viewers. It proved helpful with the first season of *Eat the Rich Before the Rich Eat You.*

"This here is a good idea," Jorge nodded. "Maybe he should do an episode on fake psychics while he's at it...."

Diego rolled his eyes and shook his head.

"The fact that I've dealt with psychopaths and savages over the years," Jorge shook his head as he slowly rose from his chair. "That I now deal with this, it is unbelievable to me."

"Well, according to her," Diego followed his lead and rose from the chair. He reached for his phone. "*You're* one of those psychopaths and savages."

Jorge merely shrugged, uninterested, and the two men headed for the door.

"I'm going to the office to talk to Marco about this," Diego reaffirmed. "What about Chase?"

"I have to go talk to him later anyway," Jorge shook his head. "I found out that Maria, she went to the bar to see him the other day to ask if he would teach her how to shoot."

"Yeah, I know, she asked me too," Diego admitted as he reached for the doorknob. "I told her no. I was gonna tell you, but I figured you'd lose your shit."

"Yes, well, tell me anyway," Jorge spoke firmly. "I have to know these things. I must talk to her again. I think maybe Chase got through to her, but this obsession has to stop. I cannot deal with this right now."

"She means well...."

"Look, I never wanted my kids into this," Jorge reminded Diego.

"She might have to learn eventually," Diego reminded him as he started to turn the doorknob. "I know that's not what you want to hear..."

A knock at the door interrupted their conversation. Diego pulled the door opened to see Paige on the other side, holding Miguel, who was playing with her hair.

"That cop is back," She spoke in a low, calm voice. "And you better come see what he wants before your daughter talks his head off."

"Oh fuck," Jorge said under his breath. "This here is all I need."

The three of them headed toward the living room, but already, he could hear Maria rattling on to him.

"....and so that seems like it would be a smart idea," She was speaking in her adult voice.

"It does seem like a good idea," Mark Hail was calmly replying. "But the police can't make those kinds of decisions. I do appreciate your concern, but..."

"Concern about what?" Jorge sharply cut him off. "Are you here interrogating my 13-year-old daughter now?"

"No," Hail immediately turned his attention toward Jorge. "She was suggesting how to help the homeless...."

"I told him they should be nicer to the homeless," Maria cut him off. "I heard they are really mean to them, but if they gave them a place to stay, they would be helping them and taking care of the problem. It's so simple! In the summer when there's no school, let them stay at the schools or like kid's camps in the winter or something...like why are they mean?"

"Maria, we aren't mean, but..." Hail attempted to explain.

"This here, we do not have time for," Jorge pointed toward the window. "Maria, you have to get to school. Juliana is waiting for you outside." He turned toward Hail. "Me? I got things to do so, what you want now?"

"*Papa,* maybe he believes that weird psychic...you know," Maria reached for her book bag. "Some people do."

"This has nothing to do with that," Hail insisted. "I wanted to talk to your father about...an ongoing case."

Maria looked ill.

"There you go, scaring my child again," Jorge gestured toward Maria as he exchanged looks with his wife.

"Maria, it's not like that," Paige attempted to explain.

"It's fine," Hail jumped in. "I...I wanted to come here to follow up on a case that's since has been resolved."

Jorge nodded toward his daughter.

"Ok," She spoke in a shy little voice that broke his heart. The two made eye contact, and she rushed back to give him a quick hug before heading toward the door.

Without saying anything, Jorge looked at Hail and pointed toward his office.

CHAPTER

23

"So this here," Jorge immediately pointed toward his office door after it was closed. "It is not happening again. I do *not* want you scaring my children over this nonsense. Do you understand?"

Mark Hail attempted to give Jorge a stern look, but the fear in his eyes was apparent.

"Now, sit the fuck down and tell me what you want," Jorge abruptly pointed toward the chair and went to the other side of his desk. "I do not have time for this bullshit today. I am a busy man. Do the police not have things to do? Arresting little old ladies for driving too slow or kicking some homeless people around? What? Nothing?"

"Mr. Hernandez, I'm not here to scare your children," Hail started to speak slowly, as if it would have a calming effect on Jorge. "I just wanted to tell you that the Maxwell case was resolved. We know you had nothing to do with it, and I wanted to apologize for…I mean, if I gave you any…"

"Is this it?" Jorge cut him off. "You want to tell me that you *now* know that I didn't have anything to do with his murder? This here, I already know."

"But because I was here previously…"

"We did not need a follow-up visit," Jorge reminded him. "This here is why crimes, they are never solved by the local police. You're too busy wasting your time on this stupid shit. I *know* I did not kill this man. It was obviously someone who knew he had a lot to say and wanted to make sure he never had a chance to say it."

Hail nodded.

"Season two of my series, it will be a huge success," Jorge reminded him. "And it is about the police. So, you got anything for me?"

"Anything?"

"Come on, Hail," Jorge shook his head. "You are not here for this reason you say. What is really going on? Will I find a listening device under my desk later? You here thinking you will intimidate me? Or maybe you got some stories to share for my series about how corrupt and stupid the fucking police are? If that's the case, *then* I got time for you."

Hail fell silent.

"You new to this department?"

"Yes, I started in January."

"So they send you here?"

"Yes."

Jorge nodded, and the two men shared a look.

"They send you here because they know I am not an easy man to deal with?"

Hail didn't respond.

"That is what I thought," Jorge relaxed slightly, enjoying his power. "Because maybe, I have a reputation of some kind? Maybe they were talking to their psychic friend who's saying shit about me all over Twitter? Do you think?"

"I think….honestly," Hail stopped abruptly. "It doesn't matter what I think. I actually should go since…"

"Nah nah nah," Jorge wagged his finger. "You come here to take my time, now I take yours. Tell me what you know."

Hail appeared hesitant.

"You got a phone?" Jorge asked.

Hail slowly nodded.

"Turn it off," Jorge instructed, taking out his phone to show he had done the same. "Then we talk."

Hail appeared ill as he did as he was told, gently placing the phone on the desk.

"Now, let me be very clear about something," Jorge started. "I do not know you, and I have no reason to trust you. And you, you don't know me and have no reason to trust me. But I know one thing, it is that *they* do not want to be in my crosshairs. So, if they send you, that tells me you are in a weak position, and no man wants to be in a weak position."

Hail didn't say a thing but listened.

"Why do you want to be a cop?"

"To protect people. To make them feel safe."

"And how is that working out?"

He didn't respond.

"That's what I thought."

"It's...not quite as I thought it would be."

"You know something," Jorge leaned back in his chair, enjoying the smell of fear in the room. "Back in Mexico, I had a very....productive relationship with the police. I helped them. They helped me. It was good. Maybe someday, you will be in a position where you need my help."

Hail considered his words and didn't respond.

"The funny thing about life," Jorge continued. "It is a lot like a sport. You know, sometimes, we pick a team because it is the team that our father or friends say is good, but really, we do not know. Maybe it is representing the place they live....I don't know, but after you watch a few games, you decide that this here team, it is not for you. And it is disappointing. And you start to look at another team and think, you know, they are better. More skilled, more prepared, more *powerful*. You do not wish to disappoint your friends and family, so you secretly cheer them on, but no one has to know."

Hail continued to listen.

"I am not sure if this here, it has ever happened to you," Jorge said as he leaned forward on his desk.

Hail looked away.

"That is what I thought," Jorge sat back again. "You know why I am doing this here series? On the police?"

Hail didn't respond but looked into Jorge's eyes.

"Because I have so many stories of the corruption, the fuck ups, the problems within the police departments all over this here country," Jorge replied. "There is a, how you say, a false sense of security and maybe some undeserved respect. We, here in this society, we put certain people on a pedestal that may not always belong there, and you know what Mr. Hail, I have met many of them and I can tell you, for a fact, that every man, no matter how powerful, at some point is caught with his pants down with his dick in his hand."

"We are all...human..."

"Yes, Mr. Hail, we are," Jorge nodded as he saw something change in the cop's eyes. "So, do not ever think that anyone is safe from being pushed off their throne. Except me, of course, because I am not going anywhere."

There was a silent, awkward moment of understanding that flowed through the room as Mark slowly began to nod.

"Do we understand each other?"

"Yes."

"So, tell me," Jorge spoke kindly. "Why are you here?"

Hail hesitated before replying.

"They sent me."

"Why?"

"Exactly what you said," Mark seemed hesitant to continue. "They thought it would be funny, like an...initiation or something. They were counting on you being pissed off. When they found out you were, they sent me back."

"This here, it seems like a very unproductive way to spend your time," Jorge suggested.

Hail bit his lip before continuing.

"They want me out."

"Why?"

"When I first started," Hail hesitated before continuing. "A woman I work with was being harassed by the male officers and I said something..."

Jorge nodded in understanding.

"I got the pushback," Hail continued. "She's out on stress leave. Some of the guys are being investigated."

"And you're being shit on..."

"Literally," Hail nodded. "It's been found in my locker."

"Ahh...such class from the police," Jorge shook his head. "Plus, you are not a white boy..."

"I'm half Japanese, half black..."

"In a white department," Jorge finished his sentence.

"I didn't think it would be a problem..."

"Think again," Jorge reminded him. "This here, it may be a multicultural country, but it is just lip service to some."

Hail appeared relieved and slightly more at ease.

"So," Jorge thought for a moment. "What you need, *amigo,* is someone in your corner, just as you were in that lady's corner when she complained."

"As I said, they want me out."

"You and I, we can work together," Jorge insisted. "But, you must pretend you are still rooting for the same team."

Hail nodded.

"You go back there," Jorge gestured toward the window. "And you tell them I told you to fuck off and get out of my house. You tell them that you thought I had a gun on me but weren't sure. You tell them that I repeated your name and said, "I will remember this conversation". Then you tell me what you need, and I will take care of it."

"The woman....that was being harassed..."

"She can talk with the man who is behind my series," Jorge replied. "We will put this on the forefront, and it will *have* to be dealt with, or the department will look like a piece of shit. What else?"

"I...I...maybe...wait, what are you going to do?"

"I can do whatever you want," Jorge replied as he stared at Hail.

"I want them to stop fucking with me."

"I can, but you know, then they might know you are rooting for a different team, and we can't have that," Jorge reminded him. "But I am thinking, that if these men might talk less if they have someone threaten to rip their tongues out. I also think that men who have broken limbs might need time away from work. I have a lot of thoughts, and they can go much darker, Mr. Hail."

He nodded in understanding.

"Leave me some names," Jorge instructed. "And I will take care of it."

"But...what...what do you want in return."

A grin curved Jorge's lips, but he didn't reply.

CHAPTER

24

"I'm going to slit her fucking throat," Jorge announced before the group even had time to sit around the table in the club's VIP room. Infuriated by recent events, the group's leader exploded when he saw that morning's headlines in *Toronto AM*'s top competitor. "Where the fuck is Makerson?"

"He's on his way, sir," Marco spoke calmly with worry in his eye. "I sent him a message, and he said he'd be here as soon as possible."

"This isn't his fault," Diego reminded him as he sat in his usual spot at the table. "It's not like anyone foreseen this *wacko* making the *real* news."

"She's a fucking psychic!" Chase jumped in as he sat across from Paige, who was shaking her head. "Why is this news?"

"Because this here," Jorge pointed at that morning's paper placed in the middle of the table. "Is news today. Nonsense and gossip. The world has gone mad."

"Or stupid," Chase threw in. "It feels like a reality show that never ends."

"Keep them dumb..." Paige muttered under her breath.

"Well, that there, *mi amor,* is hardly difficult," Jorge reminded her. "It is not like the people had far to fall."

A knock at the back door interrupted their conversation. It was Jolene.

"I thought it was Makerson," Jorge complained, still furious by the morning headlines.

"Sorry to disappoint!" Jolene snapped as she sat down. "Be happy I am here at all. We are very busy with the series, you know."

"And you're working *with* them," Jorge reminded her. "Not trying to supervise anymore."

"I cannot help," She quickly defended herself, waving her arm in the air. "It is my way."

Diego rolled his eyes.

Another knock cut Jorge off before he was able to speak. It was Makerson.

"Good! We can start," Jorge pointed toward an empty seat at the table. "Please sit down."

"Look," Makerson pointed toward the newspaper in the middle of the table. "I have no idea how this became front-page news, but it shows how unprofessional they are over there," He shook his head. "I can counteract."

"Is that going to help, though?" Paige asked with a shrug. "Aren't we feeding the fire that way?"

"Perhaps," Makerson reached for the newspaper and studied it for a moment. "I can't believe that they are using a *psychic's* recommendation to write this story on. It's beyond absurd."

"You could do a live stream saying that," Chase suggested. "Talk about how ridiculous she is."

"Sir, I did find some information on her," Marco quickly reminded him. "She has a bit of a strange history herself."

Jorge bit his lip and thought about what everyone was saying.

"She's trouble," Diego shook his head. "She's got a mouth!"

"How I will handle her," Jorge started as his eyes lit up. "I will deal with later. Right now, I must deal with her words."

"We can easily discredit her," Makerson suggested. "Or the paper. This is essentially clickbait. The article ends with suggesting going to their site for more background."

"I saw your tweet earlier today," Paige commented. "About all this."

"What tweet?" Jolene seemed eager to join the conversation.

"Tom said that….something about the quality of journalism and had an image of the front page…" Paige pointed toward the paper.

"I said that journalism had made a mockery of itself," Makerson shook his head as he threw the newspaper aside. "Because it has."

Jolene reached for the paper and squinted as she read the story in question.

"Famed psychic warns of Hernandez."

"It's not even a good title!" Makerson continued to complain.

"What does this say?" Jolene continued to squint as she read the story. "I do not understand. Is she saying you are choking Toronto? I do not understand."

"Choke*hold*," Chase corrected her. "It means he controls the city."

"It is true," Jolene looked up from the paper. "You control a lot."

"This idiot is trying to say that Jorge has a dark plan to make it into Gotham," Chase shook his head.

"What?" Jolene squinted her eyes. "What is Gotham?"

"From Batman, it symbolizes crime and corruption."

Jolene opened her mouth to say something, but Jorge gave her a warning look, and she stopped.

"It's very unprofessional," Makerson shook his head. "They're trying to validate it by saying that she's been right about several things, but let's face it, we can all predict things that turn out to be right. It's just ludicrous that this became a headlining story."

"But people will believe it," Diego chimed in. "Because they like scandal and drama."

"Not me," Jorge shook his head. "And this here drama ends now. I'm going to go see this fucking psychic and then the editor of this here paper..."

"No," Paige cut him off, gently touching his arm. "We need to focus on counteracting this article. If people think the idea has steam, they will grab onto it, but if it's being mocked, they'll stay away."

"I already have had several accounts mocking her on social media," Marco spoke up. "I was blocked a few times, but I think I got my point across, and more importantly, I think others jumped in to do the same."

"That's what we want," Paige nodded. "We want everyone to jump on the bandwagon, so she is looked at like an idiot."

"How could she be looked at any other way," Makerson shook his head and turned toward Jorge. "How about I challenge her on Twitter to meet with you, face to face, and have a live discussion."

"I will eat her alive."

"That's the point," Makerson raised his eyebrow. "I can do it right now."

"Do it!"

Makerson turned on his phone and began to type.

"Enough of this bullshit," Jorge said. "We got other things to cover."

"The series, we are doing well," Jolene piped up. "The first show is almost ready."

'I keep meaning to drop by, then this other crap comes up," Jorge shook his head and pointed toward the paper. "This here was a waste of too much of my time."

"It was a waste of the time of the person that wrote this crap," Makerson muttered as he tapped on his phone.

"End of the month?" Jorge asked Jolene, who nodded. "Good, the first episode is focused on Alwood and the way the police handled the situation and how he is now missing, and they can't figure out their ass from their elbow."

"Hit me up when it's about to come out," Makerson said as he continued to type. "I'll do a story on it."

"Sir," Marco was next. "I have some information about the police department."

"You," Jorge directed his comment toward Makerson. "You do not hear any of this…at least not yet."

"Not a word," Makerson said as he pushed his chair out. "I gotta make a call to the office. I'll be back shortly."

Once he was out of the room, Jorge turned his attention back to Marco.

"You got something for me?"

"A few things, sir," Marco nodded vigorously while his eyes casually glanced at the paper. "Mark Hail, I think you can trust him. I searched all his personal and work emails, text messages, everything. All he does, sir, is complain about how he is treated at the department, the fact that they are making his life hell. I do not think he has much loyalty to them."

Jorge nodded.

"He recently received a message from a coworker that said, 'Loose lips, sink ships' regarding something he reported on?"

"A woman, she was being harassed by male colleagues," Jorge informed the group. "He reported this, and now, they make him pay."

"Oh," Paige groaned. "Why are we always hearing about women in the police and army who are treated like shit?"

"Because, *mi amor,* these here professions, they attract a certain kind of man."

"Yeah, the kind that wants to push his weight around," Chase complained. "Feel superior."

"They can feel any way they want because they are *not* superior," Jorge insisted. "I will wait and see. But I believe this man, Hail, he will be useful."

"I don't trust the police," Diego shook his head. "I don't give a fuck what's the deal. I don't trust him."

"It will take time," Jorge agreed. "But I believe that Chase, later today, is supposed to take care of the biggest issue Hail has at the department. The man is about to have an accident that will require him to be out for some time."

Chase nodded.

"And once Hail sees that I am here to help him," Jorge continued. "I think we will see him helping us. I also think he will want to be careful. Once I have done something for him, it already seems as though we are working together, no matter if he says otherwise. After all, he comes to see me twice, having conversations with me. He told me about his problems. That is hardly...professional."

"He could try to scam you," Diego reminded him. "Say it was part of the plan."

"Then information leaks that *he* hired someone to attack the man in question," Jorge shrugged. "There is always a way to work these things out."

Diego paused and nodded.

"Trust me," Jorge continued. "This here, it is not my first rodeo."

"Also, sir," Marco continued. "Hail went back to investigate the area where Maxwell was murdered and found Alwood's gun nearby..."

Jorge smirked.

"Another revelation from your meeting?" Diego asked and nodded, looking impressed.

"You might say that," Jorge replied and raised an eyebrow. "We talked about all kinds of things."

"Sir, also, I did not want to say much before Makerson left," Marco continued. "But this psychic, you must wait months to get in for an appointment, but I've also hacked her information, her cameras, her records....she has a lot of traffic violations and insurance claims. Sir, she is a really bad driver."

Jorge raised an eyebrow and nodded. He was about to speak when Makerson returned to the room with a grin on his face.

"She refuses to do the debate saying that she's afraid your 'dark energy' will affect her and her 'special gift' therefore she has to decline," He stopped to laugh. "She's being torn apart on social media."

It would soon be the least of her worries.

CHAPTER

25

"...that's when things got even worse," She shook her head and glanced at Hail, who nodded and looked toward the floor. "It's almost like they couldn't handle a woman questioning their theory and decided they'd put me in my place."

Jorge nodded, showing signs of concern as the young woman continued to talk. Although he was only interested in the docuseries, he knew it was necessary to show compassion for her to share her story. Jorge imaged how he would react if this were Maria talking to him about the same thing. Assuming his daughter would ever work for the police department.

"I see," Jorge spoke gently. "And so, it was a combination of bullying and sexual harassment, you say?"

"I didn't even know about half of it," Hail quickly jumped in, exchanging looks with Jorge then the young woman. "I just heard when he made a very...sexual comment to you. I hadn't realized the extent of this issue."

"It started long before that day," She assured him, and Jorge noted Hail's solemn face and attempted to do the same.

"Well, I assure you," Jorge spoke up with assertion. "This here, it will be exposed in the series, if you are willing to talk. We can hide your face, do whatever...my associate Jolene is on her way here so, you can talk to her more. She's involved in the series."

"Is she the director or something?" The woman stuttered along nervously.

"No, but she is assisting the director and creator of the series," Jorge replied and glanced at the clock. "I thought you might be more comfortable talking to another woman."

The lady nodded and smiled. "Thank you."

"And meanwhile, I believe there are other similar stories to yours," Jorge encouraged. "Tony and his crew have received many emails and contacted women with the same issues as you. Being intimidated, harassed...and so on."

"I do appreciate the chance to speak out," The woman continued. "I don't think I will be able to go back, but when I made a complaint, they came after me."

"That is why no one can know that it was Hail that brought you to me."

"No," She shook her head. "I will say it was my idea. That I heard about this series..."

Jorge nodded in approval.

"I won't say I talked to you either, Mr. Hernandez," She continued to speak with some hesitation, as if nervous. "These men are ruthless. If they come after me, they'll come after you too."

Jorge threw her head back in laughter, causing the woman to jump.

"Lady," Jorge finally contained himself. "*No one* comes after me. No one."

She grinned self-consciously and nodded just as Jorge's phone chimed. It was Jolene.

"I see that my associate Jolene has arrived," Jorge pointed toward her office door. "It will be her you will work with from this point on."

"Thank you," The lady replied as she and Hail both stood up. Jorge remained seated but slowly rose from his chair too. "I do appreciate your help, Mr. Hernandez."

Jorge smiled and followed the two out of his office to meet Jolene in the living room. After making quick introductions, he noted everyone's reaction to each other, gave an apprehensive smile, then found Paige in the kitchen.

"Wonderful," He muttered as he moved close to his wife and glanced toward the living room. "Jolene, she meets Hail, and there's practically a wet spot on the floor after she shakes his hand. I do not need this drama with her."

Paige laughed. "So elegantly put."

"This is all it is with her," He muttered. "Catching a man and running his life."

"I don't think you're giving her credit," Paige glanced toward the living room. "Besides, he's a little on the young side for her."

"Like that matters all of a sudden?" Jorge reminded her. "Remember her and Chase? I do not think that is the only young one she has sunk her claws into either."

"As long as she gets her work done," Paige reminded him. "You want her out of your hair, and having a man around tends to help."

"Yes, but it is the fallout after things go to hell that I do not enjoy."

"True."

"And speaking of wet spots," Jorge muttered as he moved in and grabbed her ass. "I was thinking that after these people leave our house..."

"Latino men, such perverts!" Jolene was speaking in her usual, loud voice as she moved closer to the kitchen. "Can you not keep your hands off her for a second?"

"Jolene, you snuck up on us," Jorge turned around and glared at her, while both Hail and the woman appeared stunned. "This is my wife. This is my house. Of course, I show her affection. Now, do you have things sorted out here?"

"I decided to take her to meet Tony and Andrew before she tells her story," She replied, and Jorge found himself eager for her to leave as he glanced at his wife. "I do not want her to have to repeat it again and again. I think Mark should come too."

Jorge gave her a look and finally decided that if he wanted any time alone with his wife, it was easier not to argue, although long term, he didn't like Jolene hanging around Hail.

Merely shrugging, as if he didn't care, Jorge was relieved when Jolene finally announced they were leaving. The lady thanked Jorge again and then they were gone.

Jorge wasted no time swooping in to grab his wife, both hands on her ass, their lips met, and he automatically felt his hormones surge into overdrive. There was something about the woman's vivid details of sexual harassment that oddly turned him on. He was pulling Paige close, feeling her against his body, when the sound of his phone interrupted them.

"Jesus fucking Christ!" Jorge moved away to grab it. "Can I not have one moment of pleasure in my own house?"

"Like you never have any," Paige teased as she leaned in to read the message on his phone.

Jorge began to laugh.

"*Mi amor,* it looks like I have finally done it. Madame Anika, or whatever the fuck her name is going down," he grinned ear to ear. "She will not recover from this."

"Makerson's article about the decline of fact-based journalism with substance helped," Paige reminded him. "But if you want to prove her wrong, it looks like you did."

"Talk shows, social media, everyone is against her," Jorge grinned. "This cancel culture, it has helped me."

"People are pointing out all you do for immigrants through Our House Of Pot," Paige seemed to stop as he set his phone aside. "No one can deny that you go above and beyond. I mean, you give immigrants jobs and have your HR department help them with questions or whatever they need to adjust to life in Canada. Once people started talking about that, the psychic was out."

"Yes, who knew that a situation that started by making me the asshole," Jorge grinned, pulling her closer. "Would end up with me being a hero. I like that story much better, *mi amor.*"

"So do I...."

With that, Jorge felt pleasure rush through his body as he leaned in to kiss her neck. He heard a soft moan coming from her lips was all the encouragement he needed to move his hand over her hips and between her legs. Thankfully, she was wearing soft pants, which he caressed through. Her breath grew heavier as Jorge moved his lips toward her mouth.

"We should go in the office," She whispered. "It's getting close to the time Maria gets home."

Jorge glanced at his phone and slid it into his pocket.

"Very close, we will need to rush," He pulled her tightly against his groin as anticipation flowed through his body.

"That shouldn't be a problem."

Within minutes, they were behind the locked door of the office, and Paige was riding him on the couch. They could hear the front door opening as Maria arrived home. She was probably looking for them, which only caused a frantic rush as Jorge gasped while Paige attempted to keep quiet. She moved quickly as if trying to get that final release of pleasure, which drove him crazy.

Reaching down to touch herself as she continued to move uninhibitedly, he watched her as she lost control, gasping in pleasure as she pushed harder against him. He finally couldn't hold it together any longer as he felt himself releases all his tension from the last few hours.

Paige moved away, her face red, her body now relaxed, he stared at her, and a thought crossed his mind.

"You know, my fear was Maria would be looking for us," Jorge commented. "But I do not think she even cares that we are here."

"I know," She sighed as she reached for her clothes. "I was rushing before she came to the door and knocked."

"I noticed," Jorge commented. "It made things more...exciting, but, *mi amor,* I had a thought."

"What?"

"Why stop now?"

He moved closer and pulled her body toward his, kissing her again as his hand wandered over her stomach, his fingers caressing her softly, noticing that she was moving slightly to meet them.

"Just because I am done..."

He continued to work as she squirmed in anticipation as his fingers moved inside her. She quickly came undone as she gasped in pleasure. Fascinated by her reaction as she moved, as her head fell back, Jorge couldn't take his eyes off her.

"That was quick," Jorge commented. "Let's see if the next time is as fast..."

CHAPTER

26

"You are talking to someone who once killed a man who said bad things about The Beatles," Jorge reminded Diego later that week as they sat at the bar, while Chase stood nearby observing the two men. "It is not like it is such a stretch to kill this psychic lady too. Her mouth, it was getting a little out of control."

"If you ask me," Diego jumped in as if he only heard half of what Jorge said. "It was the newspaper that went after the story and pushed her to say more. Maybe it was *them* that you should get rid of, not just her."

"Nah, she was saying a lot on her social media too," Chase reminded Diego, who merely shrugged. "It wasn't just that the paper was highlighting the story, she was getting a lot of attention. And the more she got, the more she talked…and you seriously once killed someone who bad-mouthed The Beatles?"

He directed his question at Jorge, who merely raised an eyebrow and grinned.

"Do you think it takes that much?" Diego reminded Chase as he adjusted his tie. "We ain't talking the king of peace."

"In fairness," Jorge interrupted. "There was a whole other situation going on. That was the final straw, but can we get back on topic, please? I know it's not just this lady, but if I have learned anything in this business is that you take care of a little problem before it becomes a big problem, as little problems often do."

Chase nodded in agreement.

"We have seen it," Jorge reminded them both. "She wasn't about to stop plus, this here is a way to warn others that it is not fun to get in my crosshairs. The newspaper will be next."

"What are you going to do?" Diego asked as he leaned in closer to Jorge, his breath smelling of tequila. "Blow it up?"

"I'm gonna buy it."

"Buy it?" Chase made a face. "How will Makerson feel about you buying his competitor?"

"I'm gonna buy it to shut it down," Jorge continued. "It eliminates the competition, plus I want to start a media company, so some will stay for that, some will leave..."

"Hold up, a media company?" Diego repeated. "Don't you have enough on your plate?"

"I'm not going to run it, Diego," Jorge reminded him. "But I am already working on a docuseries. It only makes sense that I continue my work, expand it with the same messages that I put out there now. There's a huge demand for entertainment online, all these streaming sites. I'm getting in on the action. I will find more Tonys to work on their projects, but there must be an underlying message that I approve of."

"Like?" Chase was intrigued.

"Like," Jorge replied. "Well, let's just say, we will not be showcasing pro-police dramas and anything that says that Big Oil and Big Pharma are the heroes if you know what I mean."

"That seems like a big project...." Diego seemed hesitant.

"First thing first," Jorge jumped in. "I buy the paper, and considering it is worthless, I can get it for next to nothing. They're practically giving it away. It has become a gossip paper anyway, no real news. So I take hold, move people that are useful to Makerson's paper, or keep them there for my media company. The man who decided that they run a front-page article about a fucking psychic prediction, for example, he is done."

Diego grinned and nodded.

"I like that you aren't firing everyone," Chase spoke with approval in his voice. "Cause that would be a dick move."

"Exactly, the opposite of the public profile I want."

"You are a clever one, Hernandez," Diego smirked. "Very clever."

"You do realize that Maria will lose her shit when she finds out," Chase reminded him. "She won't be interested in the bar any longer..."

"Well, she might when I tell her that this will be the place that stars will hang out, where we have parties to celebrate our accomplishments, and so on..."

Chase nodded, appearing impressed.

"You do think of everything," Diego threw in. "I gotta hand it to you, this all makes sense."

"Me, I think so," Jorge agreed. "The world is changing, and we must change with it. There is no reason why Canada, or Toronto, cannot have an entertainment industry that stands out in the world. What we have now is limited, and so we must expand. I think that when I do announce this, it will create a lot of excitement."

"And if you need special permits..."

"I got friends in government who will help me out," Jorge spoke confidently. "And friends in media to help get my projects out there. See, it's nice when you have friends in many places."

"We all work together," Diego nodded with a grin on his face.

"We all work together," Jorge repeated and nodded. "Trust me, I have been thinking about this for a long time, but when the opportunity arose, I took it. It's always about taking the opportunity when it comes along. Too often, we are focused on other things and miss what is going on in front of our eyes. Me? I try to pay attention and consider how a specific opportunity will help me."

"So, a mouthy psychic ended up helping you?" Chase laughed. "Only Jorge Hernandez could see that angle."

"It is just me," Jorge reminded him. "But I do believe that it does help to stand back and observe at times, rather than get overly caught up in the moment."

"That will be the next thing," Diego laughed. "Jorge, the self-help guru, selling seats for $1000 a pop."

"No, I will leave the self-help to my wife," Jorge referred to the online business Paige had when he first met her: or more appropriately, the front for the money she made as an assassin. "But you know, there is no limit to the amount of money those places can take in. All you got to say is that you are 'advising' someone, that you are 'counseling' someone as a life coach or whatever. It is quite clever."

"And it's the same," Diego jumped in. "Most of those people, they say the same thing. They aren't exactly original."

"In fairness," Chase added. "Some are good, but there are a lot that creates hope that falls flat."

"Many fall flat," Jorge insisted. "But my wife, she knew what to say and how to say it. And really, that is all you need. It did not matter anyway. She just had to find a way to move money through legally so that the government kept the fuck away."

"They keep away now," Chase replied. "As long as you keep Athas in there..."

"If it is not Athas, it will be another," Jorge seemed unconcerned. "He is doing fine, though. He may help me move this sale along quicker, which is what I wish for. Plus, he may change some rules regarding the police that may not be popular."

"Like what?" Diego asked.

"I haven't decided yet," Jorge replied and reached for that day's copy of *Toronto AM*, which included a story about the death of a local psychic. "But I will say, it is impressive that this woman here was able to predict her death."

The other men automatically started to laugh, knowing that Marco had hacked her account. He posted on her social media accounts that 'dark times' were in her future, and she felt that it was time to keep a low-profile and meditate, but would return in a few weeks. She died in an accident shortly after this announcement.

"It is, as you say, essential to keep up the maintenance of your car," Jorge dropped the newspaper back on the bar. "It is good that Marco collected these messages between her and her mechanic. It gave us what we needed to move things along and make it simple, make it easy. Sometimes, it is good to keep the blood off your hands."

"There are some rumors on the internet that she feared her death was coming," Chase reminded him with a smirk on his face.

"That is all we need," Jorge replied. "Those who wish to cross me make the connection, and certainly, no other psychic will put their ass on the line if they *see* something in the future."

"This psychic shit is complete garbage," Diego grumbled. "I can't believe people believe any of it."

"Bad experience with a psychic, Diego?" Chase asked with a humored expression on his face.

"You might say that," Diego nodded but remained closed-lipped. "They say what you want to hear."

"That is how they make their money, no?" Jorge shrugged. "It is for entertainment only."

"Another online business that would be easy to run as a front," Chase suggested.

"Do not think it has not happened," Jorge replied as he rose from the barstool, grabbing his drink, he knocked it back. "I have a meeting with Tony. I keep trying to connect with him, but one of us always is too busy. Plus, I wish to tell him about my plans to buy the newspaper and see what he thinks."

"He could have a real office then..."

"He could now, but he likes to keep his cards close to his chest," Jorge reminded them. "And close to home."

"He might feel a little differently once you get this place."

"There is some time yet, but I am hoping," Jorge reached for his phone and glanced at the messages. "A new studio, a new office, what more could he want?"

No one replied as Jorge headed for the door.

"Don't forget to tell Maria," Chase reminded him.

"Not yet," Jorge shook his head. "It is a secret for now. My daughter, she does not keep secrets well."

"She's already talking about working here this summer," Chase directed his comment more at Diego than Jorge, who was now at the door. "I have to figure that out...."

"Three days a week, three hours at a time," Jorge said as he reached for the doorknob. "But it is barely May. Let us not jump the gun yet."

With that, he was out the door and on to his next meeting. He had no idea what was around the corner.

CHAPTER

27

"She died in her vulva," Jolene spoke loudly as she glanced at the newspaper, while the three men attempted to hide their amusement. Noting the awkwardness, she rushed to explain herself. "The psychic? She die in her car? It was a vulva?"

"*Volvo*," Tony calmly corrected her even though he appeared more frustrated than humored. "Not vulva."

"That is what I say," Jolene snapped. "I do not understand."

"A *Volvo* is a car," Tony spoke in a condescending tone. "A vulva is.."

"A lady part," Andrew abruptly cut in. "And you probably don't got one."

This caused Jorge to laugh and shake his head.

"What? I do not understand…" Jolene appeared confused. "A vulva, it is a car…"

"Ok, this here, we don't have time for," Jorge cut into the conversation. "I got a lot to do today, so can we get right to business."

Jolene continued to look confused as if she appeared to be figuring out something, which Jorge ignored.

"As I was saying, the psychic, she is no longer a problem," Jorge continued his original thought. "She had an accident and now, for this reason, and this here…it must be a secret for now…"

Everyone gave him their full attention and remained quiet.

"I am buying out the paper that printed this story, shutting it down and starting a media company."

"All at once?" Andrew asked. "Wow."

"No, it will be a process," Jorge continued. "The point is that we will have a place where this and other docuseries, shows can be created. There is a huge demand right now for programs, and why not us? Why not in Toronto? I think we have a lot of advantages that other places do not. And I plan to run with it."

"Lots of talent here," Tony nodded as he took the idea in. "I can see it."

"Of course, we here, we will not be producing Disney shows, if you know what I mean," Jorge reminded them. "But this is the future, for now, we must focus on the series."

"The first one is ready to drop….very soon," Tony nodded. *"All About Alwood.* Should make for an interesting program, especially since he hasn't been out of the media since his disappearance."

"I like the footage you sent me," Jorge nodded.

"That guy was shady as fuck," Andrew threw in. "Like, we didn't have to dig too far to find all this shit on him. Not a well-liked guy."

"From day one, he was a dick," Tony added. "And it's still a hot topic, so it's a good first show. The second one with that lady about the harassment, man, we got so many other women talking."

"It's where chauvinists and white supremacists go to shine," Andrew threw in. "They become a cop."

"Yeah, the white supremacists' show is coming up too," Tony nodded. "We're finding lots of those stories."

"Sounds like you got it under control," Jorge said and glanced at Jolene who had been oddly quiet throughout the meeting. "You got anything before I leave?"

"Me, I think we are going to piss off the police and they will come after us," She spoke candidly.

"Do I look worried?" Jorge countered and turned toward the other two. "Anything else?"

"Actually, there is," Tony chimed in. "Look, you can say no to this, but I'm thinking about ending this season with an episode on victims who never received justice due to the police not taking the proper steps in an investigation. I want to make it personal by telling my mom's story."

Jorge thought for a moment and nodded.

"And specifically," Andrew jumped in. "How the cops did fuck all. They had access to that camera from the neighbors, but never did go see her."

"And it was erased somehow…." Tony added even though they knew that the group had viewed it, then took care of the situation that the police were helpless in solving. "The point is that the lady let the police know she had something on her camera and they never did get back to her."

"Despite multiple calls," Andrew added.

"We can throw them under the bus with that, and I will talk directly to the camera….it's close to me so it will be heartfelt."

Jorge continued to nod while Jolene appeared sad.

"I like this idea," Jorge agreed. "I believe this might be the perfect end to season two."

"I know that's a few shows ahead…."

"But you are always thinking, and I like that," Jorge said as he stood up. "Ok, this sounds good."

"The only catch is that we aren't supposed to know about the woman having the camera…"

"Just say some 'insider information'," Andrew suggested. "You don't have to reveal your sources."

"I think maybe this could be leaked in the news first…" Jorge suggested. "Maybe just before the show, so that people realize that justice, it is only for some."

"By the last show," Jolene jumped in. "They will already see this."

"Oh, and you didn't tell him about the strippers and hookers," Andrew spoke up and turned toward Jorge. "We got stories about how the cops in one city had a little party last year and turns out they had some live entertainment."

"Is that so?" Jorge was amused. "Perfect, because I want you to throw these fuckers under the bus so many times that there's nothing left of them when you're done."

"Something tells me," Tony calmly spoke as he glanced at the nearby laptop. "We're just getting our feet wet. The more I talk to people, the thicker the mud gets."

"This here, it does not surprise me," Jorge said as he headed toward the door, turning on his phone as he went. "Keep me posted."

Once outside, his phone lit up with various messages, including one from Paige.

I need you at home whenever you can.

Mi amor, is this an emergency?

No, just come home.

He thought about a flirtation that ended with a crying baby earlier that morning and decided that perhaps his wife wanted some time with him. Feeling his libido going into overdrive, he jumped on the highway and headed home. Maria would be in school and Miguel in daycare, leaving them some time alone. That was what he needed.

However, his momentum dropped when he arrived home to find a solemn Maria sitting on the couch.

"What are you doing home from school?" Jorge spoke sharply, feeling his original hopes drop, and his anger moved in. "Do not tell me you got kicked out, Maria!"

"No," She spoke flatly and glanced toward Paige, who was returning to the room. "We had a half day."

"Then what is going on here?" Jorge grew irritated and looked toward Paige. "What has she done this time?"

"Well, it's not so much what she's done as what I found," Paige looked sternly toward her step-daughter. "Do you want to tell him, Maria, or should I?"

Maria's face grew red, and Jorge feared what was coming next. Drugs? Alcohol? He wouldn't even allow his mind to go any further.

"It was...it was just a gun."

"*Just a gun!*" Jorge's voice rose as he glanced toward Paige. "Where the *fuck* did you get a gun, Maria? And please tell me you didn't take this to school with you..."

"No," Maria automatically shook her head. "Of course not, *Papa!*"

"Why do you have a gun?" Jorge shouted this time. "Maria, what did I tell you? All the times you ask, to learn how to shoot? You are too young, and you go out and find a gun? Where did you get it? Did you find it in this house?"

He usually kept his guns safely stored, as did Paige. They had learned this lesson the hard way.

"I...I can't tell you, *Papa,*" Maria spoke quietly, her face a bright red. "You will be angry."

"Too late, Maria!" Jorge shot back. "Tell me now! I am not playing this game with you today, Miss Muffet. Tell me where you got the gun and why you defied me."

"I'm scared!" Maria attempted to defend herself, but she quickly lost steam. "What if someone were to break in and do something? I need to be able to protect my family. I'm old enough, but you won't listen to me!"

"You are too young!" Jorge insisted. "You are very safe living in this house. We have a security system. We both got guns. Paige and I are capable of looking after the family. Even Juliana downstairs, she has a gun and can shoot if need be, but Maria, guns are very dangerous, they are not a toy."

"I *know, Papa,*" She shot back with fire in her eyes, and he backed away.

"Maria, ok, I understand," Jorge attempted to calm down. "But you are safe. You are too young to learn these things. Maybe someday, but not now."

"*Papa,* you have to stop treating me like a baby," Maria whined. "I know what this family is, and I'm part of it too."

Jorge paused for a moment and took a deep breath.

"Maria, please," He finally spoke in the calmest voice he could muster. "Where did you get the gun? Did you find it here?"

She shook her head.

"Did you have someone buy it for you?"

She shook her head.

"Did someone at school get it for you?"

She shook her head.

"Then Maria, I do not understand," Jorge was trying to put it together. "Where did you get it?"

"Someone got it for her," Paige replied.

"Who?"

Maria looked away.

"Not your friend, Cameron?" Jorge pushed.

"No!" She shook her head. "He wouldn't touch a gun."

Jorge raised an eyebrow.

"Maria, I am not messing around here. I do not have all day. Who gave you this gun?"

"Tell him," Paige pushed.

With a small voice, Maria finally answered.

"Jolene."

CHAPTER

28

"Jolene!" Jorge hollered as soon as he walked into the empty club and caught sight of his associate at the bar. Ignoring both Chase and Diego, he slammed the door and flew through the club. "What the fuck is wrong with you?"

"I..." She started but was quickly cut off.

"If you were a man, I would beat your head into this here bar," He pointed toward the ceramic countertop while an alarmed Diego sat in stunned disbelief, two stools away from his sister. "What the fuck is wrong with you? Giving a *child* a gun!"

"What?" Diego's eyes blazed in anger, turning his attention toward Jolene. "Who the *fuck* did you give a gun?"

"I was only trying to help..."

"Jolene!" Jorge shot back at her. "Of all the stupid things you have done, this here is the worst! You gave a 13-year-old kid a gun? Again, what the fuck is wrong with you?"

"Wait, what?" Chase suddenly got up to speed behind the bar. "You gave Maria *a gun?*"

"I was only trying..."

"Jolene!" Diego glared at his sister. "You gave Jorge's *kid* a gun?"

"She was asking for help..."

"So?" Jorge snapped at her. "What next, Jolene, are you going to give Miguel a gun too, if he asks?"

"Of course not," She snapped back. "I am not a moron."

'Really, Jolene?" Jorge countered. "Because from where I stand, you seem like a fucking moron to me."

"I only give it to her because she asks," Jolene attempted to explain, but her words fell flat. "I mean, she keep asking…"

"She asked us all, Jolene, because she wanted to learn how to shoot," Diego cut her off. "But we said no, let alone give her a gun."

"But she was right," Jolene attempted to explain herself, despite being ganged up on. "You would be different, all of you if she were a boy."

"What?" Jorge shook his head.

"If Miguel were 13 and asked for a gun, you would not give it to him?" Jolene asked with a shrug. "It is because she is a girl."

"It is because she is a *child*, Jolene," Jorge quickly corrected her. "My daughter she was manipulating you and you fell for it."

"Well, she learn from the best!" Jolene started to fight back. "She is just like you. You tell me that you did not know how to shoot a gun at her age?"

Jorge glared at her, his face burning from anger.

"I just say…."

"Jolene, you gave my fucking child a gun!" Jorge began to yell again. "And now you try to justify it? This here is too much!"

"I am trying to explain if you let me," Jolene countered, her face full of innocence. "Is this why you ask me to the bar? To yell at me?"

"Jolene, right now, you are lucky that I did not have you meet me at the crematorium," Jorge shouted. "Because I cannot say for sure that I would not throw you into the oven, for what you have done."

"I can't believe you did this," Chase was shaking his head. "I mean, Jolene, common sense? She's a kid. Just because she wants something doesn't mean you give it to her."

"This is why it is good you were never a parent!" Jorge snapped at her, even though it was a very low blow. "Because you would've been a *terrible* mother."

With that, Jolene began to cry. Jumping up from the bar, she rushed off to the lady's room, leaving Jorge with blood boiling in his veins.

"Wow," Chase shook his head. "I can't believe this."

"With Jolene," Diego shook his head. "Believe anything."

"What an incredibly irresponsible thing to do!" Chase continued. "How could she possibly feel like that was a good idea?"

"We are talking about Jolene," Diego reminded Chase. "She is *loco.*"

Jorge ran a hand over his face and took a deep breath. Reaching in his pocket, he turned his phone back on.

"What are you going to do?" Diego leaned toward him. "Are you going to…"

"I do not know, Diego," Jorge shook his head as his phone beeped. It was Paige.

You raced out of the door before I could talk to you. Please keep calm. Don't do anything irrational. Please.

He slid the phone back in his pocket and glanced at the two men.

"I have to go," He nodded and spoke in a calm voice. "Because if not, I will kill that woman."

Without saying another word, he turned around and headed for the door.

Once outside, he welcomed the fresh air as he made his way to the SUV. After he was behind the wheel, Jorge reached for his phone.

I had to walk away. I was far too angry.

That's good. Keep walking away.

I am but mi amor, this is so wrong.

Wait. Just wait. For now.

I will.

Sliding the phone in his pocket, he headed back onto the road.

He wasn't sure what was more disturbing; the fact that his 13-year-old daughter felt the need to learn how to use a gun to protect the family or that Jolene was so quickly persuaded. The whole situation made his stomach churn.

With a heavy heart, he decided to go home.

Jorge started to relax as he drove along. The original rage turned into depression when he reconsidered his daughter's fears. This wasn't normal. He had made every effort for his kids to have a normal life, and yet, it was impossible. Maria wasn't even 14 but had seen too much. Sometimes he wondered if having him as a father was a blessing or a curse. A lot of days, he decided it was the latter. Maybe she would've been better off being brought up by her grandparents in Mexico when they wanted her. What if the damage she had suffered was beyond repair? What if his daughter was broken?

He continued to ponder these thoughts as he returned to the house and drove into the driveway. He felt deflated and depressed.

His phone beeped.

Jolene finally came out of the bathroom. We tried to talk some sense into her, but you know...

I do.

She stormed out of here and said she was going to your place.

Oh fuck.

Taking a deep breath, he slowly got out of the SUV, even though his body felt sluggish and uninterested in moving.

Once inside the house, he noted it was quiet. Maria would be in her room. The baby wasn't home yet, and Paige was putting away dishes when he walked into the kitchen.

"We need to expand Juliana's duties, so you do not have to do that," He pointed toward the cupboards. "You have enough with...everything else."

"It's not a big deal," Paige calmly reminded him as she stopped what she was doing and headed toward him. "You seem...calmer..."

"I know, and yet, I did *not* kill her."

"Jorge, you have to remember that your daughter can be..."

"Manipulative?" Jorge asked and took another deep breath. "I know."

"But still..."

"It does not give her reason, I know," Jorge added. "And now, after I yell at Jolene and she hides in the bathroom, then I get a message that she is headed over here. Can we not answer the door?"

"I'm afraid if we don't, she'll camp out in the front yard."

Jorge shrugged then nodded. She was probably right.

"You need them both in the office at the same time," Paige suggested. "I can be the referee."

"We may need this."

The doorbell rang, and Jorge glanced at his wife.

"Go to the office," Paige suggested. "I will round up the troops."

He followed her advice. Going to his office, he felt apathetic as he sat down. And even more apathetic when Jolene and Maria joined him, followed by Paige, who closed the door. They all sat down.

He didn't say anything.

"You are not talking," Jolene spoke nervously.

"What is there to say, Jolene?" He shrugged. "I give up. Neither of you will listen to me. I have said again and again, that Maria, you cannot use a gun, and here we are. You asked every one of my associates for help. Of course, none of them did until Jolene decided it would be a good idea. So, what is the sense of talking?"

"*Papa,* you must listen to me," Maria attempted to be an adult but quickly sunk back in her chair when faced with Jorge's dark look.

"Earlier today," Jorge continued. "Jolene, I told you, you would've been a bad parent. I should not have said that. I know it hurt your feelings but you know what? I was furious. But, I have been doing some thinking since, and maybe, you are a better parent than me."

Paige gave him a curious look.

"In fact," Jorge continued. "You have already taken over the parental duties with Maria, despite both mine and Paige's wishes, so I think you may as well take them on full time."

"I do not understand," Jolene squinted her eyes. "What do you mean?"

"I mean that if you think you are a better parent to Maria than we are," Jorge gestured toward his wife. "Then, you take her."

Jolene was stunned, while Maria looked hurt.

"Me take...what?" Jolene stumbled over her words.

"You take her," Jorge replied. "Cleary, you feel you can override me, her parent, so you take her. She can live with you. And Maria, if you do not want to listen to my rules if you do not think that they are right and feel that Jolene is more reasonable than this here, is perfect. Neither of you wants to listen to me then I give up."

With that, Jorge abruptly rose from his chair and walked out of the room.

CHAPTER

29

"You're kicking me out?" Maria came running behind as Jorge headed toward the living room. "*Papa,* just because she…"

"No, Maria," He swung around and saw the hurt look on her face and almost relented, but knew nothing would change if he did. "As I said, since you both disrespected my wishes, then I feel that perhaps you living with Jolene might be a better fit for you both. She thinks her rules overrule mine…in fact, you *both* do, so that is fine. I cannot fight this. Go live with her, and she can bring you up."

With that, he swung around and headed toward the door.

"But *Papa!*"

"Pack up your stuff, Maria," Jorge called over his shoulder and turned just in time to see an even more stunned Jolene rushing behind them both, while Paige stood back with a slightly humored expression on her face. "This here, it is perfect. I think you will get along quite well."

"Jorge, it is not that I do not want Maria at my place, but…"

"*Perfecto,*" Jorge cut her off. "Then this here will be perfect. The two of you can go out shooting all the time, maybe learn how to make bombs or something too. Like an arts and crafts project."

"I do not have room," Jolene had a look of fear on her face. "I only have one bedroom. My apartment is so small."

"You got a couch?"

"Yes, but…"

"Then there you go," Jorge shrugged. "Maria, she is very small. She will fit."

"*Papa,* I need my own room," Maria insisted. "I–

"Maria, there are children with no homes, let alone rooms," Jorge cut her off. "I am sure that whatever Jolene can arrange for you, it will work. Maybe she can give you her bedroom, and she sleeps on the couch. This here, you will have to work out between the two of you. I do not care. I have somewhere to be."

With that, he reached for the doorknob, halting for a moment. He turned around and looked at both of their worried faces.

"Oh and Jolene," He continued. "If she ends up pregnant, hurt, or in jail while living with you...."

He didn't finish the sentence. He didn't have to.

With that, Jorge walked out the door and headed toward his SUV. He smirked to himself after he climbed behind the wheel and flew out of the driveway. Let them sit on that for a while.

Deciding to head for the office, he wasn't halfway there when his phone rang. Hitting the button, his wife's voice flowed through the vehicle.

"You really started a shitstorm here."

"*Mi amor,* this was the best idea," He insisted. "Do not relent."

"Oh, I'm not," She assured him. "I explained to them both that they went behind your back, and it may take some time to regain your trust."

"And?" Jorge was humored.

"I don't think Jolene is exactly ready to be a full-time mom to a teenager," Paige spoke in a low voice.

"Where are you right now?"

"In your office," Paige replied. "They're upstairs getting some of Maria's stuff."

"Good."

"You really want her to move in with Jolene?"

"It will be temporary, but it is good that they both expect the unexpected with me," Jorge confirmed. "Maria must learn that freedom comes at a price, and Jolene, she must learn that going against me is never a good idea. She tends to think this here is ok, and it is not."

"Such an interesting situation we find ourselves in."

"This here, it is nothing new for Jolene," Jorge reminded her. "As for Maria, I guess when it comes to bringing up a teenager, it is best to be creative."

"They're going to get on each other's nerves fast."

"I'm counting on it, *mi amor,*" Jorge grinned. "Meanwhile, we will have a quiet night at least."

"Where are you going now?"

"I'm stopping by the office to see Marco."

"Oh, remember we have to plan Miguel's birthday party too."

"Oh yes!" Jorge spoke with delight in his voice. "Maybe Jolene wants to take this here over too while she's at it."

Paige laughed.

"I will be home later," Jorge spoke in a calmer tone. "Keep me posted on what is going on there. I refuse to go back until Jolene and Maria have left. I do not want to deal with their excuses anymore."

"I have one question," Paige was hesitant. "If it was Miguel and not Maria…"

"Paige, every situation is different," Jorge attempted to answer. "I cannot say for sure yes or not but I will say that with Maria, she is not someone who should have…well, she should not be in this situation."

"Just when she told Jolene…"

"No, I cannot see me allowing this with a boy any more than a girl," Jorge shook his head as he got closer to the office. "She is using this card because it would work with Jolene. It is not working with me."

They ended their call shortly after, just as Jorge parked the SUV and headed for the office. Despite his best efforts, the day was starting to wear him down. He could take down a dragon if he had to, but dealing with family issues was a different kind of battle and one where he was flying by the seat of his pants.

Marco's friendly face automatically put him at ease. He was a man who was rarely in a bad mood despite what was going on around him.

"How do you do it?" Jorge asked as the two men sat in the empty conference room. "How do you bring up a family and not lose your mind?"

"Well, sir, I am not sure about that just yet," Marco gave a bright smile and rubbed his balding head. "My hair, sir, is another story."

Jorge's head fell back in laughter, and he clapped his hands together.

"Me? I got my hair, but there are a lot of grays popping up now that Maria is a teenager."

"Sir, I do not envy you," Marco shook his head as he opened his laptop. "My children, they are still pretty young and not that it is easy, but teenagers…"

"And Maria," Jorge shook his head. "Not an easy child. Do you know she has been asking my associates to teach her how to shoot a gun? I say no, and yet, somehow, she not only persuaded Jolene to teach her but to give her one."

"What?" Marco shook his head as his fingers moved quickly over the keyboard. "This is not ok, sir."

"You tell Jolene that," Jorge shook his head. "I tell Maria that if she and Jolene both feel she can override what I say, then Jolene can bring up my daughter."

"What?" Marco's eyes bugged out, and he immediately stopped what he was doing and looked at Jorge.

"I know it will be temporary," Jorge shrugged with a grin on his face. "But for me, I am at the end of my rope with both of them."

"Sir, I am sure a few days with a teenager will be enough to make certain this does not happen again."

"I am hoping to have that effect on both of them," Jorge insisted. "Now, Marco, do you have anything new for me?"

"I continue to investigate this man, Hail," Marco glanced at Jorge who nodded. "Sir, he seems to be on the clear, but I would still be cautious. Also, he seems to be texting Jolene quite often."

"Fuck…" Jorge shook his head. "This here is a drama I do not need."

"From their texts, sir," Marco said with a shrug. "I do not think you have a reason to worry."

"Good," Jorge was satisfied with the answer. "Anything else?"

"Not with him," Marco shook his head. "The police, they are no longer looking for Alwood…"

"Were they ever?" Jorge quipped.

"Yes, at least briefly, sir," Marco replied with laughter in his voice. "It is interesting though…"

"What is that?"

"It almost seems as if they want to wash their hands of the case altogether," Marco replied and turned the screen around to show Jorge a series of emails. "They do not want to pass it on to a federal level, but they also aren't sure how to close it without having too many questions asked."

Jorge rolled his eyes.

"At any rate," Marco turned the laptop back toward him. "It seems that their biggest concern these days is your series."

"That is why I have Tony locked up tight."

"Yes, and they have noted that he is 'off the grid'," Marco giggled. "They think you have him hidden away in a rural area."

Jorge grinned. They had gone to great lengths to make Tony untraceable.

"But they are worried, sir," Marco continued. "They know that something in this series will blow up in their faces. They think it's Alwood, but they aren't sure yet."

"I hope to have many explosions," Jorge replied.

"I think they are most concerned with public reaction," Marco looked up from his laptop. "Sir, this is a bigger concern than what you actually find."

"Anything else?" Jorge asked wryly.

"Sir, I am not finding much," Marco shook his head and closed his laptop. "These days, I try to help Tony and Andrew when I can and make sure they are secure, but other than that, things are kind of quiet."

"For now," Jorge replied as he turned his phone back on. "Speaking of which, I see my daughter has text me about 17 times."

"The quiet, it never does last for long, sir."

"You are right, Marco," Jorge stood up. "You are so right."

CHAPTER

30

"This here is a good morning," Jorge announced on the following Friday as he stared at his laptop while he drank his morning coffee. "The first episode of season two drops tonight, so the police, they are shitting a brick about what will come out. I have a meeting with a local activist who is interested in creating a protest in upcoming weeks to bring attention to the racism, inefficiency, and corruption of the cops, and somewhere else, Jolene is dealing with a whiny teenage, and we have the peacefulness of a little boy."

Glancing toward his son, he noted that his wife was grinning at the other end of the table. Miguel continued to eat his yogurt, getting a great deal of it on himself and the highchair. On impulse, Jorge leaned in and kissed him on the forehead.

"Well, don't get too used to it," Paige reminded him. "According to the texts I've been getting from Jolene and Maria, I would say the countdown is on."

Jorge laughed. "It took this long?"

"Yeah, it's not going well," Paige shook her head. "Maria has completely taken over Jolene's living room, making it her bedroom, and there seems to be a lot of issues about Maria leaving messes?"

"And if she were here," Jorge reminded her. "She knows I will not tolerate that, but she thinks she can walk on Jolene. And me? I don't care? Walk all over her. This is what she gets."

"Has either attempted to text you to negotiate the terms of their punishment?"

"Yes, but for me, I do not answer," Jorge shook his head. "I do not wish to take part in this conversation. I am busy and quickly reply sometimes, asking if they've gone for shooting lessons lately."

"I don't think that the lessons were worth all this…."

"Crossing me wasn't worth all this," Jorge pointed out. "I was pretty clear on how I felt about the issue. I understand Maria's side but *mi amor,* she is too young and to be honest, my Maria, she has a lot of emotional problems. I do not think it is good for her to have a gun. I worry you know?"

"I think that's a pretty normal reaction for any parent," Paige replied, then hesitated. "Any *normal* parents."

"Well, we are not the average, normal parents either, *mi amor.*"

"I think eventually…."

"I know, but for now, let my little girl continue being a little girl," Jorge shook his head with sadness in his eyes. "Even if it is just for me."

Paige smiled and nodded.

His phone beeped.

"I have a call with Athas," Jorge said as he pushed his chair away from the table. "I almost forgot."

"It's been a while."

"All is quiet on the capital."

"For now."

Jorge shared a look with his wife before heading to his office, where he would speak to the Canadian prime minister on a secure line. Sitting behind his desk, he immediately jumped into the call.

"So Athas, what is new in the political world," Jorge had his usual, flippant attitude with the prime minister as he leaned back in his chair and glanced around the room. "You have been quiet lately. No scandals? No issues? What is going on? Are you sleeping on the job?"

"No, we've been busy with some environmental laws," Athas replied in an emotionless voice. "The opposition is making a lot of noise, but that's always the case."

"Well, that is their only job," Jorge reminded him. "To make noise, so it appears they are earning their paycheque."

"That's debatable."

"Well, some may say the same of you," Jorge curtly reminded him. "What you want today?"

"I thought we should touch base on a few things."

"Go ahead."

"To begin with," Athas continued. "The sale of the newspaper you want shouldn't be an issue. I have people making sure it goes through fast."

"Very good."

"Why do you want a newspaper?" Athas asked. "I thought you always worked with the rival, the one with Makerson?"

"I do, but I plan to close them down."

"So...those people..."

"I'm opening a media company," Jorge continued. "The people worth having jobs will find a place, everyone else can go."

"Oh, I see," Athas replied. "That's interesting...when you say media company..."

"Streaming, it is big now," Jorge continued. "I plan to make more shows, docuseries, and other things that will put Canada on the map for our media, not just our pot."

"Interesting...." Athas paused for a moment. "That gives you a lot of influence..."

"That is what I am hoping," Jorge replied. "This here, it can work for you too."

"I might have some thoughts when you do."

"I will always give your thoughts a listen," Jorge replied. "But keep in mind that this here company will share my vision of the world, of this country, and of course, will be political."

"Regarding this series, it starts again tonight?"

"Yes."

"Should I be concerned?"

"You personally, *amigo,* no."

"Will my government be put through a shitstorm?"

"You know," Jorge thought for a moment. "Remember, you mentioned trying to pass some environmental laws and getting pushback?"

"We always do."

"Well, let us say that with the proper distraction," Jorge paused for a moment before continuing. "You should have no issue passing these laws or bills or whatever, and no one having time or attention to notice a thing."

"But, I still think..."

"Trust me. I am working on it."

That was all that needed to be said.

"Should I expect Toronto to be burned to the ground?"

"No," Jorge replied. "But there will be a lot of attention in the upcoming weeks on poor policing, and you know, sometimes people may feel the need to have a...peaceful protest."

"Peaceful?"

"Well, I assume so," Jorge shrugged as if Athas were sitting across from him. "Why would someone not want to be peaceful if they can?"

Athas sighed loudly on the other end of the line.

"You must not worry," Jorge replied. "Just be prepared to do a lot of business while everyone's eyes are on the dumpster fire."

"So, what is the first episode about?" Athas finally asked. "It seems like everything is very hush-hush."

"Alwood, how he treated that indigenous child, his past crimes and complaints made about him," Jorge replied. "This sort of thing."

"But he went...missing, right?"

"*Si,*" Jorge grinned. "We will cover white supremacy in the police, harassment, and bullying within the police, how they treat the indigenous and minorities, how crimes against women are ignored...."

"You weren't joking about the dumpster fire," Athas replied. "I suspect this will create a lot of uprising. What do you get out of this?"

"If you create the disease," Jorge replied. "You can also create the remedy. When I create this here remedy, I run the fucking show."

"I should go," Athas replied after a pause. "I have a feeling this is the time to work on a few other things that I want to pass in the next few weeks."

"This is your time, Athas," Jorge replied. "Take advantage."

Jorge ended the call, and after giving his wife and baby a quick kiss, headed for the door. He had a meeting with the activist in the VIP room of *Princesa Maria.*

Naomi Brookes was a well-known figure in the activism world for her work with various groups that wanted to make their voices heard. She had created petitions, spoken in interviews as well as conferences, and of course, was heavily involved in protests. Naomi knew how to bring attention to causes. Jorge was hoping she could do the same for him.

"So, is this an actual issue for you personally?" She started to interview Jorge almost as soon as they sat down at the table. "Are you having issues with the police?"

"Lady, I assure you, I do not have issues with anyone," Jorge leaned in and gave her a dark look that didn't seem to affect her. Although according to his research, she was a woman close to forty, she was so frail and pathetic looking in appearance that she barely passed as a teenager. He didn't care as long as she could get the job done. "But I do think this here is important. As a minority, I see how people are treating by police. I see the news. And I am told you are the person I should be working with. Of course, this is to be kept quiet."

She nodded. "I understand. We have a lot of anonymous donors who want to stay in the background as much as possible."

"I want to be completely in the background," Jorge insisted. "But I can give you information, resources, whatever you need."

She appeared intrigued and nodded her head.

"So, this series, it starts tonight…"

"Yes," He nodded. "I am thinking two, maybe three episodes in, we will start to have some protests, perhaps you would be interested in discussing issues with the police."

Naomi let out a sharp laugh. "There are lots to discuss."

"Exactly, so I think we can work together," Jorge replied. "We are on the same page."

Naomi appeared guarded but nodded.

"I think we are definitely on the same page."

"Very good," Jorge said as he pushed his chair out and turned his phone back on. "I will be in touch."

After she walked out the back door, Jorge glanced at his phone.

Mark Hail contacted him.

He said it was urgent.

CHAPTER

31

"So what the fuck happened here?" Jorge automatically asked as soon as he arrived on the scene. Before waiting to hear the answer, he glanced around the small, older style house, attempting to assess the situation. His eyes then returned to the dead man on the floor. "Who the fuck is this and why you kill him?"

"I *didn't* kill him," Hail automatically jumped in to explain. "That's the problem! I got home and found him here, dead on the floor."

"Just….found him?" Jorge leaned down to examine the gunshot wound to the chest. He was a middle-aged white man wearing casual clothing. "When were you home last?"

"A few hours ago," Hail rushed to explain, clearly anxious about the whole situation, while Jorge remained perfectly calm. "I went out to…you know, get groceries, run some errands…"

"Your day off?"

"Yes."

"And this man, do you know him? Why would he be in your house?"

"I..I don't know," Hail stumbled along. "He works with me. But… he's never been to my house, I don't understand…I don't know what's going on."

"And this here…." Jorge nodded toward the gun on the floor. "Do you not take it down to your lab and see whose fingerprints are on it, who it was registered to, that kind of stuff?"

"That's the problem," Hail spoke nervously. "That's my gun."

"That's *your* gun?"

"Yes."

"And you did not shoot this man?" Jorge asked. "Because, if you did, you do realize that I don't give a fuck, right? You can tell me."

"No, I swear, I had nothing to do with this," Mark shook his head and started to cough, his face turning red. "I....I came home, found his body, saw my gun, and I knew...no one is going to believe me."

"No, you are right," Jorge agreed. "This here is a setup. And if this man is from your work, it was to fuck you over while getting rid of him."

"He creates a lot of waves...or...did..."

"And you, they do not like," Jorge added and nodded. "Ok, I got this."

"You...you can help me?" Hail asked with reassurance in his eyes. "What can we do?"

"Well, I am guessing you do not want a corpse in the middle of your house," Jorge spoke with sarcasm in his voice. "So me, I will get rid of the body."

"Where you...I mean, can I know..."

"I'm getting rid of it," Jorge reassured him as he reached for his phone. "That is all you must know."

"But my gun was used..."

"No one is going to find this here body," Jorge turned on his phone. "I will make some calls, and we will resolve this quickly, and you, my friend, you need a new lock on your door. A *good* lock because these fuckers will get in again if you don't."

"The house was left to me...the house, I never bothered..."

"Do it now," Jorge instructed. "Today."

His phone was on and ready to go. Jorge called his wife.

"*Mi amor*, I got a fun job for you!"

"For me?" Paige went along with the gleeful tone. "And what is that?"

"I have a man who needs some redecorating at his house," Jorge said with laugher in his voice. "He inherited this house, and I must say, it sure needs some work. I know this here is your...area of expertise, so I thought you might want to come by. We will need to rearrange a few things so you might need Chase for his muscle."

There was a pause.

"Sounds fine to me," She spoke calmly. "I'm looking forward to diving in. Is there anyone else to call?"

"Andrew."

"Got it."

"I will text you the address."

Hail was white as a ghost.

"Are you ok?" Jorge asked as if he were overreacting to the whole situation.

"Not really."

"You're a cop, you, have not seen a dead body before?" Jorge asked as he turned off his phone.

"Not in my *house*."

Jorge considered his word and nodded. "Fair enough."

"So, what are you going to do?"

"Well, my wife, who is an expert in a lot of things," Jorge insisted. "She will be by with some help very soon. They will remove the body."

"And then what?" Hail was confused. "How can I be sure no one will link this to me?"

"As I said, no body," Jorge reminded him. "No body, no crime, do you not know this already? Do they not teach you anything in policing school?"

Hail looked down at the body and back at Jorge.

"But, where…."

"If you must know," Jorge started but stopped. "First, we must have a conversation."

Jorge pointed toward the kitchen.

"Let us sit down."

The two men headed for the next room, leaving the body behind. There they sat down at an older style table and chair set. The room was small, compact, and didn't appear to have been renovated in many years.

"So," Jorge started immediately. "You do realize that I am helping you with a big problem."

"I know," Hail seemed to relax slightly now that he was away from the body. "You have the power now."

"Oh, no, *amigo,* I *always* had the power," Jorge quickly corrected him. "But now, I own you. *You* work for *me*. I do not care who pays you because you work for *me*. I will pay you more. No one fucks with you with me on your side, but again, I own you. If I need something, you give it to me. You have access to information at your station, you know what is going on behind the scenes, so you can let me know. And of course, you have that there uniform and the car you drive around. From time to time, I may need this too, but you will always be protected. But we work together. You do not go behind my back and tell your little cop friends, or your boss, or any fucking one anything. You got it?"

"Yes, I understand," Hail nodded vigorously. "I do."

"No second thoughts or change of hearts tomorrow," Jorge continued and leaned in. "No conscience when this fuckers family comes looking for him, you got it? You know nothing."

"But, obviously someone knows…"

"Yes, so you will be fucking with them," Jorge reminded him. "This person will wonder what happened to the body and will grow paranoid that you have figured him out. You have the power."

Hail sat up straighter.

"Do we understand one another?"

"Yes," Hail nodded nervously. "Whatever you need, please help me. I know if I call this in…"

"They will railroad you," Jorge finished his sentence. "I know. That was the plan all along."

"But what if they somehow trace him to being here?"

"There is no car outside, is there?" Jorge asked. "Other than yours, in the driveway?"

"No."

"Is this man's car nearby?"

As if he hadn't thought of that, Hail jumped up and rushed to the window.

"I…I can't tell, but most of the cars on the street, I'm pretty sure belong to neighbors."

"If he is traced to here, well, you weren't home, so maybe he stopped by, but you don't know why…"

"Yes," Hail said as he stared at the floor as if his mind were racing.

"But my guess, he came here in a car with someone else, his murderer. Are there cameras around here?"

"I doubt it," Hail pointed toward the window. "The people here are mostly older. They…I mean, I haven't seen any."

"I will have my people look into it," Jorge commented. "But unless someone saw him come in, then you are fine and again, no body, no crime."

"But the body…"

"I own a crematorium."

Hail nodded in understanding and appeared relieved.

"Oh, ok…"

"Does this make you feel better?"

"Yes," Hail nodded. "I mean, as long as…"

"I assure you," Jorge stood up. "Whoever did this, they do not want to say a word, and this here is what you want. Let him spin."

Paige arrived shortly afterward, along with Chase. He was driving the unmarked van from the bar.

"So, what happened?" Paige asked with no judgment in her voice, while Chase examined the body then glanced at the door.

"Our friend, he comes home to find this body," Jorge pointed toward the gun. "His own gun nearby."

Paige didn't respond but nodded.

"I need something to put him in," Chase suggested. "We need to get him out without anyone being suspicious, and the rest is nothing. Andrew's heading in now."

"I have a huge box in the basement," Hail attempted to help. "I got a new freezer…."

"Do you still got the old one?" Chase cut in.

"Yeah…well, I have junk in it, but…"

"Take it out," Jorge instructed. "If the nosey neighbors see us remove it, they will think nothing of it."

"Oh, yes," Hail seemed to get back up to speed. "Yeah, sure, I'll show you where it is."

While the police officer rushed toward the basement, the three of them shared a look. This couldn't have worked better if Jorge planned it himself.

CHAPTER

32

"Why do you have so many lime trees?" Jorge pointed toward the row of plants that stood in the large sunroom, off of the living room. Nearby sat a large dog bed where Diego's Chihuahua Priscilla slept. "Each time I come into the house, you seem to have more."

"Don't you worry about my lime trees," Diego complained as he pointed toward the bar area at the back of the room. "When you have one of my homegrown limes in your tequila and tell me it's the best, then we'll talk."

"Diego, you can buy these things at the grocery store," Jorge pointed out to mock him. "You know, they have this thing called the produce section now."

"Whatever," Diego swung around and made a face while Jorge laughed at him. "Leave my lime trees alone."

"Is it not hard to grow in this climate," Jorge asked as he sat at the bar and Diego rushed to the other side to prepare them a drink. "Right temperature, you know, these things."

"Difficult but not impossible," Diego reminded him. "I have a moisture meter in each one and…."

"A what?" Jorge asked as a tall, tropical drink was pushed his way. "What is this?"

"Never mind," Diego shook his head. "The point is that there's a precise way to grow them and get it right."

"I see," Jorge nodded. "Kind of like children."

"Ah, I said precise, not complicated," Diego wagged his finger at Jorge. "I would rather look after lime trees than raise children."

"This is a fair statement," Jorge nodded and took a drink of Diego's concoction. "This here is good. What is it?"

"I invented it myself," Diego spoke proudly. "I might introduce it to the bar. I call it 'Diego's Madness'."

"This here, it seems appropriate," Jorge teased and took another drink. "But you are right about children, Diego. Nothing in my life has been as difficult as bringing up kids. And as you know, I've been through some dicey situations throughout the years."

"True," Diego scrunched up his lips and nodded. "You have."

"It does not get easier," Jorge replied.

"Is that why you shipped Maria off to Jolene's?" Diego asked, and before Jorge could answer, he leaned in. "You do know that Jolene doesn't make a good mother, don't you?"

"I think in looking after Maria," Jorge replied. "She now knows that she does not want to be a mother at all."

Diego laughed

"It was not so much fun for her," Jorge continued. "That is why she is bringing Maria back tonight."

"And that's why you are here?" Diego asked.

"I cannot deal with either right now," Jorge admitted. "It has been a long week, and I need a break."

"Well, you got a break here," Diego reminded him. "Unless they come to find you."

"Paige has already said that she told them I am out," Jorge replied. "And she will give no further explanation. I need to collect my thoughts."

"It has been a busy week," Diego said as he took a drink of his cocktail. "Getting rid of a dead body, corrupting the world….isn't this like most weeks for you?"

"In fairness," Jorge laughed. "This is true. The Hail situation was easy to resolve. He's still a mess but, I thought it was simple to deal with. Also, Maria, I can deal with her tomorrow. But the series…."

"*All About Alwood*," Diego shook his head. "I love that episode. Man, people couldn't stop talking about it the next morning."

"Forget the next day," Jorge shook his head before taking another gulp of his drink. "Try that same night. In a world of social media, things happen fast. People were talking about corruption in the department. There's a lot of anger."

"You always know how to start a shitshow."

"Me, I don't start anything," Jorge insisted. "I just know when to stir the pot."

"This pot has been stirred," Diego said with raised eyebrows. "People are pissed that so many things he did were let slide. It's almost as if he had a free pass to do what he wanted and get away with it."

"I think it is important that people know the truth," Jorge insisted. "And the truth is that this here happens all the time. So many things are hidden. So many things are made look pretty to the public when in fact, the truth is that this same department killed a man in Hail's house and left him there."

"I wonder what the next day at work was like for him...."

"He says he could tell who was behind it as soon as he walked in the door," Jorge insisted. "Faces don't lie."

"He's fucking with them now."

"That is what he should be doing," Jorge finished his drink. "These people who did this, who planned this, they are wondering where the body is, why Hail didn't report it and realizing that whatever plan they had just went very wrong. Everything is now up in the air."

"Yeah, whoever tried to fuck him over," Diego muttered. "They got one hell of a surprise this week."

"Ah and Diego, there are more surprises to come," Jorge insisted as his friend poured them a shot. "And you know me, I like surprising people."

It was early the next morning that he was about to deliver one of these surprises, this time to Makerson, over breakfast at a diner near his office.

"So, let me get this straight," Makerson stopped eating and his whole face turned red as he watched Jorge, who continued to eat. "You're buying out my *competitor.*"

"Yes."

"But...I mean, I thought we had a good working relationship...." Makerson appeared ill. "I've always done everything you asked."

Surprised by his reaction, Jorge stopped eating and sat back.

"This here isn't about you..."

"You aren't seriously giving me the 'it's not you, it's me' speech about my paper..."

"What?" Jorge was confused. "I do not understand."

"I thought we worked well together," Makerson repeated, this time appearing slightly emotional.

"No, you do not understand," Jorge attempted to explain. "I'm not breaking up with you, Makerson, I am trying to get rid of your competition."

"Oh…." Makerson appeared confused. "So, you're…"

"Dismantling the paper," Jorge replied after glancing around him first. "I'm buying it to kill it."

"But….why?"

"Because they fuck me over and that is the only reason I need," Jorge reminded Makerson. "Also, it eliminates your main competitor, while potentially giving you your pick of any staff you might want. I also plan to start a media company."

"Oh," Makerson appeared intrigued.

"I want to do more of these docuseries, maybe some different kinds of shows," Jorge shrugged. "I want to connect with people. Sometimes, this here means a docuseries, and sometimes, it means something much more light."

"I see," Makerson slowly began to eat again. "So, for me…"

"Nothing changes," Jorge reminded him. "You will be a much stronger voice in the city though, once I have eliminated your competition. I think we can work together to make sure this new company is a success."

"This is…a lot to process," Makerson appeared somewhat overwhelmed. "So, if my main competitor is gone…"

"It means you pretty much have the monopoly," Jorge leaned in. "So tell me, how does it feel to be king?"

"I'm not sure I am," Makerson seemed doubtful.

"But you will be," Jorge reminded him. "This is a dying industry, and you've kept this paper afloat and in fact, thriving. This here is not a small feat. You must recognize it and others, they will see it too."

Makerson nodded slowly.

"You do not look happy with this news."

"But people…." Makerson seemed hesitant. "They know that we work together. I mean, they see it. So, they might see this as a move to help me so I'm…I'm not sure that they think I've done this on my own and maybe I haven't, you know?"

"You, *amigo*, you think too much," Jorge reminded him. "This here world, it works this way. It is never just hard work, nose to the grindstone that pushes people ahead. That is a story. It's a story that we like to tell ourselves, but in reality, it is the connections you make that put you on the top of the mountain. Do not think that this here is a bad thing. Having a powerful name behind you, it can only help. It will never hurt you."

Makerson took in his words and nodded.

"It's just that….you know, I had this thing for people in the media recently," Makerson admitted. "It was a dinner and someone said…"

"It does not matter," Jorge automatically cut him off. "You must not listen to what others say. This here is a way to tear you down because they see you are getting too high up. That is what people do. It is easier to pull others down than it is to lift themselves. I tell my daughter the same thing all the time."

Makerson didn't respond but continued to listen.

"In this world, you must make your own rules, and you must make others abide by them," Jorge instructed. "Until you recognize your power, others will cause you to doubt yourself, no matter what you accomplish."

Makerson was still young. He had so much to learn.

"You take what is yours to take," Jorge continued and reached for his coffee. "Accept it, Makerson, in a very short time, you will *own* this fucking industry. And once you own it, you can make all the rules. You just tell me where to point the gun, and I will shoot."

CHAPTER

33

"Miguel's second birthday party is much livelier than his first," Diego commented to Jorge. The two men stood aside as a real-life version of the two-year-old's favorite character danced around the awestruck child. All around was a collection of Jorge's friends and associates as well as Marco's children. "I can't believe you let in some stranger in a costume to play with your kid."

"It's Andrew," Jorge replied and pointed toward his abandoned backpack in the corner. "Like I'd let some random fuck in my house. As it turns out, this here is not his first time putting on a costume. I do not care. It makes my son happy. He is having fun."

Appearing impressed, Diego nodded as Jorge pointed toward his office.

"Let us go speak about a few things while the party is on," Jorge gestured toward the many guests. "Before Athas gets here."

Diego twisted his lips, his face grew serious, and he nodded. Following Jorge away from the others, they discreetly went into his office. After closing the door, Jorge began to speak again.

"We got a lot of irons in the fire."

"Second episode coming up...."

"It's going to heat things up more than I originally expected."

"People are pissed about Alwood like I said the other day."

"I got a call from my riot girl," Jorge said as he removed his phone and turned it off, while Diego did the same as the two men sat in their usual seats. "This Brooke's woman. She's having a hard time keeping a harness on everyone because they want to get on the streets now. She's planning something, maybe next weekend?."

"That's when the episode about the harassment within the department drops?"

"Yup."

"Why would that cause riots, though?"

"Technically, protests, not riots," Jorge reminds him. "This particular one demonstrates how harassment is allowed in the police. What does this mean to everyday people? Well, shit, it rolls downhill to the public. They eat the weak."

"I would think you would appreciate that method," Diego pointed out with a grin on his face.

"But the weak, Diego, they always have their place," Jorge said and sat back in his chair. "The difference between me and the police is that I only have an issue with disloyalty. The cops, it seems, like running things in what you might say is an 'old boy's club,' which means the women are lower ranking. You should hear the stories in this next show. It will be called *Loose Lips Sink Ships,* which seems to be a common reminder to women who want to speak out when their coworker sends them videos of them jerking off. Funny how women, they do not like this."

"Fuck."

"Pathetic men, Diego, they become police to feel powerful, and nothing makes these kinds of people feel more powerful than carrying a gun and degrading others," Jorge said as he took a deep breath and shook his head.

"Yeah, but they do shit to Hail," Diego pointed out. "He's not a woman."

"See, it is different with men," Jorge said as he leaned forward and glanced toward his window. "With men, they want to make them feel like pussies. This here is something they do when someone is new. All this harassment in the police department, it is their way to break them down because it is easier for them to control. That is why the people at the top, they allow it."

Diego nodded and didn't reply.

"Once this gets out," Jorge continued. "Their whole world will go up in smoke."

The two men discussed more details before ending their meeting and heading back out to the party, where the children continued to play and the adults socialized. Jorge noted that Maria was glaring at him from across the room but quickly looked away. This didn't bother him. He knew she was still angry because he had sent her to live with Jolene. It was only briefly, but he made his point.

"Your daughter," The Colombian woman was approaching him. "She is a pig."

"Is that right, Jolene?" Jorge replied and looked away as if to dismiss her. "She is not here, but we do not allow such."

"She was a guest," Jolene started. "And I..."

"I do not care," Jorge abruptly cut her off. "It is done and over. I do not wish to speak of this again. You know how I feel about everything, and you know that this time, you got off pretty easy, Jolene. So, I would not exactly complain if I were you."

With that, he walked away, leaving her to stand alone. She was lucky he let her live so many times, and yet, she continued to push her luck. It was time that Jolene saw that there were consequences to her actions.

"I think Alec just arrived," Paige spoke in a low voice as she approached him. "Is he here for the party or a meeting?"

"Both," Jorge replied and pulled her close. "But right now, I could make him wait, and maybe you and I...."

"*Mama!*" Miguel suddenly called out as he waved his hand in the air to get her attention. "Look, *Mama!*"

The costumed Andrew appeared to be doing a booty dance, which their son thought was hilarious for a vasty different reason than the rest of the room. Everyone was laughing at the large, cartoonish character as he attempted to entertain everyone, while Paige appeared awestruck.

"I think it might be time to open the presents," She announced and pointed toward the gifts in the next room, just as Alec walked in the door. Paige turned her attention toward Jorge. "Before things get more out of hand."

Grinning, Jorge winked at his wife before starting toward Athas, who held a present in his hand.

"Thank you for coming," Jorge said as he grabbed Chase's attention as he walked by. "Can you put this gift with the others? Athas and I must talk."

"Sure," Chase replied, glancing at Athas before taking the gift to the next room, following the rest of the party.

"Once again," Athas commented as they made their way to the office. "A child's party hardly seems like a time to be talking about your line of business."

"On the contrary," Jorge argued with him as they entered the office, and he closed the door. "I think this here is the perfect time. I have everyone together in one room, and we can talk for a few minutes to see where everything is. My son, he is busy with his party, so this here, it is fine."

Athas grimaced as the two men sat down.

"So, the protests, they are coming," Jorge warned him. "So warm up your pencil and write out whatever you need to slip past the people because they will be too preoccupied with this sideshow."

"I don't want the city burnt to the ground, Hernandez."

"It won't be," Jorge ignored the attitude in his voice. "This here, it will be fine. I cannot promise there will be no destruction, but we do not want to give the police an excuse to break out the riot gear."

"They might anyway."

"Not if you tell them no," Jorge instructed. "The point is to make the police look like fucking assholes while you get your bills passed. End of story. That way, we both win because the people, once they do not trust the police, it will be a long, hard road to win them back. That will give us lots of time to do whatever it is we need to have done."

"I don't want all the local police to go missing..."

"So far, I believe there's only two...."

"Or dead," Athas continued.

"Well, you know, you make a lot of demands for a man who needs my help," Jorge reminded him. "I think you should take what you can get and declare it a victory."

Athas didn't reply but appeared unsettled.

"Is this all you have for me today?"

"I got more for you."

"Regarding...."

"The police," Athas appeared almost hesitant to continue. "I hear a lot in my office that never hits the media."

"What you got for me?"

"It's disturbing," Athas finally replied. "A lot is kept quiet. Cops buying underaged prostitutes, pocketing money and drugs they find at crime scenes, taking bribes......it's even worse than I originally thought. I think we need to overhaul the police altogether."

"That there sounds like a lofty goal," Jorge said as he leaned back in his chair. "However, if you are holding this over their heads, you can snap their necks if they don't keep in line. Even just the threat...."

"Funny how you can turn anything into a power game."

"That's because, *amigo,* everything is a power game," Jorge reminded him. "Do not think it ever is anything else."

"You and I have different goals here," Athas reminded him. "I want to make things better. You, you...."

"I..I am realistic," Jorge cut in. "I do things that make sense, and this here, it makes sense to me. You are the most powerful man in this country, at least, in theory. Act like it."

Athas didn't reply.

"Meanwhile," Jorge said as he leaned back in his chair. "I am feeling generous because it's my son's birthday. What do you want, Athas? I will make it happen."

"That's very *Godfather* of you," Athas replied and moved ahead on his chair. "But I don't want anything from you. Everything you touch is tainted."

With that, Athas rose from his chair.

"It may be tainted," Jorge reminded him as he stood up. "But it gets resolved. Do we not at least agree on that?"

Athas didn't reply but headed toward the door, leaving Jorge behind to ponder their conversation. He texted Chase to meet him in the office.

"What's up?" Chase automatically asked as he closed the door behind him.

"I got an unusual job for you."

"Ok," Chase grinned. "Will I need a weapon for this?"

"No, but not all problems can be solved with guns," Jorge grinned. "But I do think we may have a solution to a couple of my problems. But this here, it cannot leave this room."

Chase nodded.

"You got my word."

"Good because Paige, she can never know about this."

"What?" Chase shuffled in his seat and tilted his head slightly. "You want me to what?

"Please, you are the only person I can trust with this," Jorge insisted while carefully watching his reaction. "It is very important you do this for me. No one can ever know about this conversation."

"But I don't understand," Chase seemed confused. "Why...why do you want to do this exactly?"

Jorge raised his eyebrows with a smooth grin on his face.

"You do not believe this is out of the goodness of my heart?" Jorge teased. "That I do not just want Alec to get laid or for Jolene to be happy?"

"Jolene will never be happy," Chase insisted, then made a face. "And isn't she a little crazy for the prime minister of Canada?"

Jorge laughed.

"I don't know, Chase, is she?"

"Why do I have a feeling that you have something more in mind here?" Chase asked. "And hey, I don't care, but be straight with me. I want to know what I'm being a part of."

"Fair enough," Jorge nodded and pulled his chair closer to the desk. Leaning toward Chase, he looked into his eyes. "It occurred to me today that a couple of problems are lurking in the background, and if there is one thing that I have learned in my life, it is that you take care of a small problem before it becomes a big problem. You have heard me say this many times."

Chase nodded. "Yeah, I mean, that makes sense to me."

"And the problem lately is that there is an….unrest with my people," Jorge gestured toward the wall to indicate the party on the other side. "I am having issues with Athas and his attitude. He is doing what I ask, but he is not as compliant as he once was. I am seeing a fighter rising in his eyes, and my concern is that this fighter is for me, not for the people. Not for his job. I need him to be passionate again, less cynical because the people, they see these things. They sense the cynicism, for example, when what we need is for people to see a passion in him. I know that the election is not exactly around the corner, but we are at the point where people are paying attention."

"Ok," Chase nodded. "I see what you mean."

"Right now, they are seeing a kind of cranky, middle-aged man," Jorge replied. "And this here, I understand, so I wonder to myself, what would spark his passions again, what will make him manageable? What will make him seem more voteable in the next election? What will improve his profile?"

"And you think Jolene will do it?" Chase appeared skeptical. "I mean, no offense, but couldn't we find someone else to…"

"We could," Jorge nodded and raised a finger in the air. "But we must also find someone we can keep in line. Jolene, she knows the consequences of not doing as I say."

"But, you're going to make her…"

"Please, neither of them are even going to know what has happened," Jorge insisted. "This will be their idea or…so they think. We must find a way to connect them. I am wondering if this is something you can help me with."

"Well, they are both at the party now….unless Alec is leaving?"

"No, he is not," Jorge shook his head. "He plans to stay so he can hang around my wife…"

"Oh."

"What?"

"You don't want him…" Chase hesitated. "I mean, I understand."

"Athas is a thorn in my side," Jorge insisted. "He may have been a part of Paige's past, but I do not want him around her. I do not want him to get any ideas."

"I don't think that will happen," Chase insisted. "And even if he did, he's not going to cross you, and besides, Paige, she's dedicated to you."

"This is true," Jorge nodded with some hesitation. "The problem with Athas is that he is the boy scout, the hero of the movie, whereas I will always be the villain. And yes, Paige is dedicated to me, but still, I feel better if he was tied up with someone else. Besides, he's cranky, so perhaps his dick needs some attention. Jolene has too much time on her hands, even with this film project. I need her out of my hair, and this kind of kills two birds with one stone. You know? Who knows? It might enhance his public profile as well...."

"Yeah, I mean, the media will be more interested in what he's doing in his love life than political..."

"Because people are fools," Jorge nodded. "That is my expectation. The celebrity will win out over the political side because people are dumb, and they want everything dumbed down to wedding dresses and babies. But, if it works....I need Athas to stay on his game."

"If he has Jolene wrapped up in his life," Chase reminded him. "That might be difficult. She is demanding."

"Which means she will take what she can get," Jorge grinned. "That means she will be hanging around him for every second she can, even if that means sucking him off in a closet between meetings, or whatever she does. She's desperate and pathetic. These kinds of women, they hover and fixate. Again, this here solves two of my problems at once."

Chase grinned and couldn't help but mention the obvious.

"I'm thinking...maybe this might have a strain on Jolene and Paige's friendship," Chase wondered out loud.

"Oh? I had never thought of it," Jorge commented quickly, which caused Chase to laugh.

"Ok," He finally shrugged. "I think you know best, and I also think you've given this a lot of thought."

Jorge nodded.

"But what about...the downfall," Chase asked. "When they break up?"

"The country will feel bad for Athas because he had his heart broken, and yet he continues to move ahead."

"And if they *don't* break up?"

Jorge swung his head back in laughter.

"Chase, do you think this here is realistic?" Jorge finally asked. "Do you think, with what you know of Jolene, that she will not self-destruct within weeks or months of all of this?"

"Fair enough."

"There are no drawbacks."

"But what if…she does something stupid?" Chase appeared concerned.

"I do appreciate your concern," Jorge replied as he tapped his fingers on the desk. "But you must also know that I will have full control over this situation. If I see too many fires along the road, I will put them out. Do not worry. I will have Makerson write some fiction that will make her appear intriguing to the public. An immigrant who worked hard to rise up and become a Canadian. Not that this matters. She's attractive and dresses nice. People, they may not get past those details."

"Ok," Chase nodded. "What do you want me to do?"

Jorge grinned and nodded. "This here, it will be easy."

A few minutes later, Chase returned to the party while Jorge sat alone with his thoughts. A dark grin crossed his face. This would work out perfectly. If you wanted to get even with someone, you had to hit them where it hurts. And if you wanted to control a man, you did so with lust. This would be too easy.

Once he received a text from Chase, Jorge returned to the party. He did so just in time to see Paige leaning down next to her son while everyone sang Happy Birthday and the little boy gushed from the attention. His son would one day rule the world, and already, he was ruling that very room. Pride filled his soul.

Jorge slowly allowed his eyes to drift around the room. Jolene was standing beside Athas, and they were talking. A glance at Chase, who gave a slight nod which indicated that their plan had worked. The two had no idea that this was even going on. Chase would be smooth, careful and no one would be suspicious. Jorge let his eyes wander back to his wife, who seemed oblivious to the new connection being made elsewhere at the party, her eyes instead focused on their son, who laughed as he received a piece of cake. *Perfecto.*

He continued to observe the room. Marco and his family were very enthused about Miguel's second birthday. Diego was taking pictures, while Andrew was now out of costume and hanging close to the cake. Tony was nearby, checking his phone because he never stopped working. Athas and Jolene continued to have an enthusiastic conversation. Juliana was talking to Maria, who was giving Jorge a sheepish look.

"Maria," He spoke in a low voice while he indicated for her to come to see him.

Rising from the seat, she apprehensively made her way toward her father, who showed no signs of anger or frustration. He said nothing but put his arm around her and pulled her close.

"Maria, your birthday will be soon too," He reminded her. "I cannot believe you are almost 14."

"I can't believe I'm *only* 14," Maria complained. "I feel like I should be 16."

"Maria, do not push time ahead. You will be 16 soon enough."

"I hate being a kid."

"Well, Maria, sometimes I hate being an adult."

She laughed, and he pulled her closer, leaning in to kiss her on the head.

"*Papa,* I am sorry."

"I know, Maria," Jorge spoke quietly while the others moved closer to Miguel, and on the other side of the room, Jolene pushed her breasts out as she talked to Athas. Jorge had to look away, or he would've laughed. "But you must know, I worry that you are safe. I worry about making the right decisions for you. I do not want to be a terrible father like my own was to me."

"You're not a terrible father," Maria insisted, and he looked down into her eyes and saw sincerity. "My *abuelo,* he did not care. But you, I think sometimes you care too much."

"Of course, Maria," Jorge leaned closer to her and spoke in a low voice. "You and Miguel, you are my life. I only want better for you. Please, in the future, do not go to Jolene for anything. She is a very unstable woman, and I do not feel she is a good role model."

"But she's my Godmother."

"I know, Maria, and she would do anything for you," Jorge replied as he glanced at her tarting it up to Athas. "But, I want you to...*not* be like her."

Maria glanced across the room and nodded.

"I understand, *Papa.*"

"Maria, you are better."

The crowd around them was laughing, clapping, and enjoying the moment with his son. But Jorge, he was enjoying the moment with his daughter because he knew that she needed it more.

CHAPTER

35

"What?" Paige began to laugh as soon as she heard the news while standing nearby, Maria giggled as she hoisted up her backpack. "Is this a joke?"

"Exactly!" Diego spoke dramatically while Priscilla sniffed at his shoes. "That's what I said!"

"Diego, that there dog," Jorge pointed toward the chihuahua fidgeting around his owner. "He isn't going to piss on my floor, is he?"

"It's a *she*," Diego automatically corrected him. "And no, she's well trained. And she just did her pees and poops outside."

Jorge rolled his eyes.

"She's so cute," Maria dropped her backpack and rushed over to pet the dog, while Jorge glanced toward his wife.

"So, Alec and *Jolene?*" Paige continued to look humored. "That seems like an odd pair."

"Everything about Jolene is odd," Diego complained. "She'll make his life hell."

Jorge held back his laughter.

"Oh, I don't know about that, Diego," Jorge shrugged. "Who knows what brings people together?"

"I have a pretty good idea in both their cases," Diego quipped while shaking his head. "We got to break them up because she'll drag us down with her."

"Nonsense," Jorge shook his head. "They'll…spend some time together and eventually part ways. It will be fine."

"Nothing is ever fine with Jolene," Diego argued. "You know that better than anyone."

"And I also know that eventually, she moves on," Jorge attempted to explain. "All these men, they eventually go on their way, and she freaks out and then moves on to her next….whatever."

"Lover?" Maria looked up as she continued to pet the dog.

"Maria!" Jorge snapped. "Please!"

"I'm just telling you the truth," Maria spoke in a very adult-like tone. "She told me that all men want is to sleep with her, and then they don't want to…"

"She tell you this?" Jorge cut her off. "Maria, do not listen to her nonsense. She makes her own decisions *and* her own problems."

"She's going to make his life hell," Maria insisted as she stood up, while the dog continued to sniff at her feet. "Even I see that, and I'm 13."

Diego made a face and shot a look at Jorge.

"What?" Jorge shrugged. "What do you want me to do, Diego? Your sister is her own train wreck. I cannot help."

"I'm going to tell her to not fuck this up," Diego complained. "We can't have her out there bringing attention to us."

"She won't, Diego."

He shot Jorge another warning look as he ushered his dog out the door. In the driveway, Juliana was waiting in the car.

"Maria, off to school," Jorge pointed outside before leaning in to kiss the top of her head. "Be good, *chica.*"

"I will," Maria said as she went outside and Jorge closed the door behind her.

"Now, I must meet with Makerson and…"

"So, this is the first you heard about this?" Paige asked suspiciously. "You had no idea about Jolene and Alec?"

"I suspected, but *mi amor,* I suspect a lot of things," He shrugged.

"You didn't set them up?"

"Oh, Paige, I am hardly cupid," Jorge joked as he held up an invisible bow and arrow in the air. "A romantic, yes, but I do not set up people. And why would I do that to Athas?"

Paige gave him a look.

"Do not worry, *mi amor,* this will be another train wreck, but it will be over soon."

"Diego's right," She reminded him. "If this train wrecks, we might have a lot of debris to clear up."

"You know me. I am good at cleaning up debris. Now, let us not worry."

"Why do I feel like you want them to be together," Paige quietly asked as she moved closer to him. "Because with Jorge Hernandez, there's always more than meets the eye."

"Well, this here, it is true," Jorge flirted with his wife. "But you know, this here has nothing to do with me. But I won't lie, *mi amor,* I have no sympathy for either of these people when it blows up in their faces. And it will."

Paige seemed slightly unsettled with this comment but didn't reply. Jorge took this opportunity to depart, announcing he had a meeting with Makerson. He did, but first, he had another stop to make.

Hail appeared surprised when Jorge arrived at his door. A cup of coffee in hand, he gestured for his guest to come into the house. Jorge held back, inspecting the two locks on his door.

"I see you took my advice," He commented as he walked inside, noting his casual attire. "You don't work today?"

"Later," Hail replied and gestured toward the next room. "Can I get you a coffee?"

"This here isn't a social call," Jorge replied as he fixed his tie. "I got a meeting shortly. I wanted to touch base. Anything new?"

"Nothing," Hail admitted. "A few of the guys at work appeared surprised when I came back the day after we found…"

Jorge nodded as if to rush him along.

"That's it."

"No problems?"

"No," Hail shook his head and gestured to the place where a dead body lay only a few days earlier. "They're out looking for buddy."

"Another wild goose chase…"

"Well, I guess we're also looking for Alwood too, but yeah, it's freaking people out why these officers keep disappearing."

"I bet," Jorge raised an eyebrow. "Sometimes, people, they disappear."

Hail didn't reply. Jorge studied his face.

"Am I going to disappear?" Hail finally asked.

Jorge shook his head.

"Why would you?

"I just thought…"

"I would not overthink this," Jorge reminded him. "You had a problem; we fixed it. We will continue to fix problems together. You work with me. You are invincible as long as you continue to do so."

"I feel like….I feel like I'm going against what I always believed."

"And what is that?" Jorge was curious.

"Justice."

"But tell me something," Jorge asked. "In your time at the police station, did you see a lot of justice?"

Hail didn't reply. His expression said it all.

"This is what I tell you," Jorge continued. "You gotta make your own justice in this world. Would it have been justice if you were getting raked over the coals for a murder you did not commit? The world, it does not work as you want to believe, but it works, how it works."

On that note, Jorge decided to leave, allowing Hail time to consider his words. Jorge was confident he'd see his side of things.

At the coffee shop close to the *Toronto AM* office, Jorge found Makerson waiting for him. He was staring at his phone when Jorge slid into the booth.

"I made sure the news broke regarding you buying out my competition," Makerson commented breezily. "Interesting, I hadn't considered that this would take off some of the heat from the people saying you control our paper."

"Ah, never underestimate me," Jorge reminded him with a smooth grin on his face. "Nothing I do is ever for one reason, but many. I knew that this here would cause people to separate our connection…how little they know."

"Trust me, I never underestimate you," Makerson clarified while shaking his head. "I know better."

A waitress approached, and Jorge ordered a coffee. After she left, he continued.

"And so, there may be some protests after the next episode drops…"

"*Loose Lips Sink Ships?*"

"Yup, lot of info coming out. People are not trusting their local police so much anymore."

"And I suspect that's not going to improve as the series continues?"

"The next episode after this one," Jorge nodded toward the waitress as she approached with his coffee. After thanking her, he continued.

"Is about white supremacy in the department. And the next show is about the unfortunate relationship between the police and the indigenous community. A lot of bombs will go off for both."

"So, you said protests?"

"Do you know a lady, Naomi Brookes?"

Makerson raised an eyebrow. "She's very...dramatic."

"I like dramatic," Jorge commented. "She has some people lined up."

"She always does," Makerson commented breezily. "They're referred to as the Naomi cult."

"I do not care," Jorge clarified. "They can be anything as long as they cause some tension in the media."

Makerson grinned.

"And Athas, he's about to start a new relationship," Jorge continued. "With Jolene Silva. Make sure it gets lots of attention, create a love story for the people."

"People like love stories."

"That's what I'm counting on, especially as we get closer to the summer," Jorge replied. "Summer love and all that."

"He's been down in the polls lately."

"His polls are about to rise," Jorge said with laughter in his voice. "That is all that matters. People need to be inspired from time to time."

"How far will this relationship go?"

"Not far, trust me," Jorge insisted. "But far enough to satisfy all parties."

"How did you manage that?" Makerson was intrigued.

"I got my ways," Jorge replied. "I think that's all."

"That's pretty good for a Thursday morning," Makerson shook his head and reached for his coffee. "But for a change, I got something for you."

Jorge was intrigued.

CHAPTER

36

"*Loose Lips Sink Ships*," Jorge repeated the banner underneath the live coverage of a protest taking place near Young and Dundas, in the downtown area of Toronto. Although it looked relatively peaceful from the footage, there was a sense of frustration in the air that could only grow. "This here, it is good."

"Isn't that the name of the new show?" Maria asked as she collapsed in a nearby chair, her backpack in the middle of the floor. "I heard people talking about it in school today."

"About my show?" Jorge looked up from his laptop.

"Yeah, the teachers," Maria confirmed as she shrugged apathetically. "They were trying to act like they were talking about school stuff, but I heard them. One was complaining because her boyfriend is a cop, and she said your show got it wrong."

Jorge rolled his eyes, and Maria laughed.

"I'm just telling you the truth," She shrugged. "*Papa* is it true that the police are mean to one another at work?"

"Maria, a lot of people are mean to one another at work," Jorge insisted as he glanced back down at the monitor. "But the people protesting today, they are mainly former cops, family members, people who have seen harassment ignored inside the police and RCMP. This is on top of all the stuff we are hearing on the news about the lack of professionalism by the police."

Maria looked slightly bored but nodded.

"*Chica,* we need to talk about something," Jorge looked up from the monitor.

"Did I do something wrong?"

"No, not this time," Jorge shook his head and laughed. "At least, I hope not."

"What is it?" Maria asked as Jorge closed his laptop and pushed it aside.

"Maria," Jorge hesitated. "You know that I do not like the idea of you learning to shoot a gun however, since *Jolene,* she already go ahead to teach you, I decided that both me and Paige, we will take you for lessons."

"Oh!" Maria's eyes widened. "Really?"

"Yes, but Maria, this is not a toy," Jorge spoke sternly. "And I do not like to teach you at all but, I know, it is necessary. I do not want to think that you will ever be in a dangerous situation, but I want you to be prepared if you are. This here, it is important. You cannot take a gun out and show Cameron or your friends how to shoot or show off with it. This is very serious."

"I know," Maria insisted as she nodded vigorously. "But I want to know to protect my family."

Jorge felt his heart warm, and he leaned forward and kissed her on the top of the head.

"I know, Maria, because family, it is the most important thing."

Paige came downstairs a few minutes later, just as Maria was rushing past. With a heavy backpack over her shoulders, Maria excitedly ran upstairs.

"She looks happy," Paige commented as she joined Jorge in the kitchen. "Did you tell her?"

"Yes," Jorge took a deep breath. "I hope this is the right decision, *mi amor.*"

"I know, and I understand why you're hesitant," Paige sat beside him, and he reached out to touch her hair. "But in this family..."

"I would do anything to make sure my family is always safe," Jorge insisted. "I do not want any of this for my Maria or Miguel."

"Well, I hate to point out the obvious," Paige muttered. "But stoking the fire probably isn't helping."

"I know, but we must play tough in this world," Jorge reminded her. "We must be a lion so people can hear us roar."

"I think they've heard it," Paige confirmed. "So, what was it you wanted to tell me about your meeting with Makerson?"

"We went over a few things," Jorge replied as he glanced toward the stairs to make sure Maria wasn't within earshot. "He said this woman that does the protests, she has what is called the 'Naomi cult' because they must follow whatever she says."

"A powerful woman."

"That is what we want," Jorge nodded. "Already, there is a small protest downtown. But they will grow with each episode, but I can put a stop to them at any time. First, I must make sure the police, they are crippled and are in a weak position. They must know their place."

"I think you're well on your way."

"Makerson is going to cover it and make sure it gets the voice it needs," Jorge insisted. "The other paper, I will have control over by next week. That is when I will start to make cuts, and Makerson will hire the valuable people if they are interested."

Paige nodded.

"And I guess he is going to cover this new romance with Athas and Jolene," Jorge rolled his eyes. "We think it is something that will 'humanize' Athas and something people will find far more appealing than politics."

Paige gave him a skeptical look.

"It is...how do I say," Jorge shrugged. "A surprising thing, but we must use it to our advantage, the short time they are together."

"You assume it will go up in flames?"

"Do you *not* assume the same, *mi amor?"*

Her expression said it all.

"But there is more," Jorge continued. "I was talking to Makerson, and he had a little bit of news for me."

"He did?"

"His journalist ear must be to the ground to hear this one," Jorge continued. He glanced toward the stairs before he continued to speak. "There is a huge division within the department. One side against the other. This is why Hail comes along and is getting pushed out already. He is not someone they can put on a side."

"He seems to be on *your* side," Paige commented.

"I make a more compelling argument," Jorge grinned. "Cleaning up the body they left for him, that would be the most compelling of all."

"So we know that was a setup to push him out?"

"They would see him as the do-gooder, who will go to the top with any concerns," Jorge reminded her. "Which means they had to get him out of the way and fast since they could see he wasn't about to play ball."

"So that's why they were bullying him," Paige nodded.

"And sending him to the door of the most ruthless person in the city," Jorge pointed toward himself. "They were hoping I would take care of him, and when I did not..."

"They put a dead body in his house."

"That of another man who was also not playing ball," Jorge said. "That is what I think. Not that Makerson knows this, of course, but because he knows this other man is missing. He assumes they did something to him to send a message."

"So corruption in the police department," Paige spoke sarcastically. "What a concept."

"There is a lot," Jorge replied and took a deep breath. "I do not know. I guess payoffs to keep quiet, the usual thing. This here was normal in Mexico, but at least there, the people know this fact."

Paige nodded but didn't reply.

"In Canada, people make heroes of the police," Jorge said. "Because in Canada, people, they only want to see the side that makes them comfortable."

"So, is this why you decided to teach Maria how to use a gun?"

"*Mi amor,* she was already taught by Jolene," Jorge complained. "I will teach her the *right* way, and so will you."

"Jolene is a good shot though," Paige reminded him.

"But, unfortunately," Jorge replied. "Everything else with Jolene is *wrong.*"

As the days moved forward, the press went crazy with the story about Prime Minister Athas and his new girlfriend. Although some of the media were highlighting the attractive couple, it didn't take long for the vultures to move in and uncover some of Jolene's unsavory past, which included running a sex club a few years earlier.

"They do not seem to care it was my club she ran," Jorge laughed about it with Chase the following week at *Princesa Maria*. "They only care that she was involved. Of course, then the rumors come out that she, herself, is a freak show, so this here it has helped me."

"People are laughing at Athas," Chase reminded him.

"So, it is what it is," Jorge grinned as he reached for his drink. "We did not force them to get together, Chase, we merely got them close and allowed their hormones to do the rest."

"It wasn't a tough sell," Chase grinned. "For either."

"Athas was horny, and Jolene, well, we are not sure if it was the same or desperation."

"I'm thinking both," Chase grinned as he leaned over the bar. "You were right, this is a pretty reasonable punishment for them both. Diego was saying how Jolene was basking in the media attention until it turned sour."

"Jolene, she thinks Athas is such a prize," Jorge insisted before downing the rest of his drink. "Until the media rips her to shreds, then the fun, it has ended."

"I think it will cause a strain on their relationship."

"Good, they can both fucking suffer," Jorge spoke sharply. "Me, I do not care. They can both burn until I decide to put the fire out."

"On the plus side," Jorge continued. "It has helped Tony and Andrew work more successfully with Jolene out of their hair a few days. I thought she would be helpful, but in the end, she made more work for them."

"And the next episode?" Chase asked.

"This Friday," Jorge said and raised an eyebrow. "It is called *White is Right* because this here is what a cop once told a new guy when he was a rookie."

"Here?"

"No, this was in Vancouver or somewhere that way," Jorge waved his arm in the air, indicating the western provinces. "The point is that it will create even more issues. We have proof some of the top people in the police department were part of a white supremacist group and that they were groomed to move up the ranks. It is not a coincidence. This is where shit hits the fan. If you thought we had protesting before, wait until this comes out."

Chase didn't reply but gave a sad nod.

CHAPTER

37

"What a pleasant surprise," Jorge allowed the sarcasm to ring through his voice as Athas sat across from him in his office. "You, here, at my house, unannounced, I love when that happens."

"You know I can't have this stuff on the official itinerary," Athas attempted to explain in a quiet voice as if he were a man in a weak position. "Plus, I had to take care of this right away, and I didn't know what else to do..."

"Oh, what is it?" Jorge played innocent as he leaned back in his chair and felt the power shift to his advantage. "I thought your life, it was perfect right now. A new woman in your life, all this positive media attention, a rise in your poll...your polls. Isn't this what every man wants?"

"Ok, you don't have to be sarcastic," Athas responded in a quiet voice. "I know what you think of Jolene."

"Really? Is this right?" Jorge continued to enjoy the moment. "You knew that I thought Jolene was a loose cannon, and yet, you choose this person to parade around town with for the media to see and spend your nights..."

"Ok, we don't have to get into this," Athas put up his hand. "I didn't intend for any of this to happen."

"No one ever does with Jolene," Jorge reminded him. "She is, after all, what you say? A femme fatale? Is that the expression?"

"She is...very sexy, but that wasn't why I got involved with her."

"Right," Jorge spoke sarcastically. "It was all the work she did with the church that inspired you."

Athas ignored his remark.

"So," Jorge continued. "What do you want from me?"

"I need to clear this up in the media," Athas waved his hand in the air. "You control it, don't you? I can't have them digging up this dirt about her, and I would think that you'd appreciate that because it affects you too."

"Not really," Jorge shrugged.

"She's connected to you."

"Not in the same way she's connected to *you*," Jorge reminded him. "And also, I don't hold the highest office in the country."

"You know what I mean."

"So, what?" Jorge shrugged passively. "What you want me to do? Try to make her into a Disney princess?"

"I need the media to back off," Athas insisted. "That's all."

"This here is impossible," Jorge countered. "You are the prime minister. People are interested in who you are dating."

"That's the thing," Athas said before letting out a tired sigh. "We aren't anymore."

"Oh, you dump her already?"

"Does it really matter?" Athas snapped back.

"Oh…so she dumps you," Jorge made the assumption and thought for a moment. "Well, you know, I do have this newspaper that I am taking over. I plan to disassemble it, and God knows, Jolene is good at ripping things apart, so maybe this would take up her time. It would make her a bitch in the media, but it would take the attention off your…*former* relationship and also give people who are still in the media some compassion for you."

Athas nodded with enthusiasm.

"It would also help me," Jorge continued. "Maybe she will find a new victim at the paper, no?"

Athas didn't reply but looked frustrated.

"So, if she comes back knocking at your door…"

"I won't be answering," Athas shook his head. "Look, I don't mean any disrespect to her. She's a bit erratic, which is great if you work for someone like Jorge Hernandez, but it's not so great if you're in the public eye, and you never know how she will react."

"True,' Jorge nodded. "Ok, so this here romance is over. I will send her to the paper. Meanwhile, you give an interview to Makerson and talk to him about what you do and do not want him to write. He will find a way to slant this in the media, and I will find a way to get Jolene out of your life."

"Thank you," Athas looked relieved.

By the time the prime minister left his house, Jorge felt reassured that he had him back under his thumb. The fallout of his relationship with Jolene had shaken things up and allowed Jorge to move in to fix them in a way that only he could. Athas needed to know that he could burn in hell if Jorge Hernandez decided to light the match.

He texted Jolene.

I have a new job for you.

What is it?

I bought out a paper. I need you to oversee things.

I know nothing of papers.

This is fine. It will not be a paper for long.

Sitting his phone on the desk, he looked up to see Paige entering the office with Miguel in her arms.

"What was Alec doing here so early?" She asked as Miguel successfully struggled to get out of her arms. "I didn't think you had a meeting."

"I didn't," Jorge replied as their son started to wander through his office with a curious expression on his face.

"What's going on?"

"Him and Jolene have parted, and he wanted to put out some of the fires."

"Oh?" Paige showed no reaction, something he noted. "So, what are you doing?"

"Since Jolene, she is already hated, I am going to have her dismantle my newspaper," Jorge paused for a moment. "Meanwhile, Makerson will put a good spin on the story, make Athas seem the victim, that kind of thing."

"I'm not sure he wasn't," Paige commented as she sat down, glancing at their son as he continued to walk around with interest. "Jolene tends to have a track record."

"That she does,' Jorge was already bored with the topic. "Before he arrived, I was watching the new episode of *Eat the Rich*. It is very powerful, emotional. I have information on white supremacists moving up the ranks with the RCMP. It is not going to go well."

"Should we be rattling their cages?"

"It is a docuseries," Jorge shrugged. "This is what we do."

"You keep talking about a quiet life," Paige reminded him. "But it's not going to happen if we keep provoking the wrong people. We need to watch it."

"No, we must let them know who runs the show," Jorge insisted. "Trust me, I do not see any danger in doing so. They will be too busy trying to recover their image that they will not care if it was me behind all of this."

Paige didn't appear convinced.

"Trust me, this here is important, and don't the people deserve the truth?"

"I'm not saying that," Paige reminded him. "I don't think you need to jump in with both feet. Stay in the background as much as you can."

"You have nothing to worry about, *mi amor,*" He assured her. "This here is fine."

"The quiet before the storm makes me nervous."

"There is nothing to be nervous about," Jorge replied. "The police will be too busy trying to fix their image and trying to stop the protests that the Naomi cult will have in full swing by the weekend. They will not have time to look further than that."

"What's your goal here?"

"I want someone who has all the power sitting right there," Jorge pointed to a seat on the other side of the desk. "Telling me that it is *me* who holds all the power. Until that moment, we will never be at complete peace. If we have the police on our side, we have added protection."

Paige continued to appear skeptical as she glanced at their son as he made his way to Jorge, who leaned forward and picked him up. Sitting the toddler on his lap, he received a hug.

"You see, Paige, this here is for my family," Jorge insisted as he snuggled with Miguel. "If the police work for me, then I know that my children will always be safe because they will be a priority. This here, it is what I want. If I control the puppet strings, then everyone knows their place. That is all most people want, *mi amor,* it is to know their place. Once they do, everything, it tends to go smoother. People do not want to have to figure things out. They want the solution handed to them."

"So, you feel that they will..."

"Will be extra security," Jorge continued.

"This isn't Mexico," Paige gently reminded him. "I don't think you can control things quite as you did there."

"On the contrary, *mi amor*," Jorge insisted as Miguel finally sat still and closed his eyes. "Once again, you assume that the Canadian system is pristine, that people are honorable and follow the rules. I promise you that this is not the case. Someone's always is in control of the puppet strings. If it is not me, it is another powerful, rich, probably white man that runs the show. So why not me?"

The question hung in the air with no answer in sight. The two continued to speak of things relating to the home, their children, and plans for the day. However, before Jorge was able to get out of the house, Jolene showed up at the door.

"Jolene, I do not have time for this right now...." He attempted to explain as she walked into the house. "I tell you about the job more later once I have taken possession of the newspaper, and..."

"This is not about that," She insisted as she walked to the living room and sat on the couch. Jorge closed the door and followed her into the room, sitting in the chair across from her.

"What you want, Jolene?'

"Did you set me up?"

"For what?"

"With Athas, did you set me up?" She asked suspiciously. "At Miguel's number 2 birthday, did you set me up?"

"Jolene, I was taking care of business that day, and also, it was my son's birthday," He reminded her. "I do not have time to play matchmaker."

"You did it to increase his polls."

Jorge let out a laugh.

"Oh, Jolene, it was you who did that," Jorge stood up. "But for me, the last thing I want is you to create havoc in his life. So, no, Jolene, I did not set you up. What? Did you not enjoy the celebrity attention?"

Not answering the question, she rose from the couch. Appearing small and embarrassed, she didn't reply.

"Jolene, take a few days off," Jorge insisted as they walked toward the door. "We no longer need you with the series, this newspaper I bought, it will need your full attention soon. Trust me, this here is for the best."

After she left, he stood by the door, and he laughed.

CHAPTER

38

"Maria, you are to stay home from school today," Jorge insisted as soon as their daughter joined them for breakfast. "There is too much going on."

"What?" She appeared confused as she approached the table. "I have a test today in…"

"Maria, this here is important," Jorge pointed toward the laptop, where he watched a live protest against the police that was taking place in the downtown area. Although no violence or crime was being committed yet, there was a sense of tension that was difficult to miss. "I do not trust that this here won't explode. I want you to stay at home."

"*Papa,*" Maria leaned in and stared at the screen. "That's not even near my school."

"Maria, it is still early, and a lot of people are angry," Jorge reminded her. "I don't want you out, period. I want you at home where you are safe."

"But, my test…"

"Let's relax," Paige commented as she sat beside Miguel's highchair. "Your test is this afternoon. We can make sure you're there in time for that unless something changes."

Paige gave Jorge a look, and he replied with a nod.

Maria appeared skeptical as she glanced at the laptop.

"Is that the Tom guy you know, *Papa?*" She pointed toward the reporter who was live-streaming the event. "Wow…"

"Yes, Maria, he saw what was taking place and wanted to get out among the people to learn more," Jorge commented. "He is a smart reporter."

"People seem really mad."

"Well, Maria," Jorge turned toward his daughter. "Our new episode shows that there are white supremacists infiltrating our police departments and RCMP. They are mad because Toronto, of course, is a city of the world. We have people here from so many places, and many have been harassed by police or ignored when they needed help."

"Speaking of which," Paige chimed in as she wiped some mushed up cereal off of Miguel's chin. "Isn't the indigenous episode next?"

"Yes, *mi amor* and the police, they never help those people," Jorge ranted. "Missing and dead indigenous women and children, the police do nothing."

"Because they don't care," Paige muttered.

"Chase talks about that a lot," Maria mused.

"Well, Maria, that is what he is," Jorge reminded her. "His mother, she was from a reserve. This is his people."

"Have you seen any footage?" Paige asked.

"Some," Jorge nodded as his eyes landed back on his laptop. "It is not pretty, but then again, neither is this episode."

"Your show, *Papa,* it was trending on Twitter," Maria reminded him. "I watched it."

"Really?" Jorge turned to his daughter, impressed. "What did you think, Maria?"

"I think that it's scary," Maria admitted and made a face. "I don't trust the police, *Papa.*"

"Maria, if I teach you anything, it is not to trust anyone, no matter what kind of fancy uniform they wear or how well educated they are," Jorge spoke honestly, as he placed a hand on his heart. "Trust you."

Maria nodded.

"Not all police are bad," Paige gently countered.

"But they are not all good either," Jorge jumped in. "As you saw from my show last night."

"So, these white supremacist guys," Maria finally sat down beside him. "So, they hate people because they aren't white?"

"Well, they aren't crazy on Jews either, Maria," Jorge reminded her. "They hate a lot of people."

"I don't understand," Maria shook her head. "What difference? Who cares?"

"Exactly, Maria, who cares?" Jorge complained. "But these people, they would not even believe that Paige and I should have had Miguel because he is a mixed-race baby. They would prefer if Paige had a baby with a white man."

All eyes were suddenly on Miguel, who continued to eat with no cares in the world.

"Ok, let's just let this go," Paige calmly warned. "The point is that there are some people out there who are...."

"Fucking racists," Jorge jumped in.

Maria laughed.

"Jorge, can we.....tone it down a bit?" Paige gently, but sternly, reminded him.

"Maria," Jorge calmed slightly. "The point is that everything in this show last night was true. There are white supremacist groups out there, and they try to have their people in the police, in government because these here are powerful positions. They can create havoc from the inside."

Although he didn't want to scare his daughter, he also knew it was important to inform her of the truth.

The protest remained peaceful, but as it turned out, Jorge's instincts weren't wrong. A late afternoon phone call would confirm this fact.

"Jorge," Hail spoke sheepishly from the other end. "I think there's something you should know."

"Yeah?" Jorge leaned back in his office chair.

"On my way out of work, I heard them complaining about the show last night," Hail spoke in a low tone as if he thought someone would overhear him. "They want the protests to stop immediately."

"It is not illegal to have a peaceful protest," Jorge stated as he glanced at the window. "Or has this suddenly changed?"

"Supposedly, the concern is about how it could get out of control like protests have in other places," Hail hesitated before going on. "They want the police to show up or have a 'presence' if they're out again tomorrow."

"They will be," Jorge replied.

"There's talk of riot gear."

Jorge fell silent.

"They do that on purpose to send a strong message for people to go the fuck home," Hail insisted. "Nothing is official though."

"Thank you for this here information," Jorge replied. "We will be in touch."

Ending the call, he sat behind his desk and thought for a moment. He found Naomi's number.

There's talk of a police presence and maybe riot gear.

Bring it on. This will only work against them.

Jorge grinned and thought for a moment. He messaged Makerson.

Are you going to the protests again tomorrow?

Not sure.

There's talk of police, riot gear.

I'll be there. I'll alert my friend at the news channel too.

Perfecto.

As he considered his options, Jorge's thoughts were interrupted when Paige and Maria walked into his office.

"First shooting lesson is complete," Paige announced as Maria pranced in with a grin on her face. "And very successful, I might add."

"Really?" Jorge was surprised. "I did not know you were going."

"After her test, for a bit," Paige calmly replied as they both sat down. "She handled herself well, took it seriously, had some pretty good shots."

"Wow," Jorge nodded toward his daughter. "I am impressed."

"I'm super excited," Maria danced in her chair. "It was fun."

"Maria, it is not a game," Jorge warned. "This is for emergencies only."

"I know, *Papa,* I know."

"I am serious, *chica.* I understand you want to learn, but it is not something I want you to use unless necessary."

"Remember, a gun can be grabbed and used against you too," Paige reminded her. "And it's not a video game. This is real life."

"This is true, Maria," Jorge spoke solemnly, even though he was secretly proud of her enthusiasm. "You must be careful however, I am very happy that you did well today."

"I was awesome, *Papa,*" She bragged. "A natural."

"Well, Maria, this here is in your blood," Jorge reminded her. "So, I am not that surprised."

"We talked about how she can't tell Cameron or any of her friends," Paige told Jorge, and Maria nodded vigorously. "It's better that few people know."

"But I can tell Chase, right?" Maria asked, directing her question toward Jorge.

"Yes, Chase, he is fine," Jorge replied with a grin. "That would be fine."

"I'm gonna call him now," She bounced off the chair and headed for the door. "Thank you, Paige."

After she was gone, the couple exchanged looks.

"As I said," Jorge finally replied. "It is in her blood."

CHAPTER

39

"As it turns out, my series has affected the country," Jorge announced to the group the following morning. Leaning back in his chair, he noted the expressions on everyone's face before continuing to glance around the VIP room. "The people, they will soon realize that the police, they are not to be trusted."

"Most people will continue to believe in them," Paige interjected. "This series or the protests won't change their mind."

"Yeah, the sheep," Diego spoke up.

"But it will cause some serious doubts," Jorge reminded them. "Just as I tell Maria, you must never have blind trust in anyone. I do not care what their title is or what kind of uniform they wear."

"That's for sure," Chase agreed. "The whole system is a joke."

"So, the protests," Jolene piped up. "Did you start?"

"I had a hand in it," Jorge replied. "Just as I will have a hand in when they will stop."

"But there are more protests across the country, right?" Chase asked.

"No, these here," Jorge pointed toward the laptop on the table. "This was not me. All the people need is one place to lead, and they soon follow. It is our natural way."

"I don't know," Diego seemed uncertain. "I don't like the idea of police being around with riot gear."

"That is to scare us, Diego," Jorge reminded him. "To put us in our place. It is more about appearance and intimidation than it is to do anything. They want people to go home."

"But how far do we want this to go," Paige asked. "I just…I don't see how this will help."

"Trust me, *mi amor,* we must put the police in a weak position," Jorge reminded her. "Specifically here in Toronto because that is the only way to have control. They must know who has the power."

"I don't get it," Diego shrugged. "What's the plan? We keep the series going…it's only got a few more episodes, and we keep the riots going? And then what? What's the point?"

"As I keep saying," Jorge reminded them. "We must let them know who has the power. We want the police to work for *us*. We want to be untouchable. If they know that we have the power to drag them down, to cast doubt, to make them valueless, then they will keep out of our way but be there when we need them. I want to run the police. That is my plan."

"I hate to say it," Diego shook his head. "But if anyone can do it, it's Jorge Hernandez."

"So, if that's the case?" Chase jumped in. "That means….."

"It means we are protected," Jorge replied. "We cannot get arrested. My children will be kept an eye on. If I need help, I get it. As long as all goes smoothly for me, all will go smoothly for them. The minute anyone steps out of line, it is a whole other story."

"We, all of us, will be protected?" Jolene appeared confused. "They cannot arrest."

"It means if they stop you because you are speeding, you just say you work for me," Jorge replied. "And they leave you alone. There are benefits to all of you for this. You will be, in essence, above the law."

"But why should they do this?" Jolene asked. "They do not have to."

"Because I can make their life hell if they do not," Jorge answered. "And they are already getting a taste. They do not want all their corruption coming out."

"Yeah, there's a lot of talk about that," Chase assured them. "On social media, around the city, people are starting to feel free to talk about problems they've had with the police…"

"I've opened a floodgate," Jorge replied. "And I am the only person who can close it up again."

"So, for now, we…" Diego leaned in.

"Just wait," Jorge reassured him. "Something big is around the corner. But until then, Jolene, you start at the paper tomorrow. You have your instructions on what to do?"

"Fire the editor?"

"There are other things, Jolene," Jorge reminded her. "But yes, that is your first move. I will have Makerson proposition the people he wants, and the rest get laid off in the next couple of weeks. When Tony is finished with the series, he will be helping me create a media company, hiring people, that kind of thing. You will be his assistant to help him with what he needs, keep an eye on things, you know..."

Jolene nodded.

"And Chase, I think I told you, all our parties and the hangout for the studio people will be at the bar," He continued. "They will have incentives to go there, of course."

"Maria will love to hear that," Chase said.

"And yes, she will help you soon on a limited basis," Jorge reminded him. "But only when the bar is closed, of course, make her work. It is a real job. Whatever you need, even if that means cleaning the toilets. I do not care."

Chase appeared surprised.

"I am serious," Jorge continued. "Do not make her a princess. She must work and see the real truth about running a bar, and everything involved."

"Ok," Chase agreed while beside him, Jolene made a face.

"By this fall, we will be even more powerful than ever before," Jorge reminded them as he pushed his chair out and stood up. "We will rule this city."

"Sounds good to me," Diego replied as he started to stand. "You know, I was thinking...

Diego's voice suddenly sounded so far away. Jorge could hear him, but there was a hollow sound so, he couldn't make out his words. A cold sweat swept over him, and he felt a heaviness in his chest, causing him to lean against the nearby chair. Everyone's voices sounded strange as if they were in a different room, and yet, he could sense them moving in closer almost to the point that he felt trapped, unable to breathe. His tie was too tight. There was something wrong with him.

"Jorge...."

Was that Paige? Did he imagine her voice? He felt someone helping him into a chair, just as he felt his body coming back down to earth. Slowly, the words were making sense again, and his vision returned to normal. Slowly, he could recognize the fear in everyone's eyes. His stomach suddenly felt nauseous, and a shot of cold air seemed to enclose his body as he reached out to touch the nearby table and took a deep breath.

"We're going to the hospital!" Paige insisted. "Now!"

"I am not...Paige. I am fine," Jorge corrected her. "I feel a little woozy for a minute, and now, I am fine. It is nothing."

"It's your fucking heart," Diego spoke in a panicked voice. "Jorge, you had a minor heart attack before and now...."

"Diego, please," Jorge put his hand in the air. "I am still not feeling too wonderful. Could you please calm down for a moment? I do not need this right now."

"Jorge, you are sick, go to hospital!" Jolene insisted.

"Please, can I have a moment?" Jorge put his hand up and noted the genuine look of concern on their faces, and his heart felt heavy. "I appreciate, I do appreciate that you all care, but I need a moment alone. I cannot have this much talking."

With reluctance, the group slowly started to disperse, heading out of the VIP room and into the main bar. Paige stayed behind, with obvious worry in her eyes that caused him to look away. He didn't want her to see him like this.

"How many times has this happened that you didn't tell me?" She asked, with no judgment in her voice.

"Paige...it is not often I feel this way."

"How many?" Her voice was small this time, and he immediately felt guilty.

"Just...you know, a couple of times lately," Jorge admitted with shame. "But it is a panic attack. You know me, I have a lot on my plate and this here...I feel overwhelmed at times, and that is all. It is nothing."

"But what if it's not?" She asked, and he looked up. He hesitated to reply.

"I am fine, Paige. Do not worry. It is just stress. This is not like the last time when it was more serious. I remember how that felt. It is not the same."

"But why not check, just in case," She pushed. "For me, please."

"Paige, I do not have time," Jorge pointed toward his phone. "I have a meeting with Tony and then...

"Cancel them," Paige spoke up with determination in her voice. "This is your health. Your family wants you here. We don't care if you have power over the police or whatever. This doesn't matter. You need to let it go."

"But Paige...."

"Please, Jorge, we can't keep doing this," Paige insisted as she sat down beside him. "We need to back off. We need to figure out what is most important to us. The fact that we're teaching our 13-year-old daughter how to shoot a gun, that says something about our lifestyle."

"Paige, what are you saying? We walk away from all this because I had a panic attack?"

"I think it's more than this panic attack," She reminded him. "This is your body telling you something is wrong. Whether it's a heart attack or a panic attack, you have to listen. It's only going to give you so many warnings."

Jorge considered her words and didn't speak.

"Please, can we ease off at least," Paige suggested. "I don't mean that we have to completely disregard everything here, end the series, and move to the middle of nowhere, but can we at least step back a bit. Maybe let things play out and not cause more chaos than is necessary. Put the rest of the series out. Tell Naomi not to push the protesters so much. Just back off, please, and let's take a breather after this."

Jorge nodded and took a deep breath. She was right. It was time. It wasn't worth it anymore. He would message Naomi and stay in the background. It was time to walk away.

Except of course, when he turned on his phone, Jorge discovered that this might not be so easy.

CHAPTER

40

"I tell you that it was nothing," Jorge reminded her as they left the hospital. "They do the tests, they do all this here funny stuff, but in the end, I was right."

"You weren't completely right," Paige was quick to remind him as they reached the SUV. "He said your blood pressure was up."

Of course it was," Jorge insisted with laughter in his voice. "You take me to a hospital. Of course, I am going to get upset. This here, it is ok. It shows that I am still alive and full of fire."

"It shows," Paige corrected him as she reached the passenger side of the SUV. "That you need to calm down."

"Paige, you know me. It is my natural state to be in the center of the excitement," Jorge insisted as he got in the SUV and watched Paige do the same, with skepticism in her eyes. "This here is normal. The doctors want me to be afraid, and Big Pharma wants me to take their pills. It's all part of the machine, Paige. I assure you, I am fine."

She didn't look convinced and remained quiet for the drive home. Jorge's phone beeped just as they arrived in the garage.

"What is it?" Paige leaned over as Jorge bit his lower lip. "What's going on?"

"The protests," Jorge said and took a deep breath as he automatically began to tap on his phone. "They are growing angrier."

"What?" Paige spoke sharply. "But Maria....she's..."

"I will have Chase get her at school," Jorge insisted. "I am sure she will be fine, but the protests are getting close to her school."

"I don't like this," Paige confessed, and Jorge gave her an assuring look.

"Paige, it will be fine, I..."

His phone began to ring, interrupting their conversation. It was Makerson.

"Hello," Jorge answered as he and Paige got out of the SUV. "What is it?"

"We got a problem."

"What?"

"Things are picking up fast....it's getting pretty dicey."

"Oh?"

"And I'm checking around other places," Makerson continued. "The protests are continuing across the country, but they're getting violent here......some far-right..."

His phone cut out. Jorge stopped on the spot.

"What is it?" Paige asked as she reached the garage door.

"Makerson," Jorge shook his head and attempted to call him back. "He disappeared."

"Maybe his phone died?"

Jorge made another attempt to call back as they walked into the house, but with no luck.

"I sent a text to Chase for you."

"Oh yes, I was going to," Jorge attempted to call Makerson again. "But..."

"Is that your secure line in the office?" Paige asked as a faint sound could be heard. "I think it is."

Jorge rushed to the office, closing the door behind him. It was Athas.

"What the fuck did you do?"

"To what?" Jorge asked with a sharp return. "What are you talking about?"

"The fucking protest downtown," Athas snapped. "I thought you were handling it. I thought you were going to keep it under control."

"So, it is picking up steam, so what, Athas?"

"Picking up steam?" Athas countered. "There are cars on fire, and a far-right group is attacking protesters. Is that what you consider *picking up steam*? Are you hoping to have the entire city burn down because of your attack on the police?"

"The police, they are useless," Jorge snapped back. "If they weren't so useless, these protests would not be happening in the first place."

"They were brought on by your series…"

"Which tells the truth," Jorge snapped. "Athas, what do you want from me? The people are expressing their views."

"Do something about it!" Athas snapped.

"So, you are admitting that I am more powerful than the police," Jorge pushed. "That I am more powerful than *you?*"

"Just do something," Athas sounded defeated on the other end. "I have the Toronto mayor and the police chief both coming to me for help. What the fuck am I supposed to do?"

"Change the police altogether. That is what you need to do," Jorge snapped back. "Announce that because of these protests…"

"Riots," Athas sharply corrected him.

"That these *riots* demonstrate that people are dissatisfied and that my series, it shows that there are a lot of problems to solve with the police…"

"Yes, I admit that," Athas snapped. "Will you please help me."

"I am trying," Jorge snapped back as his heart began to race, and he took a deep breath. "I am telling you that you must announce right now that you plan to start an investigation into the police, both locally and federally with the RCMP. You are going to put a stop to the blatant racism, that you will screen prospects more closely and that you will also punish the cops who break the law more severely because they are supposed to represent the law, that you hold them at higher esteem. Now, Athas, are you getting all of this in your little notebook?"

"I got it," Athas seemed to relent. "But this isn't going to stop what's going on now."

"You will ask…..*beg* the people to step back," Jorge continued. "And meanwhile, I will see what I can do."

"Make it fast."

"Athas, I do not take my orders from you."

As if he suddenly realized where he stood, the prime minister stepped back.

"Please, Jorge, I need your help."

"And you will get it," Jorge assured him.

Ending the call, he quickly messaged Naomi.

End it. Now.

She didn't reply, and of course, he knew it was out of her hands. He turned on his laptop to look for live footage while trying to contact Makerson.

There was no answer.

A knock at the door grabbed his attention. It was Paige.

"Things are really bad...."

"I know," Jorge snapped. "I am sorry, Paige, but this here..."

"Is why I worry about you," She cut in. "This is too much."

"I know," Jorge typed in his laptop. Finding live footage, he grimaced.

"There's talk of getting the army in," Paige gently told him as she sat across from him. "This can't continue."

"I know," Jorge replied as he found the footage he was looking for. "I know this, Paige."

His phone beeped. It was Naomi.

We can't stop now. We need to get our message out.

I am telling you to stop. It was not a suggestion.

It isn't that easy.

I don't care. Stop it. Now.

Sitting his phone down, Jorge didn't want to admit that he didn't have control of the situation. He felt his heart pounding furiously and attempted to hide his discomfort from Paige. Taking a deep breath, he opened his mouth to say something but stopped.

Jorge's phone beeped, and Paige looked down at it and gasped.

"What? What is it?"

"Chase has Maria, but he said they're trapped within the protests. They had to get out of his car and run away because Maria was scared."

Jorge didn't reply.

He felt trapped.

His heart continued to pound.

"Jorge...."

"I know," He replied with frustration in his voice. "Where are they now?"

"He said they're making their way back to the bar."

"Ok, so....they are close?"

"I think so."

His phone beeped again. It was Diego

Are you ok?

Yes, amigo.

What the fuck is going on downtown?

He didn't reply. He wasn't sure what to say. For the first time in his life, Jorge felt powerless. He had no idea what to do. He didn't think things

200 | MIMA

would get this out of hand, and yet, he couldn't let the others know the truth. They were counting on him to handle everything, but in reality, he couldn't handle this situation.

Paige's phone beeped.

"They made it to the bar," Paige said with relief before they both turned their attention back to the commotion on the screen. It was difficult to tell the protesters from the authorities or far-right group. Everything was such a mess.

"We can't do anything," Paige gently commented as if reading his thoughts. "You can't control this one, but you can make sure it stops here."

"I have already told Naomi…."

"I don't think it's going to be that easy."

"Athas, he is going to make an announcement soon…"

"You have ripped the bandaid off and shown everyone the scab," Paige reminded him. "You can't cover it back up again. People are angry, and rightfully so. Even if Athas announces changes and even if Naomi hauls things back, there's still some who will be out there."

"Paige, my intention…."

"I know, this wasn't your intention," She assured him. "I know."

He felt like a rat in a cage. Text messages were coming in, and he felt unable to deal with them. There was no answer.

"This needed to happen," Paige spoke gently. "Now that the truth is out, they can't avoid it."

As the day passed, the protests slowed down and eventually ended. Many arrests were made while other people were hurt. Jorge had no luck getting back in touch with either Naomi or Makerson. He contacted Hail to see if he had any information.

Naomi was arrested. I have no information on Makerson.

It wasn't until much later that night that the news arrived. Makerson was in the hospital.

CHAPTER

41

Just a drunk Indian, out for some fun. So I gave it to her. That's all they ever want anyway, you know?

Paige tensed up as soon as she heard the audio from the upcoming episode of *Eat the Rich Before the Rich Eat You*. Glancing toward Jorge, he gave her a sad smile and shrugged, unsure of what to say. It made him angry to hear the voices of two RCMP officers speaking so casually about raping an indigenous woman, but he had to push those feeling aside and instead focus on his wife's reaction. Ranting and raging wasn't what she wanted to hear right now.

"I...it's not that I can't believe this happened," Paige sadly shook her head. "It...it makes me sick. That's how they saw this...what? Teenaged girl?'"

"Tony, he says she was 17, so yes," Jorge replied, his eyes scanning the laptop screen that he just paused. It was a black image with the words frozen along with the audio of the secretly taped recording. "She was really...not much older than my daughter and Paige, if this were Maria that they were speaking of, I would kill this man with my own hands."

Paige nodded with pride in her eyes. They both knew that nothing came before family with Jorge, and he had proven it many times. If something so vile were to happen to his daughter, no prior rage would ever match the one he would expose as a result. The person responsible would suffer to their last breath.

"So, this is how the next episode starts?" Paige gently asked. "With this recording."

"Paige, I know this here is harsh," Jorge leaned forward against his desk. "But it is necessary for the people to hear this. Many of these women, as you know, go missing or are murdered, and the police do not care. And in this recording, we hear that the police are sometimes involved."

Paige shook her head and looked away.

"This woman that they talk about, she was raped in this policeman's car," Jorge continued. "He let her out on the side of the road afterward and she was never seen again. At least, that is the story he tells."

"Why would he even confess this?" Paige shook her head. "I don't understand."

"This other man suspected the cop knew something and got him drunk so he confesses," Jorge pointed toward the monitor. "This here was something that the police, they ignored because they claim that the audio, it is not clear enough to distinguish that it is him plus because he was drunk."

"It sounds pretty clear to me."

Jorge nodded.

"Unbelievable," Paige shook her head. "And Tony didn't fix it up with some...I don't know, audio tricks?"

"Nope," Jorge shook his head. "Paige, this man, he says these things about an indigenous woman, but who is to say he wouldn't see my people as the same. What if one day, that were Maria?"

The two shared a look.

"Paige, the viewers, they must see this," Jorge went on. "In this episode, Tony finds people who say that the men who sometimes work on these pipelines, they are near reserves and may be responsible for some of these women going missing. And the police, they turn the other way."

Paige shook her head.

"This will be the most powerful episode yet," Jorge predicted. "This here has been an issue, and the government, they have done little. Maybe investigate or have an inquiry, but what is that? What does that do? Nothing."

"They never intended to do anything," Paige quietly added. "But maybe Alec can make a difference?"

"Maybe," Jorge shrugged. "Maybe, he will not have a choice."

Paige didn't reply but looked uncomfortable.

"At any rate," Jorge continued. "After this show airs tonight, we are not sure how the people will react. Considering how they have in the past..."

"You don't have Naomi doing anything this time?" Paige referred to the person heading the protests in prior weeks. "It doesn't mean it won't happen anyway."

"I believe it will," Jorge reminded her. "Remember when that reserve, it burned down?"

Paige remembered. It was during a particularly bad forest fire season. The people died because help was sent elsewhere, and the indigenous community was left to burn. Originally, it was thought that the government didn't save them on purpose. Later, it was learned that it was someone in the government responsible for the fire in the first place. An uproar of protests broke out throughout Canada, and the prime minister at the time had to step down. Alec Athas eventually stepped in.

"Paige, this here will make the people very angry."

"As it should."

"And this episode, it plays tonight."

The two exchanged looks before Jorge hit the play button for them to continue watching the show.

It was later that morning that Jorge stopped by Makerson's condo. Since being attacked at the previous week's protest, both the doctor and Jorge agreed that he should stay out of the line of fire.

"You look well," Jorge commented even though his eyes were focused on a scar on the editor's face. "All things considered."

"All things considered," Makerson repeated as he closed the door and gestured toward his couch. "Can I get you anything?"

"Should it not be me asking you the same question?" Jorge asked with a grin. "You are, after all the patient."

"I'm better," Makerson admitted as they both headed toward the couch and sat down. "Not going back to the office better, but I'm better. I've been doing a little work from here, but..."

"You had a concussion," Jorge reminded him. "Not a little thing."

"It is what it is," Makerson admitted. "I still don't know who hit me."

"Probably a cop," Jorge sniffed. "They were in the mix, I heard some were not in uniform."

"I heard that too," Makerson nodded. "It was funny that I was the only reporter that was hit."

"That's 'cause you're the only reporter making a lot of noise," Jorge reminded him. "They knew what they were doing."

"I keep trying to remember...to think who did it, but I didn't see it coming."

"Well, if you follow the rat, you'll find the cheese," Jorge commented. "I would not be surprised if it was the police that did this...."

"Or the far-right group," Makerson snuffed. "Which, I'm told, sometimes work with the police."

"This, it does not surprise me," Jorge admitted as he glanced around his place. "And you are still safe here, no problems?"

"No," Makerson shook his head. "I'm fine."

"If this changes," Jorge reminded him as he stood up. "You call me right away."

"I think I'll be fine," Makerson insisted as he stood up. "I'm working from home for the rest of the week and back to the office on Monday."

"Very good," Jorge headed toward the door.

"I do have one request though," Makerson caught him by surprise and he swung around. "You said that your daughter was there during the protests?"

"She was caught in them, yes."

"Could I interview her...not as your daughter, but as an anonymous source, from a teenager's perspective?"

"I do not see why not," Jorge grinned. "Maria, she is very dramatic, so I believe she would like this..."

"If you don't mind...."

"Not at all," Jorge confirmed with a smile as he turned back toward the door. "I will be in contact."

He headed downtown to the club, where he was scheduled to meet Naomi. When he arrived, she was talking to Chase at the bar.

"People come from all around," She was saying as Jorge made his way across the room. "Because they see the importance of the cause. You have to make noise if you want people to listen, and sometimes, this is the only way."

"I don't disagree with that," Jorge commented as he sat beside her. "This is, after all, the way of the world."

"Hello Mr. Hernandez," Naomi spoke with respect in her voice. "Thank you for meeting me."

"Thank you," Jorge nodded. "So the episode for tonight, have you watched it?"

"I have," Naomi nodded with hesitation. "And I can't promise that people won't break out on their own over this one. It's pretty contentious."

"I know, I'm furious," Chase admitted. "But I'm not surprised."

"Is there any word?" Jorge asked Naomi. "Are there plans?"

"It's hard to say," She shook her head. "I tried to calm the waters, but I don't know...after watching that episode, all hell could break loose when it's released. I might not have the control that you think I have."

"But what difference?" Chase cut in. "If there are protests, does it matter? Isn't that a good thing, because it will bring attention to what is going on..."

"I promised Athas I would not have the city burnt to the ground," Jorge admitted. "And I am not so sure I can keep this promise."

"So, let it happen...." Chase suggested.

"The problem is," Naomi cut in. "Is that the police get into it with riot gear on and that causes people to get more agitated."

"Which is what they want..." Chase nodded.

"They want to say that the people were out of control, and that's why they attacked them," Jorge reminded him.

"Can't Athas stop this?" Chase asked.

"He has tried," Jorge replied. "They do as they want."

"You would be surprised how little control they have over municipalities," Naomi shook her head. "The Toronto mayor is pushing the police on the scene because they don't want their city destroyed, and that's the justification they need."

"To hit my key reporter over the head..." Jorge added. "This is what I suspect."

"But we can't prove it," Naomi replied. "That's the problem I run into. People don't believe me because I'm just a *crazy* activist, but I have seen it happen in the past, and I've been told to keep my mouth shut...or else."

Jorge raised an eyebrow.

"You don't understand how dangerous these people are," She spoke dramatically. "They have the law protecting them, but what do we have?"

"You have better than the law," Jorge boasted with arrogance in his voice. "You have me."

CHAPTER

42

"But he said it was better to not use my name," Maria informed both Paige and Jorge after they read the online interview that came from an anonymous source who got caught up in the riots. "But he said it would be cool to have a young person's point of view."

"It is, Maria," Jorge nodded as they all leaned in to read some of the replies made underneath. "It is safer not to expose your identity, especially with what you said about the police officers who were on the scene."

"They *were* scary!" Maria stood up straighter and, her brown eyes grew in size. "I mean, the people, they didn't scare me, but the police that wore those….what do you call it? The face shields and…"

"Riot gear," Paige calmly answered.

"Yeah, like *that* was scary," Maria confirmed. "I thought they were going to hit me, and all I did was happen to be there at the wrong place and time, you know?"

"This here, Maria, shows you how police, they like to control us," Jorge warned her. "You must always be careful."

"I know, like, that show from last night," Maria made a face and glanced at the laptop to indicate the streaming series. "That was creepy. Is that true? Did that cop really do that to the indigenous woman?"

"Yes, Maria," Jorge nodded. "And she was not much older than you."

"But she was just a kid."

"And yet, nothing was done," Jorge reminded her. "Maria, you are a smart young woman, and you must always trust your instincts and be careful. You trust your family and be cautious of everyone else."

Maria nodded.

"Jorge, we don't want her to be scared of the world," Paige reminded him.

"Maria, it is as I alway say," Jorge jumped in, touching his chest. "Listen to yourself."

"I will, *Papa,* I promise."

It was after she left the room that Jorge confessed his fears for his daughter.

"Paige, she is so small," He spoke in a quiet voice. "So frail. I worry about her. We try to get her interested in martial arts, self-defense but she quickly grows bored. The only way to protect herself she has cared for so far is learning to shoot a gun. And this here, it does not fill me with confidence."

"I know," Paige nodded, glancing toward the stairs to make sure her step-daughter was out of earshot. "But we have to trust that she is more powerful than she appears. And we have to wait until she wants to learn these things before we can effectively teach her."

Jorge reluctantly agreed. He glanced at his phone and stood up.

"I gotta go. Tony is expecting me."

"He must be happy over last night's ratings," Paige commented as Jorge grabbed his phone.

"Best ones yet," Jorge replied before leaning in to kiss his wife. "But the locals, they are restless."

Jorge was barely in his SUV and out of the driveway when his phone rang. He was surprised to see it was Athas.

"Good morning, Mr. Prime Minister," Jorge spoke flippantly. "Did you mix up your lines? This here is my cell."

"There are more protests downtown," He spoke bluntly.

"Ah, thank you for the update," Jorge mocked him. "But I'm actually going the other way."

"What are you going to do about it?"

"I already spoke to Naomi," Jorge replied.

"Yeah, well, she's there."

"She might be, but she didn't start them this time," Jorge informed him. "I tell her not to."

"I find it hard to believe."

"That I told her not to?"

"That she would listen to you at all," Athas replied. "She doesn't listen to anyone, and as I said, she's there now. She started this shit."

Jorge felt his anger build up.

"I will take care of it."

"I think I should go down there."

"And what?" Jorge started to laugh.

"I could make a speech."

"What? Stand on top of a car and call order to the group?" Jorge mocked him. "Stay the fuck where you are."

He ended the call then attempted to call Naomi. There was no response. He called the bar.

"Are there protesters outside?" Jorge asked Chase. "Around the bar?"

"No, I mean...I don't think so," Chase replied and could be heard shuffling around. "I don't see anything here, but that doesn't mean they aren't in the area."

"I am told Naomi might be involved even though I tell her not to."

"She did say she wouldn't start the fire, but she'd jump in if she had to."

Jorge felt his heart race.

"Tell me if this here changes."

"Will do."

By the time Jorge arrived at Tony's place, he was fuming. This automatically concerned the young filmmaker when he met him at the door.

"The ratings are good..." he stumbled on his words as Jorge walked inside. "I was just checking..."

"Yes, this here is great," Jorge automatically shifted gears. "Everything with the series, it is fine. Lots of great comments."

"I wasn't expecting more protests this soon," Tony pointed toward the laptop on a nearby desk. "I stopped to watch before I got back to work."

"Yes, well, there weren't supposed to be any, but the people, they already had the fire in them," Jorge commented as he moved closer and examined the screen. "It does not look too bad so far."

"I heard there could be more across the country," Tony replied as he looked at the screen. "But I think that's natural considering the information we are putting out. I sent Andrew down to check things out."

"I do not care if the people want to protest," Jorge informed him. "My concern is how far these protests will go and how the police will react. They may get out the riot gear again."

"I assume they will," Tony spoke with some hesitation as he moved closer to Jorge. "A lot of people are mad. They've heard about missing and murdered indigenous women but, this episode gave them more facts and that recorded conversation with the officer…"

"He claims it is not him."

"We proved that it was."

"And yet, he will get away with his crimes," Jorge assured him. "They always do."

"Thus, the protests….." Tony pointed toward the screen. "Can you see at the back?"

"Nah," Jorge shook his head. "Just more people."

"I think that's riot gear," Tony pointed out as he sat down in the nearby chair and did something to the monitor to increase the size. Jorge watched but didn't see anything. At least, not at first.

"Yeah, it's the cops," Tony spoke excitedly. "In riot gear…"

"No way…."

"I wonder if Andrew is there yet…"

Tony grabbed his phone and hit some buttons. It could be heard ringing, but with no answer.

"He may not hear," Jorge suggested as he sat down beside him.

Tony didn't reply. He left a message for Andrew.

This here," Jorge pointed toward the screen as the police started to move in. "This is too much. The protest, it looked peaceful."

"They're pissed off that we are exposing them…."

Jorge continued to watch while his mind raced. Grabbing his phone, he quickly texted Paige.

Stay home with the kids. Downtown is a mess.

The cops again?

Yes.

That's when Chase texted him.

Diego just got here. He said the protests are getting closer.

"It's finally on mainstream news," Tony announced after tapping on the keyboard of another laptop. "Before this, only the independent journalist was talking about it."

Jorge didn't comment but felt his chest tighten.

"Jesus, what a difference," Tony commented as he glanced from laptop to laptop. "The mainstream media is mentioning it while they stand away from it, but the independent journalists are in the middle of things."

Tony's phone rang, and he calmly answered it. Jorge noted that his face paled, his mouth fell open, and he looked like he couldn't speak.

"What….are….are you sure?"

He paused for a moment, nodded, and finally said.

"Get back here right now."

CHAPTER

43

"What the fuck is this?" Jorge repeated his question while Andrew fumbled with the phone, and Tony shook his head in disbelief. "Were the police shooting?"

"She was shot," Andrew spoke bluntly, his face pale, his eyes full of horror. "I was looking for her, and she was shot right in front of me."

"What are you talking about?" Jorge remained calm, while Tony hastily grabbed the phone from Andrew's hand and rushed toward his computer. "So, you go to the protests and..."

"I wanted to get footage," Andrew spoke excitedly. "I thought it would be helpful for the series. We were thinking of doing an episode on the actual protests later on. I wanted it to be very amateur looking as if it just happened to be caught..."

"Ok," Jorge spoke calmly and pointed toward a chair at the desk, encouraging Andrew to sit down. "And?"

"When I got there, I heard that Naomi chick was supposed to be there," Andrew continued as he sat down, and beside him, Tony had the footage on a monitor. "I wanted to find her to interview her for the show, and I saw her. I was headed toward her, and then it happened."

"She was shot?" Jorge asked and glanced toward the screen, but instead caught Tony nodding solemnly.

"Yes, I couldn't believe it," Andrew continued. "And...I..."

"Holy shit," Jorge said as he glanced toward the monitor and back at Andrew.

"I wanted to get my first-person perspective for the show," Andrew rambled nervously. "I didn't think I would capture anything like that."

"Would anyone else record it?" Tony asked.

"There were a lot of phones out, but mostly, people were caught up in the insanity," Andrew replied as he stared into space, shaking his head. "Everything happened so fast."

"I can see it here," Tony gestured toward the screen, and they both moved closer to view what he was pointing at. "I can see where she was shot, and I might be able to capture who did it."

Jorge could see the crowd, and when he finally was able to identify Naomi, it was as she fell to the ground. People surrounding her could be heard screaming, in a panic, attempted to help her, while others ran with the sound of a gun.

"She was targeted," Jorge automatically summed up the video. "This was not random. She was picked out of the crowd by someone who is a good shot. They got her, while missing the others."

"Like an assassin?" Andrew asked.

"Or a cop," Tony replied before Jorge had a chance.

"I do not know," Jorge said as he pointed toward the screen. "But this here, it was done by someone who knew what they were doing. Not a random, everyday person who has little or no experience with a gun."

"I'm trying to see who did it…."

"Well, all those cops with riot gear have guns," Andrew pointed out.

"It would not be one of them because it would be too easy to pick out," Jorge automatically shook his head. "It would be someone dressed like everyone else, so they blended in the crowd. I am almost positive."

Neither said a thing.

"So, what do we do with this?" Andrew asked while Tony continued to play with the computer, trying to see where the shot came from. "I mean, like….we can't use this in the series, can we?"

"The police would see this as evidence," Tony shook his head. "But people need to see this. We have to let them know that she was targeted. Otherwise, they'll make it sound very random."

"Can you see who did it?"

Tony shook his head.

"I wonder if there would be any other cameras around?" Andrew asked. "That would have caught something or a person who caught it."

"I bet someone did," Jorge replied.

"But the police," Tony shook his head. "They'll get to that footage right away."

"Yeah, and if it's one of their own," Andrew snuffed. "To erase it."

"We have to get to it first," Jorge replied as he reached for his phone and messaged Marco.

I have something I need you to do.

Sure, sir.

Perfecto.

He then called Diego.

"Come to Tony's," He quickly instructed. "Bring Marco too. We need your input for the series."

"Gotca," Diego replied. "Anything else?"

Jorge thought for a moment.

"Bring Jolene, we might need her."

"Are you sure about that?" Andrew asked skeptically as Jorge ended the call. "Do we *really* need Jolene?"

"It is possible," Jorge considered. "Marco, he can hack into nearby cameras and see what there is….."

"What about the footage?" Tony asked.

"I feel that we need to get it out there now," Jorge considered. "But we cannot let anyone know that we have it."

"And point out that it was someone who could hit a target through a crowd," Andrew piped up. "As you said, that isn't something most people can do."

"It also suggests it was planned," Tony added.

"Oh, it was planned," Jorge replied and tapped on his phone and held it up to his ear.

"Hello?" Paige was on the other end of the line.

"*Mi amor,*" Jorge spoke with enthusiasm in his voice as he walked away from the others. "We may need your help. I'm with Tony and Andrew."

"Ok," She replied. "On the film project?"

"Something like that," He glanced over his shoulder as he walked into another room. "We found some footage we need your thoughts on."

"I see," Paige calmly replied. "Well, Juliana will be back soon. I can leave after that."

"*Perfecto.*"

"Do you want me to get the others?"

"I have contacted Marco and Diego…" Jorge thought for a moment. "Maybe check in with Chase at the bar, but I would rather he stay there and keep an eye on things downtown."

"I just heard that the police are trying to shut the protests down," Paige told him.

"They sure are…."

"Ok…" She hesitated for a moment. "I will be there shortly."

After ending the call, Jorge made his way back to Andrew and Tony as they continued to inspect the video.

"Anything new?"

"Nothing," Tony shook his head. "It was directed at Naomi, and it was only for her because no other shots were fired, no one else was hurt…"

"Except maybe a few people who were stampeded on when everyone rushed to get away," Andrew threw in. "People are like fucking animals in these cases. They'll stomp on their fucking mother."

"Panic, it does this to people," Jorge considered.

"So who wanted her out?" Tony wondered.

"Who didn't?" Jorge asked. "She was causing an uprising and this here, many do not like."

"The police, especially," Andrew suggested. "This is them, I'm sure of it."

"Politicians don't like it either," Tony pointed out. "She was shaking things up a little too much, and it forced politicians to do something."

"My money is still on the cops," Andrew shook his head. "They wanted to shut her down and scare others into backing away."

"People are sheep," Jorge threw in. "They cannot think for themselves so this here might be enough for them to stop."

"Or come back stronger," Tony suggested. "Not everyone is a sheep."

"I'm wondering what kind of spin they'll put on this," Andrew asked, appearing more relaxed now. "That some random person in the crowd shot her for no reason?"

"They will say it was too hard to tell in that crowd," Jorge shrugged. "And call it a day."

"Well, they can't be that casual about it," Tony shook his head. "People will complain."

"At first," Jorge corrected him. "People will complain at first, and then they forget. The police, they count on this."

All three men agreed.

"It will go nowhere," Tony suggested. "Like those missing cops."

Andrew grinned and him and Jorge shared amused looks.

The doorbell rang.

"I will get it," Jorge said as he headed to the door, first glancing out the peephole to see Diego's beady eyes staring back. He opened the door.

"What the fuck is going on downtown?" Diego pointed outside. "Jesus fucking Christ, did you order more protests today?"

"That there, I had nothing to do with," Jorge stood aside as the two men walked in the door. He noted that Marco had his laptop bag. "That's the problem."

"Jolene is coming later," Diego answered the unasked question, as Jorge shut the door.

"What is it you need?" Marco asked as he glanced toward Tony and Andrew. "Something for the show?"

"Hey," Tony called out before Jorge could answer. "There's a news releases about the shooting."

The three men headed toward the makeshift office.

Andrew's face turned white, and he looked away.

"They just confirmed it was Naomi that was shot," Tony informed them. "And she's dead."

CHAPTER

44

By the time Paige arrived, everyone was locked in their tasks. There was an uncomfortable silence that was hard to ignore.

"What's going on?" Paige quietly asked as Jorge ushered her aside. "Did I hear correctly? Naomi was shot?"

"Yes, *mi amor*," Jorge spoke in a quiet voice as the two walked into the kitchen area. "Andrew, he was downtown trying to get footage while attempting to find Naomi. He found her just as she was shot. He got it on video."

"Oh wow," Paige's eyes widened. "Did he see who did it?"

"That is what we are trying to figure out now," Jorge pointed toward the next room. "Marco, he is hacking all the cameras to see what he can find."

"And the others?" Paige gestured toward the men surrounded by computers.

"They are helping him," Jorge replied. "But also, Andrew, he is creating an anonymous Twitter account to share the video he has and point out that it was done by someone who was trained because she was only one hit in a crowd and well, she died. So this here suggests it wasn't the usual crackpot with a gun."

"No, that's someone trained," Paige nodded. "Highly trained, who had the right angle. Someone who knew where she would be and could plan accordingly."

"They often take the same route," Jorge pointed out. "This here might make it easier."

"Someone who studied her well enough to know her natural inclination," Paige added. "She caused a lot of trouble. This was planned. Probably long before today."

"That is what I was thinking too, *mi amor*," Jorge nodded. "This here, it is a mess."

"So are they finding anything," Paige asked.

"Not yet," Jorge replied. "I need you to go home on my secure line and tell this information to Athas. And Paige, do you think he…"

"No," She automatically shook her head. "He wanted her stopped, not dead."

"What if someone in his office took it upon him or herself…"

"If I had to guess," Paige thought for a moment. "This is more local government, the city or the police. This wouldn't be his office. This doesn't affect them, other than pressure being put on Alec to do something about it."

"Can you believe he wanted to go there today to make a speech?" Jorge shook his head. "I said, 'stay the fuck where you are'."

"You talked to him?" Paige asked.

"He called my cell, which is not like him," Jorge replied. "He wanted to help, but I told him I would take care of it."

"Hopefully, he doesn't think you did…"

"I would not shoot the girl," Jorge replied. "I have been good, Paige. No blood on my hands this time."

She grinned and headed toward the door.

"Good thing he wasn't there," Paige commented as she reached for the doorknob. "He might have been a target."

Jorge didn't reply as she opened the door to leave, only to find Jolene standing on the other side.

"You need me?" She asked as she stepped in, and Jorge sighed.

"Paige, can you get her up to speed?" He headed toward the others. "I must check on progress."

Before she could answer, Jorge made his way across the room to see the others tapping on computers or staring at a screen.

"Sir, it looks like the cameras, they were already turned off," Marco complained as he shook his head. "I was looking, and there is nothing so far."

"Maybe there's one you missed?" Jorge suggested.

"Not yet," Marco commented. "It is like when we do something and turn off the cameras."

"They are copying us…" Andrew looked up from his screen. "But I got the video on Twitter and tagged a lot of people, so it will go viral. It can be removed or the account suspended, but it won't matter because it'll be spread."

"That is all I want," Jorge replied. "At least, we can let others know that this was a target."

"But who did it?" Tony shook his head. "I still think it was the police. She was causing way too much noise. And she was always leading protests, so it's not like she hasn't ruffled feathers before."

"But this time," Diego cut in. "It was the wrong one."

"Me, I think it was the police or someone higher up that didn't want more attention brought to things," Jorge insisted as Jolene made her way across the room and Paige left. "They did not want to be forced to do their job or explain their misconduct."

"These people," Jolene spoke up. "They are dangerous. We do not want to piss them off too much, you know?"

"When did I ever piss off the police?" Jorge countered, and everyone laughed. "This here is their problem. Not mine. I want to shake their cages up a little bit more."

"I think you have done that lots with this series," Tony commented. "And lowered their approval rating. I was going to tell you that today until everything went to shit."

"I still cannot believe she is dead," Jolene replied. "That woman, just because she protests?"

"She made too much noise," Diego shook his head. "They don't like that."

"It was us that caused the noise," Jorge gestured around the room. "She took it a step further."

"A little too far…." Andrew commented under his breath.

"Sir, I have this camera," Marco spoke up, pointing toward the monitor. "But it does not show much."

"So, the person who did this," Jolene cut in. "They must have a hacker too. Who would that be?"

"Anyone can be a hacker," Andrew countered.

"Police have hackers," Tony replied. "How do you think they get the evidence they need sometimes? They find a crafty way to explain it, but they got hackers."

"Fucking police," Diego shook his head.

Time seemed to go slow as the afternoon dragged on. The group was growing tired and frustrated.

"Sir, this is going nowhere," Marco eventually confirmed and leaned back in his chair as he stared at the screen. "I cannot find anything. This was well planned."

"What about someone on the ground?" Tony asked. "Would they have footage? Would someone maybe catch something?"

"Put that on Twitter," Diego directed Andrew. "Ask if anyone else has footage or information?"

"We're going to get a lot of garbage," Andrew reminded him.

"We could get something good too," Diego hurriedly pointed out. "Do it!"

"Diego, relax," Jorge shook his head. "This here..."

"You should see the comments I'm getting," Andrew cut him off. "This video is going viral. People are saying....shit!"

"What?" Jorge asked.

"Shit! My account was suspended."

"Start a new one," Diego instructed. "Keep doing it."

"I knew it would happen, just not this fast," Andrew shook his head. "Fuck."

"It doesn't matter the video is everywhere," Tony commented. "And spreading like crazy."

Jorge's phone rang. It was Paige. Walking away from the others, he answered it.

"*Mi amor!*"

"I talked to him," Paige spoke smoothly. "He knew and suspected the same."

"He had nothing to do with it?"

"Nope. He was upset that this happened at all."

"He have any ideas?"

"The same as yours," Paige confirmed. "He felt that certain individuals were putting pressure on him to condemn it. The same people who called for the riot gear and insisted this had to stop immediately."

Jorge fell silent.

"Did you find anything?"

"Everything is shut down."

"You mean…"

"Yup, we got nothing."

"So well planned."

"Exactly," Jorge replied. "A little too well planned."

"So, they're making sure that nothing is found."

"Unless someone on the ground recorded something?"

"If there is, they'll make sure that disappears fast."

"We were going to put a call out for it," Jorge commented as Jolene approached him. "But the account was suspended, so now, we gotta start a new one or find another way."

"It's almost like they work together, isn't it?" Paige commented.

"Maybe they do," Jorge replied and glanced at Jolene. "You got anything else?"

"No," Paige replied. "I'm doing some research here."

"Thank you, *mi amor.*"

"Talk soon."

Jorge ended the call.

"What is it, Jolene?" He asked as he slid his phone into his pocket.

"It is about Athas."

"What?"

"He is in the media saying that we were just friends," Jolene complained. "That is not true…"

"Jolene, I do not have time for this right now," Jorge spoke sharply. "What do you expect for me to do anyway?"

"Just ask him to be honest," She whined. "It is hurtful, and since you set this up in the first place…"

"Jolene, I do not know what you are talking about," Jorge insisted just as his phone rang again. "You must let it go."

"But…"

"Hello," Jorge answered his phone and turned away from Jolene.

"I gotta talk to you," Hail was on the other end. "About today."

"I am all ears," Jorge replied. "What you got?"

Hail took a deep breath.

"We gotta talk in person."

CHAPTER

45

"Let's just say," Hail explained himself to the others shortly after arriving at Tony's place. "I heard something but wasn't sure what it was about, but had a feeling something was up."

"Then Naomi was shot?" Jorge asked with interest.

"Yeah, I mean it seemed like they only wanted specific officers to investigate, and that made me a bit suspicious. But even then, I didn't think much of it until I overheard a conversation with your name, Jorge."

"So, they out and out said they were going to frame Jorge?" Diego quickly countered. "That seems unlikely."

"Nah Nah, I heard his name so it alerted my attention," Hail quickly corrected him. "But no one was directly telling me anything, so I found a way to get my answers."

"Why would they tell you anything?" Diego asked suspiciously. "That doesn't make sense."

"Relax, Diego," Jorge spoke with laughter in his voice. "Just relax."

"It don't make sense," Diego insisted. "Why the hell would you trust this guy? He's a fucking cop."

"He works for me," Jorge reminded the group with his attention specifically on Hail.

"Look, they don't tell me anything," Hail countered. "But that doesn't mean I can't find out things. I put a listening device where it needed to be and I got your answers."

"Don't you guys check for that kind of thing?" Diego made a face. "We do."

"No, and even if they did and found it," Hail shook his head. "They have no way of knowing it was me."

"So, you overheard them talking about shooting Naomi and setting up Jorge?" Tony jumped in. "Specifically?"

"They were talking about having a suspect," Hail explained. "But, then I heard them talking about setting 'Hernandez up' and I put it together. Anyway, they're pissed because Jorge is exposing so much in his series and feel it's a direct attack, so they wanted to attack back."

"How exactly do they plan to do this?" Jorge asked. "I was not even near downtown."

"They're gonna say you hired the person who was."

"Wouldn't they have to catch this person first?"

"They will," Hail replied. "From what I understood, they know whodunnit and plan to set up a deal with him if he says you hired him."

"Is this a fact?" Jorge raised an eyebrow.

"But why now?" Diego shook his head. "The cops left you alone all along."

"Because he's getting in their faces now," Hail replied.

"So they're gonna make something up," Andrew jumped in. "For fuck sakes."

"Who is it?" Jorge asked. "We need to find him first."

"That's what I'm trying to find out," Hail shook his head. "They didn't give a name."

"But this here, it was the first time they spoke about this?" Jorge asked suspiciously.

"That I heard," Hail replied with a shrug. "I'm not always listening, and I just got the device there, so chances are they did before, and I missed it."

"We gotta find this guy before they do," Diego insisted. "But how? We don't even know who it is."

"And sir, I cannot find anything," Marco shook his head as he pointed at his laptop.

"If they think they are going to pin this on me," Jorge grumbled. "They can think again! I will burn them all."

"How high up does this go?" Tony remained patient while the others grew anxious. "The police chief? The mayor? If we know that, Marco can hack them, or we can find some way to shake them up."

"They *will* get shaken up," Jorge insisted. "That is for sure."

"If I had to guess," Hail cut in. "I would say the chief of police. He's been pushing to keep these protests contained. When they aren't, it makes us look bad."

"But, is that because the mayor is breathing down his neck?" Diego countered. "Shit runs downhill."

"I can look into them both," Marco volunteered. "As soon as I find out something..."

"I gotta go," Jorge suddenly headed for the door.

"When you talk to Athas," Jolene followed him. "Can you talk to him about..."

"Jolene, let it go," Jorge shot back as he reached for the doorknob. "I don't got time for your soap opera."

With that, he was gone.

Glancing at his phone on the way to the SUV, he felt panic in his heart. Paige wasn't going to like this one.

Rushing through traffic, he considered everything that Hail had told him. Something didn't feel right. Could he trust him? He called Marco as he drove along.

"Hello."

"You aren't talking to me," Jorge automatically said. "Go into another room."

"Ok, yes, that sounds good," Marco replied while a shuffling sound indicated he was moving away from the others. "What is it?"

"I want you to make sure I can trust *him*," Jorge said. "I do not think he is working with the police, but look into him as well."

"I was already thinking the same," Marco said in a low voice, clearly aware he meant Hail.

"It would be of no advantage to lie to me," Jorge said as he neared his house. "But others, they have tried this in the past."

"Will do, sir," Marco said. "I will be in touch."

Jorge arrived home shortly after and swung into the driveway. As much as he dreaded telling Paige what Hail had revealed, Jorge was relieved that she took it in stride, calmly nodding her head.

"I don't think they can say you had anything to do with it," Paige reminded him. "I mean, why would anyone trust the shooter? Besides, there's no way to link the two of you."

"It does not matter," Jorge reminded her. "I want to find him before they do."

"They probably won't have to look as hard," She suggested. "It sounds like maybe…"

"I know, *mi amor,* I know."

"So, what do you want to do?" She asked. "Is Marco looking into this?"

"Yes, that and Hail, to make sure he's even telling the truth."

"He probably is," Paige predicted. "But it doesn't mean he got it right either. Maybe they're playing around with framing you, but it's not that easy. They know you can tear them apart, so do you think they want to push their luck? After all, a few cops have…disappeared lately."

"A few more might be disappearing very soon," Jorge complained. "If they don't watch it."

"See, this was the kind of thing I worried about when you started this season of the series," Paige reminded him. "I don't want you to get on their radar."

"The worst part, Paige, is that I have not killed in a long time," Jorge reminded her. "And yet, here I am, getting blamed for something I did not do."

"And it doesn't make sense," Paige added. "Why would you want to kill Naomi? She was helping you."

"The police, they will spin things, so it makes sense," Jorge shook his head. "That is the thing, they like stretching stories. Maybe she was not taking my directions."

"And the protests got worse, not better," Paige added. "Have you turned on the news?"

"No, I have been so busy with…"

"They got way worse because people felt like the attack on Naomi was an attack on them," Paige pulled out her phone. "So, if this was a way to slow things down, it didn't work. People are furious, and protests are increasing across the country."

She showed him the news alert and images of crowds on social media.

"Is that….a statement from Athas?" Jorge pointed to another news alert on her phone. "What does it say?"

"It says 'we are extremely active trying to resolve this issue' and," Paige continued to scroll further down into the story. "He says, 'We are expecting the RCMP and police services to do their job and keep people safe'."

Jorge rolled his eyes. "Politician talk."

"Pretty much," Paige slid the phone back into her pocket. "What do you expect?"

"When you talk to him earlier, did he say anything more?" Jorge wondered. "Did he have any thoughts on the shooting?"

"He was pissed that it happened," Paige replied and shook his head. "But didn't really say anything else."

Jorge raised an eyebrow.

That's when his phone rang.

It was Marco.

"Sir," He began to speak rapidly. "I did some research, and sir, he is fine however, I do need to come and see you."

"Did you…"

"I have all the information you need."

Jorge paused for a moment.

"I'll be here."

CHAPTER

46

"So he shot her over a….personal issue?" Jorge asked as he leaned back in his chair, watching Marco on the other side of the desk. "It was *not* the police that set it up or maybe someone else that was mad at her? But a boyfriend?"

"That is correct, sir," Marco nodded his head. "It was not over her activism at all, but over a relationship that did not end so well. This man, Tommy Borish was married, and when it did not work out with Naomi, she told his wife, who left him with the kids and moved to another country…."

Jorge shook his head.

"I know, sir," Marco began to laugh. "No 'soap opera' for you! I understand. The point is that it was over a personal issue and nothing else."

"But what I don't understand," Jorge was already shaking his head. "Is how they thought they could blame me over this? And who turned off the cameras?"

"They knew the details and even who did it," Marco replied with wide eyes. "But hesitated to arrest him because they wanted to figure out a way to blame you. Hail overheard a conversation today…well, actually, we both listened in from Tony's, and they were saying that they would suggest that you learned of this man from Naomi's past and that you were manipulating him to kill her. As for the cameras, I think maybe they just have not worked in a long time."

"I would do all of this because, why?" Jorge appeared confused. "This does not make sense."

"They are claiming you are mad because she wasn't following your instructions regarding the protests," Marco waved his hand in the air. "That you considered her 'out of line' and felt the need to get rid of her."

"Nothing about that makes any sense," Jorge shook his head. "Anyone who knows me knows that I would not shoot her over such a thing. And if I did, *I* would shoot. I would not do something as ridiculous as find an ex-lover, or whatever the hell he was."

"It is flimsy, sir," Marco said and started to laugh. "But you also must remember, this division does not have the best track record in solving cases either. You must keep things very simple."

With that, Jorge's head fell back in laughter while Marco joined him.

"Yes, this is true," Jorge finally agreed. "But I would hope that they could figure out something slightly more....intelligent."

"I think they were grasping at straws," Marco admitted. "As usual, they have greatly underestimated you."

"*Perfecto,*" Jorge grinned. "That way, I keep them out of my hair. What else you got?"

"Sir, I do have a possible location of the man in question."

"This, Tommy Borish? Naomi's ex-boyfriend?"

"Yes," Marco replied as he leaned forward in his chair. "However, I am not sure if he is still there. The problem is that he has...mental health issues, so he has been moving around rapidly, different locations, and that kind of thing. But the police, they have not made an arrest."

"Because it was more important to frame me?"

"Basically," Marco nodded before continuing. "And the mayor, I found nothing so far. However, I did see a lot of text messages and emails from the new chief of police to various people, complaining about the riots 'getting out of hand' and how it was time to 'take control of the city again'. If I had to guess, that would be the person you should focus on."

"And you should do the same," Jorge suggested as he rose from his seat, and Marco followed. "Continue to look into this and also, look into this Tommy Borish some more. See if you can hack anything of his..."

"Already did, sir," Marco shook his head. "There was nothing. I suspect he is paranoid and destroyed his phone and is keeping off the radar."

"Then how do you know where he is?"

"His address, as well as some family member's homes," Marco replied. "My understanding is the police have seen him in both places since the murder. But they aren't doing anything about it."

"Of course not Marco," Jorge stood tall. "What do you think? The police, they do their job? Not fucking likely."

"They are spending a lot of time trying to set you up, sir," Marco shook his head as both headed toward the office door. "This here, I do not understand. Over protests? Riots? I understand they want to bring peace to their city, but..."

"Do they?" Jorge countered. "Do they *really* want to bring peace to the city? Are we sure of that?"

"This, it is a good point, sir," Marco nodded. "But I think that there is a lot of pressure to do such. We are making international news, and more protests are breaking out across the country, places with fewer resources, so perhaps government pressure too."

"Either way," Jorge shook his head as he turned the doorknob. "They've picked a very bad enemy."

Immediately after Marco left, Jorge messaged Makerson. He called within minutes.

"You were looking for me?"

"Want to do an impromptu, surprise interview with me online?" Jorge asked with a grin on his face as he headed back to his desk. "Regarding the protests?"

"Sure, what's your angle?"

"My angle," Jorge replied. "is for me to talk about what a great idea it is for people to express themselves. That I have met Naomi and was devastated by her death."

"I can anytime," Makerson replied.

"Now," Jorge replied.

"I'll tweet that we are about to go live."

By the time both men got online and started the interview, people were already buzzing about it on Twitter, in anticipation of what was about to be said. Jorge Hernandez had a reputation for not holding back his opinion on government and other issues, so people tended to perk their ears up in expectation of anything. They wouldn't be disappointed.

"It's great to talk to you again," Makerson started the interview on *Toronto AM's* YouTube channel. "I'm always interested in your perspective on hot topics here and around the world."

"Yes, Tom, you know that I'm always more than happy to share my point of view," Jorge replied, and he smiled. "Especially in these difficult times."

"Today, I wanted to start with your docuseries, *Eat the Rich Before the Rich Eat You,*" Makerson continued to speak in his usual, calm tone. "The second season is perhaps even more controversial than the first. Were you expecting this kind of reception?"

"Well, the thing is," Jorge began to speak in a relaxed manner. "I cannot take credit for this series. It is Tony Allman and his staff that you can recognize for such great work. However, I support whatever Tony chooses to do, and this specific season on police issues, I think, is an important topic. I had not expected the reception we did receive. I do understand because, like most of those watching at home, I was upset with what I was learning. The most recent episode regarding the relationship between the police and the indigenous people was very, very disturbing to me."

"Do you know what's coming up in the shows before they are aired?" Makerson asked. "Do you have any input?"

Jorge hesitated for a moment before shaking his head.

"No," he lied. "I knew the general topic, but not the specific details, no."

"What was your impression when you did see this episode?"

"Well, like with most of the episodes," Jorge shook his head solemnly. "I was disheartened by this treatment. People should be able to trust the police, and when they cannot, it is a heartbreaking situation. And specifically for women to be put in a vulnerable situation. You know, I have a wife...I have a daughter, I would like to think that if they were ever harmed that they could trust the police to help. The fact that the indigenous people, they do not have this luxury that other Canadians *might* have...it is truly upsetting."

"What else has stood out to you in this series so far?"

"So many things," Jorge replied. "The white supremacy, this here, to me, it is truly disappointing. I like to believe that Canada, that Canadians, are better than that so I am disappointed to learn that we have so many flaws in our system."

"Do you know what encouraged Tony Allman to choose the topic of police issues for this second season? Was there a reason?"

"I do not know," Jorge replied. "I am assuming stories of these kinds of issues with the local police perhaps made him look into it further, but you would have to ask him."

"What are your thoughts on the protests?"

Jorge hesitated and stared into the camera.

"I believe that it is the people's right and freedom to do this," He spoke with a solemn expression. "I believe that it is powerful to speak out. I believe that we, as Canadians, have the right to protest when it is believed that something is wrong and must be addressed."

"Would you say that you encourage people to protest?"

Jorge paused for a moment, his eyes narrowed, and a smooth grin touched his lips.

"I fully encourage people to protest," Jorge insisted. "It is important to scream as loud as necessary until your voice is heard. Freedom is what makes this country beautiful."

"And what are your thoughts on the recent death of Naomi Brooke's, who was famous in the GTA for organizing various protests and working with others who wished to do the same?"

"I believe she was very strong, very brave," Jorge lowered his head slightly. "I was saddened to hear of her death. She was a woman who wanted to inspire change, who knew the true meaning of activism, and I hope that whoever did this to her is found."

"Do you have any final thoughts before we wrap up this interview? A message to our viewers?"

Jorge sat up straight and looked into the camera.

"There is the power behind a voice, and it is necessary to use it," Jorge spoke with strength as he stared into the camera. "We shall overcome."

CHAPTER

47

"What the fuck are you doing?" Alec blasted Jorge through the secure phone line. "What the fuck was that with Makerson? Are you trying to have more riots across the country?"

"I encouraged people to protest, to have their voice heard," Jorge insisted. "I did not say anything about riots. There is a big difference."

"There is," Athas agreed and seemed to calm down slightly. "But one can quickly turn to the other. You know this."

"I see, so if there are riots, rather than protests," Jorge hesitated for a moment before continuing. "This here is my fault?"

"I didn't say it was your fault," Athas immediately insisted and backed down. "I just...I don't understand why you did that."

"Does this here matter?" Jorge countered and heard no reply. "This is not your problem."

"It is *my* problem," Athas insisted. "I've had seven calls today from everyone from the mayor of your city to the chief of police."

"Is that so?" Jorge's mind slipped into another place, and a smile curved his lips. "And what is it they want? You to wave your magic wand and make everything great again?"

"They want," Athas seemed disgusted that he even had to explain himself to Jorge. "For this shit to stop. Everything is getting out of hand, and then you come along and stir the pot. 'We shall overcome' is a hashtag on Twitter. That's you, by the way, and everyone is jumping in with both feet to support you."

"Oh, is this so?" Jorge asked with arrogance in his voice. "Imagine that people listening to me?"

"Can you just find a way to make them back off?" Athas suggested in a calmer tone.

"I will see what I can do," Jorge replied sharply, as he looked up to see his wife walking into the room. Without saying another word, he ended the call.

"Is everything ok?" She asked innocently, and Jorge merely shrugged.

"Everything is *perfecto, mi amor,*" Jorge grinned. "Why don't you come over and sit on my lap, pretty lady?"

"I would love to, however," Paige tilted her head toward the wall. "You have visitors."

"Do I want to know?" He said under his breath as he rose from the chair and followed her out of the room.

"Diego."

Jorge shrugged.

"And Jolene."

Jorge started to raise an eyebrow, but his question was quickly answered, upon entering his living room to find the siblings in an argument. Diego's eyes were red with fury.

"Why can't you keep your mouth shut once in a while, Jolene?" He was yelling at her. "Get over yourself!"

"What is this here?" Jorge cut in, and Jolene jumped back in surprise. "Why must you come to my house to argue? Do you not have a house of your own, Diego?"

"Tell him," Diego directed his comment at Jolene. "Tell him the stupid thing you did this time."

"It was not stupid," She whined. "Jorge, he say that we should express ourselves, so...."

"What did you do, Jolene?" Jorge asked and shook his head. "I do not have time for this nonsense, so tell me."

"I did nothing wrong," She insisted, but her face paled. "I just do an interview."

"A podcast with some big shot on the internet," Diego jumped in. "Told her life story about Athas."

"What?"

"I tell him that we weren't just friends, like Alec said," Jolene complained. "He made it sound like I was nothing to him."

"You probably were nothing to him," Jorge snapped back. "Why the hell would you do this?"

"I wanted the truth…."

"You wanted his attention," Jorge countered and glanced over his shoulder to see Paige standing nearby, with a blank expression on her face. "Enough of this nonsense, Jolene. You better not say anything that will give me a headache."

"She said that she met Athas through you," Diego complained. "Like you want the world to know that."

"He asked me!"

"If he asked you who you shot last, would you tell him that too?" Diego snapped back. "What the fuck is wrong with you, Jolene? We don't need this kind of attention on us."

"Was anything that serious said in the interview?" Paige jumped in. "This doesn't seem like…"

"I was just talking to Athas, and he didn't mention it," Jorge cut in. "So either he doesn't know, or he doesn't care. And you know what, Jolene? Neither do I, but I do not want you doing fucking interviews talking about this kind of thing again. We do *not* want to bring attention to our organization."

"You do," She complained.

"Not the same thing," Jorge complained. "I think about what I am going to say before I say it."

"I don't see the big deal…" Paige cut into their conversation. "With everything going on right now, I don't think anyone will be talking about this."

"You better hope for your sake," Jorge pointed his finger at Jolene. "That Paige is right. That better be it, Jolene!"

"She talked about how she worked for you, including when she ran the sex clubs for you, back in the day," Diego divulged.

Jorge turned and gave Jolene a stern look.

"Jolene, how many warnings do you need?" Jorge complained. "How many times do I have to tell you that you do *not* talk about me, this organization, any of this in public. Is there anything *else?*"

"That's it," Diego confirmed. "Trust me, I was listening."

"Why would you tell him these things?" Jorge snapped. "What is wrong with you?"

"He asked!" Jolene defended herself. "It was already in the media that I used to do this, and so I could not deny it."

"Actually, yes, Jolene, you could have," Diego countered. "You could've laughed and said you were a party planner or anything else."

"He is right," Jorge agreed. "But you know what, I don't got time for this now, Jolene. And it is lucky for you that I don't because I worry that if you say this much in public, then how much are you saying to smaller audiences?"

"I do not talk..." Jolene spoke nervously. "I swear, I do not talk. I...I promise I will not do any more interview..."

Jorge's phone beeped and he checked it.

"I gotta go," Jorge raised his hand in the air as if to indicate for her to stop. "I don't got time for this Jolene. I got other things on the go."

He started to walk toward the door.

"Oh, but Jolene, if you want to fix this mess," Jorge stopped midway and turned around. "If you want to make my life easier right now, you can go distract Athas, so he gets off my ass about these protests."

"Riots," Diego corrected him, but Jorge wasn't listening.

"I cannot," Jolene said as she shook her head. "He will not see me."

"Then, I guess you are no good to me," Jorge spoke sharply.

"Riots, not protests," Diego repeated. "At least here in Toronto, they are riots now."

"Since when?" Jorge reached for his phone. "I just talked to Athas..."

"Well, while the two of you were on the phone gossiping," Diego started toward him. "Apparently, things picked up their pace, and...."

"Your secure line," Paige cut in and pointed toward his office.

"Oh fuck," Jorge complained as he backtracked. "What the fuck does he want now?"

"I think this is obvious," Jolene murmured as he passed her, which he ignored.

Back in his office, he slammed the door and rushed across the room. Grabbing his phone and drew in a breath.

"Yeah?"

"Your protests that were merely to *let people's voices be heard* have turned into riots," Athas complained. "I'm going to have to get the army involved if they get much worse."

Jorge didn't speak but turned on his laptop to watch the live stream as Athas continued to rant. The first thing he saw was a car on fire as people ripped through the streets, screaming and fighting. There was so much chaos that he slowly sunk into the chair, unable to stop staring at the computer. His heart raced in panic, unsure of what to do next, he took a deep breath and heard himself speak.

"Let the police do their job."

"Oh, now you want the police to do their job?" Athas snipped. "But yet…"

"Athas, first you need to calm the fuck down," Jorge cut in. "But then, you must think about what you want right now."

"I want this to stop."

"No, what do you *really* want?" Jorge questioned him. "You want these people to stop calling you, complaining. Just as I want you to stop calling and complaining to me. Shit, it rolls downhill, *not* up."

With that, he hung up the phone on the prime minister for the second time that day, and he closed his eyes.

This was not how it was supposed to happen. Jorge thought he had everything under control. The joke was on him. Nothing was under control.

The phone rang again. This time, the number was unfamiliar.

"Hello," Jorge answered calmly.

"Mr. Hernandez?"

"Yes."

"This is Ronald Evans."

"The new chief of police," Jorge responded. "Yes, I know who you are."

"I was wondering if we could meet?" Ronald Evans paused. "Preferably as soon as possible."

Jorge considered this for a moment. A smooth grin spread across his lips as he realized that the devil always won. And so would he.

CHAPTER

48

"We met before," Ronald Evans said as he followed Jorge into his office. "I believe you had some involvement with politics at the time?"

Jorge turned abruptly to face the overweight man and gave him a stern look before walking behind his desk.

"I do not remember."

"It was..some time ago,"

"I see," Jorge didn't bother to hide his boredom as he sat down. "So, you have taken over for Maxwell?"

"Yes," Evans replied as he sat in the chair across from Jorge. "They needed a quick replacement..."

"What do you want?" Jorge cut him off, his words slicing through whatever the Toronto chief of police had to say. "I don't got all day."

"They said you were....to the point."

"I do not see how it is good to be any other way," Jorge replied as he stared at the older, white man across from him. "So, what can I do for you?"

Ronald took a deep breath, looking down, his eyes finally rose again to cast on Jorge.

"This is regarding the protests."

"Yeah?"

"I need them to stop."

Jorge didn't reply.

"They are getting dangerous."

Jorge titled his head as if he were somewhat interested.

"I know you can help."

"How?"

"I believe you helped to instigate them," Ronald Evans seemed to sit up a bit straighter. "And I think you have the power to help eliminate them too."

"First of all, I am not sure how I started these riots," Jorge leaned ahead and continued to glare at the man across from him. "And also, why do you think I am so powerful? Who am I supposed to be, Che Guevara?"

"You do have a certain amount of power," Evans spoke earnestly, as he leaned forward in his chair. "People listen to you. That's why I'm hoping you can do something to calm all of this down. And let's face it, the protests started after your series came out on the streaming service. I mean, you painted a very dark picture of the police that I don't think is..."

"Hold up right there!" Jorge put his hand in the air and shook his head. "Let us get something straight right now. That series you are referring to, I did not *paint* a bad picture of the police. I painted the picture that was already there."

Ronald Evans leaned back in defense.

"This here fairytale that you might tell yourself about the police being heroes,' Jorge leaned in, his voice growing louder. "It is just a story. It is fiction. Not true."

"It's not fair to say that all police are corrupt," Evans attempted to argue.

"I do not have time for this nonsense argument," Jorge shook his head. "I do not care what you think. The stories in this series, they are the truth. We have proof and, if people decided to react, this is not my fault. I did not know such things would happen. This is not my problem, and I do not understand why you feel that I should give you a solution on a platter. This...this is you, not me."

"Look," Evans suddenly grew rigid in his seat, his face tightening up as if he were fighting the bright sun from his eyes. "Regardless of what you say, I know what your true motives were."

"Oh! Is this so?" Jorge commented. "It would not be to make money on a popular series, would it? It would not be to expose the *truth* to people, would it? No, you think that my reasoning for all of this here was to make your life difficult? To start protests or riots? You, are out of your fucking mind."

"You can say whatever you want, but..."

"If that is all, you can leave," Jorge spoke sharply. "I am not taking responsibility for what is taking place out there. This is not my circus, not my clowns, get the fuck out of my office!"

Jorge stood up, and Ronald Evans jumped from his seat.

"No, please, we need your help."

"Why should I help you?" Jorge challenged. "When you were attempting to set me up for Naomi Brookes' death? Tell me that."

Ronald Evans went pale.

"I heard earlier today that the man who did shoot her," Jorge continued. "This...Tommy....something, her ex-boyfriend, that he was suicided. That is the correct term, *si?* When someone is killed, but it is made to look like a suicide?"

"I..."

"Don't even bother," Jorge shook his head. "I am not listening."

"We know about you..."

"What is it exactly you know about me? Jorge asked as he narrowed his eyes. "Please, I am curious what it is you know about me?"

"You have been involved in a lot of crimes."

"Oh, is that so?" Jorge started to laugh. "This is funny because I have never even got a traffic ticket here in Canada."

"We know you are careful."

Jorge continued to glare at him.

"We know that one of your associates, Jolene Silva was in a relationship with Alec Athas," Evans continued. "And that he works for you."

"He works for the people," Jorge corrected him. "Not me."

"That's not what we hear."

"Maybe you hear wrong."

"Look, Mr. Hernandez," Evans continued. "I need your help with this situation. Regardless of whether or not we agree on your status or even on your series doesn't matter. What matters is that we have protests right now, but in *my* city, they have gotten out of hand. People are getting hurt, and others might die. Businesses, properties, will be damaged or destroyed. I can't have this going on."

"And what is it you want me to do?" Jorge asked without showing judgment.

"Send a message," Evans shook his head. "Let them know that you don't support riots. After all, you have a business in that area, don't you?"

Jorge recognized a threat when he heard one.

"Doesn't...." Jorge thought for a moment and pointed at the police chief's chair, indicating he sits back down. "Doesn't your daughter work in that area...."

Ronald Evans went pale.

"That is what I thought I heard," Jorge said as he sat down. "Probably from the same people that tell you that I'm a criminal and that I own Alec Athas and that I created a series against the police only to make your life difficult."

The chief of police looked ill as he sat back down.

"You know, *they* sure like to talk."

Evans didn't reply.

"And speaking of the series, there is one particular episode coming up," Jorge continued "It is this weekend. The topic is women in the police force, specifically the local police."

Evans continued to be silent.

"The episode is called, *Know Your Place, Bitch,* and this here, it is the words from the mouth of someone years ago," Jorge continued. "He tells a woman, a coworker, these words when she started. In the end, you know what? She quit for some reason. Said the harassment was too much. The man? Do you know what happened to him?"

Ronald Evans sunk in his chair.

"He moved way...way...*way* up in the department," Jorge continued as he pointed toward the ceiling. "And now, he thinks he is something important, but I am here to tell him he's not. And I am here to tell him that if he doesn't shut his fucking mouth and do what I say, that I will expose this information on the series. Right now, we do not say names, but that can change."

Evans looked away.

"You walked in my office today, thinking that you were going to make me *your* bitch but instead, you will become *mine,*" Jorge lowered his voice as he leaned forward on his desk. "Because that pension, it is coming soon and if you fuck up, well, you lose everything including your job...and maybe...maybe something even more valuable, if you decide to fuck with me because Mr. Evans, no one.....no one fucks with Jorge Hernandez and if you didn't already know this, I am telling you now. Do you understand?"

Ronald Evans nodded in silence.

"Now, this next episode, it may not be as sexy as white supremacy or raping indigenous, teenaged girls," Jorge continued growing more fierce with sarcasm with every word. "But I do think that the people would have something to say if they knew who you really are...."

"I understand."

"Do you?" Jorge countered. "Now you and I will be working together. You were right, I can stop these riots, but you gotta do something for me, or this here will not happen. In fact, I will make the riots ten times worse if you don't play by my rules."

"You've made your point."

"You may be high up," Jorge pointed toward the ceiling. "But I'm higher than you. I have power. Real power, and unlike you, I don't gotta carry a gun around to know I have it. And never question this."

"I won't," Evans agreed as his face turned red.

"Now, we must set some ground rules," Jorge insisted. "And those rules, they are mine, not yours."

"I'm sure...I'm sure we can come to an agreement."

"This agreement," Jorge countered. "You do not have a choice. And it never leaves this office. If you ever say anything about this conversation to anyone....that daughter of yours?"

Ronald Evans shook his head.

"Exactly," Jorge said as he leaned back in his chair. "Let us agree that we both would do anything to protect our children and believe it or not if we work together, all our children, they will always be protected."

"So if I..."

"If you need anything, you call on me," Jorge nodded and eased back in his chair. "But if I want something, you don't fucking question it. You don't even ask why."

The two men fell silent, but there was an understanding. And it was an understanding that would follow them that day forward.

CHAPTER

49

"*The crown did not prove beyond a reasonable doubt...*" A woman's voice came from the laptop, while Paige shook her head and glanced across the desk at Jorge.

"See, this is why women don't report violence from men," She spoke over one of the final episodes of *Eat the Rich Before the Rich Eat You,* and Jorge hit pause. "Why would they? That woman did everything she was asked and told every degrading detail about the rape, and they automatically believed him, claiming she had no *substantial* proof that it wasn't consensual."

"Meanwhile, the police, they did not make any effort to help her with the case," Jorge added as he leaned back in his chair. "But quite the opposite. They almost ganged up against her."

"Of course they did because he was a relative of one of the cops," Paige shook her head. "But even the fact that the women on the force were as bad makes me sick. We live in such a patriarchal society. Even the women fell in line."

"I guess they had no fear that they too might be in that situation one day," Jorge observed. "They felt overpowered and influenced. It is such a shame."

"Welcome to the world of being a woman," Paige commented. "So, is this the last show of the season?"

"Second last," Jorge answered as he glanced at the laptop. "Now that everything is calming down, even the riots, so is the series."

"Well, you did work your magic, Jorge. That announcement that your new media company will be very involved in the community and will give more power to voices without going on the street to protest, that helped. And considering the work you've already done on the docuseries, they know you're the real deal."

"I'm the real deal, baby," He insisted as he reached for his phone. "I have calmed the people, assured them of a voice while gaining power over the police. Everyone gets what they want, and I have control over everything. This here, it is my dream."

"Just be careful," Paige warned. "You tend to get too close to the fire. I'm not sure if I trust the police, regardless of what power you have over them."

"Oh, Paige, trust me," Jorge leaned back in his chair. "They know their place with me, and also, they may need my help in the future too so they best not try to cross me, or I will cross them out."

Paige considered his words and appeared worried, but didn't reply.

Little did he know that the police would reach out to him later that same day for help. Although he had been expecting it and was aware of the details, he had assumed it would be weeks into the future. Excitement filled his soul when he realized that he now would have complete control over the local Police because what they asked of him put them in a weak position and if anyone knew how to take advantage of such vulnerabilities, it was Jorge Hernandez.

He arranged a meeting with Diego, Chase, and Jolene at the bar. Although he briefly considered letting Paige know, something held him back. He would discuss this with her later, in private.

Arriving at the bar, he discovered Chase was alone, preparing a pot of coffee.

"You dare do that and not leave it for the great coffee maker, Diego instead?" He teased as he walked across the club and sat at the bar. "He will be heartbroken."

"He'll get over it," Chase shrugged with a grin. "So, what's going on? You made it sound like it was urgent."

"I have something that we must do tomorrow," Jorge replied. "I will wait for the others before I tell you more."

Chase nodded in understanding.

"So, my daughter, she is looking forward to starting her new job next week," Jorge reminded him. "As I said before, do not be easy on her."

"So, the show we did," Diego said. "This was just scratching the surface."

"All the shows," Jorge waved his arms in the air. "Don't you see, they are connected. The indigenous show, the show about Alwood, all these shows are really about racism and discrimination, about people in position of power trying to control others."

"Evans, he met with me again earlier today," Jorge continued before anyone had a chance to jump in. "He told me that he knew a meeting was coming up because these people gather every few months to discuss plans, problems, that kind of thing. Today, he learned the next meeting is tomorrow, and it is here in Toronto. It is the most problematic white supremacy group that is infiltrating the police right now."

"And we're going to?" Chase shook his head.

"We are going to eliminate the problem," Jorge replied. "You must know, this here group is very organized, very strategic. We must help the police take care of them before they grow. They are like *rats*. If you do not take care of them fast and hastily, they only double in amount."

"So, the rats are going to get in a trap?" Diego asked.

"The rats are going to be eliminated in one, giant swoop," Jorge insisted. "Those fuckers won't even know what hit them."

CHAPTER

50

Imagine a world where you no longer had freedom of thought. It sounds silly until you consider the increased censorship on the Internet, the attacks people receive when expressing an unpopular opinion, or even the freedoms lost during a worldwide pandemic. We often take it for granted that the beautiful freedoms we enjoy will always be there, and yet, many people are willing to surrender them with almost no hesitation. What would you do without your freedom, and even more important, who would you be?

Jorge Hernandez cherished his freedom. No one would ever take him prisoner, and if they ever tried, he would claw his way out and destroy anyone who tried to stop him. To Jorge, his voice was his most powerful tool, only coming second to his inner strength and a sharp, powerful instinct that had saved him a million times over. He didn't take his freedom for granted.

When he first got the call from Ronald Evans, Jorge was hesitant to meet. If it were not for the desperation in the man's voice, Jorge would've laughed at him and hung up the phone. However, it was clear that this was a man in need, and a man in need carried a vulnerability that allowed his powers to be taken away. How quick he was to give that up, Jorge mused. All in exchange for this problem to be taken care of with no traces to the police.

"So this here should be easy," Jorge informed the group. "These people are meeting in the hotel conference room and have asked that no staff interrupt for any reason. The food is provided, and the drinks are plentiful. That is all they ask, but unfortunately, their meeting will not be as they wish."

"How the hell are we going to carry this out in such a public place?" Diego countered as the group sat together in the bar.

"There will be a lot of people at this meeting," Jolene seemed unsure. "How can we kill every one of them? I do not understand."

"And in a *public* place," Diego repeated his earlier remark.

"Let me explain," Jorge said as he raised his hand in the air to indicate that Diego calmed down. "I have thought this out, and also, I have discussed it with Evans to see what would be the best method. We have all the bases covered…"

"There's going to be people all over the goddam place," Diego cut him off.

"The conference room doors, they will be locked,' Jorge directed his comment at Diego. "The staff, they are warned to keep good and far away. This here will help us."

"But, why help them?" Jolene was concerned. "I just…"

"Maybe if you guys listened," Chase cut in. "He could explain. He obviously knows what he's doing. He didn't get this far because he's stupid."

Jorge laughed at Chase's remark and clapped his hands together.

"Thank you, Chase," Jorge continued to laugh. "I have given this some thought and remember, the police, we are doing this *for* them so even if there was an investigation, they will let us go free."

"It could be a trap," Diego warned. "To get rid of these assholes and *us* at the same time."

"You must have faith, Diego that I have thought of everything," Jorge insisted. "And this here, it is no different. Let us just say that the chief of police has a good reason to keep in line. I made a very clear threat to his family."

Diego considered his words and nodded.

"Now, can I finish?" Jorge asked and didn't wait for an answer. "As I said, no staff will be around, no cameras will be on, and the police, they won't be near. Why would they? The people in this meeting *are* police so they do not need protection."

The room was silent as he continued to speak.

"Trust me," Jorge assured them. "This here will be simple, they will not even know what hit them."

"How many are there?" Diego asked.

"Diego, these are people from all over the country, different levels of the police who are white supremacists," Jorge attempted to answer. "So there are a lot."

"What do we have to…." Jolene started.

"Just bring your guns," Jorge replied. "The rest will be easy."

"But how?" Chase asked. "Isn't that a lot for us to take on at once?'

"Trust me, it will be like shooting fish in a barrel," Jorge had an evil grin on his lips, as he tilted his head down. "I would not want to be part of the cleaning staff at this here hotel."

The four gathered outside the hotel on the night of the meeting. They had managed to slip into the concealed door with no issue. There was no one in sight; no employees, no guests, and the only proof of life was a conference room door with a 'meeting in progress, do not disturb' sign outside.

"When I talked to Evans," Jorge gestured toward the door. "He tells me that his grandmother, she managed to escape a concentration camp in Germany. He tells me that these same people meeting here tonight, they would've condoned her dying in such a cruel way, and for that, he would like them to suffer the same. So we decided that carbon monoxide poisoning seemed appropriate."

"Wait, what?" Diego halted his steps as Jorge opened a cabinet door with a red tag on it and pulled out four gas masks. "Then what the fuck are we doing here?"

"I said we are gassing them," Jorge reminded them as he passed out the masks. "I didn't say that we weren't going to shoot them."

Everyone appeared confused.

"Do you not see," Jorge continued. "They will be powerless against us…"

"I think it's risky," Diego shook his head. "We should keep our hands clean…"

"Diego, this must be a bloodbath," Jorge explained. "Because Evans wants to send a message to others. It will be revealed tomorrow morning that these people are white supremacists. There will be proof in the room. It will also be proven that they are cops. If they are just gassed, then it seems like an accident. They must know that this here, it was not just a suspicious accident."

"But the gunshots…" Jolene started.

"The room is soundproof," Jorge informed them as they stopped in the hallway. "And the staff are to keep far away. I assure you, we got this, but these masks only give limited protection, so we must act fast."

The group made their way toward the room, and Jorge ignored the insecurities the enveloped them. It was his job to lead with strength. There was no other way.

Taking out his phone, he touched an app that showed him a view of the conference room. Men were leaned over in their chairs, some were on the floor or close to the locked door, but most of them were still showing signs of life. They could still be saved. But they wouldn't be.

Opening the door, the group entered the lifeless room, giving the exhausted group a sign of hope. That was until they noticed the four people were carrying guns and all wearing a gas mask. That's when they knew their lives were over.

Each of the four focused on a point in the room. The gunshots were continuous as blood began to seep out of the many bodies that fell to the floor. The room that had once encompassed hate and bigotry was now a stream of crimson flowing along the floor, filling the room as sounds could be heard from the dying bodies. The smell of gun powder and death was undetected through their protective gear, but they had all experienced it many times before, so it was deeply ingrained in their brains causing them to believe they could smell it anyway.

Jorge stood back for a moment and looked at the bodies that lay on the floor. To make sure that no one escaped alive, he would insist on closing the door again when they left, sneaking out into the hallway, they removed their masks and glanced around. No one was around. It was easy.

It was when the group piled back into his SUV, that a phone call stole away their brief moment of shared glory.

"*Papa*," His daughter's voice sounded so small as it echoed through the SUV.

"Maria!" Jorge felt his heart race. "Maria, are you ok?

"*Papa, someone is here….*"

"What? Maria, who is there?" Jorge shouted into the phone and attempted to calm himself. "Maria, lock yourself in your room. Where are Paige and Miguel?"

"I don't know…I'm scared…"

"Oh no," Jolene was sniffing from the backseat. "The poor baby."

"Maria….I am on my way!"

"I have to go," She whispered into the phone before ending the call.

Jorge felt panic in his heart as he tore out of the parking lot. Once on the highway, he passed every car in sight, going at a speed that would've frightened most people under normal circumstances. But he wasn't most people.

"Jorge calm down," Diego was saying from the passenger side. "She is going to be ok…"

Jorge didn't hear another word as his mind raced. He would later not even recall the drive home or how he got there so fast. Normally, it would've been impossible, but that day, nothing would stand in his way.

When he pulled into the driveway, he barely had the SUV in park, when he jumped out and ran into the house.

The first thing he saw was a man lying in a pool of blood. He felt his stomach drop until he turned to see Paige looking equally horrified as her eyes turned away, and he followed them to see Maria with a gun in her hand. With tears running down her face, she stared at the man on the floor as blood poured from his head. Someone behind him let out a gasp.

"Maria!" Jorge felt himself starting to calm down. "Maria…did you…. did you.."

She couldn't answer, her teeth were chattering as she nodded and she started to cry harder.

"Maria," Jorge rushed toward her and swooped her into his arms with Paige right behind him. "Maria…it is ok."

"Jorge," Paige spoke anxiously. "This man got into the house. I…I was upstairs with the baby and Maria….she must've heard something…"

"Maria, what happened?" Jorge tried to hold back the panic in his voice.

"Threaten…" She managed to whisper through her chattering teeth. "Because of the hotel…"

They had just left a hotel.

"She's in shock," Paige spoke up as she touched the child's shoulder. "Can someone get her a blanket?"

"Maria….you heard him threaten Paige? Me?"

"Us," She answered in a small voice as she continued to shake. "He said….a hotel…kill us too."

They had just killed people at a hotel.

"He had a gun…" Paige was trying to explain. "Before I could reach for mine…." She turned her attention to Maria. "She shot him. I don't know how he got in."

Jolene brought a blanket and wrapped it around Maria, giving her a quick kiss on the top of the head. But the child continued to shake. Jorge watched his daughter start to teeter, and automatically picked her up into his arms.

Turning to the shocked faces around him, Jorge quickly instructed.

"Someone call Andrew," He gestured toward the man on the floor. "Paige, can you get some water for Maria? Diego, we need to ah….clean things up…."

Everyone went right to work while Jorge carried his daughter upstairs. Although she was almost 14, his *Princesa* was so small and delicate at that moment that she was his baby girl again. Walking into her room, he pushed the door halfway shut and sat her on the bed. She pulled the blanket closer to her while he passed her some tissues.

"Maria, I know you are in shock," Jorge started as he leaned in and kissed the top of her head. "But I understand what you did, and I am very proud of you. You protected your family, and you know me, family is the most important thing."

Nodding, she began to calm, her eyes watching him closely.

"I know you are scared, but it will be ok, Maria."

"But the police…jail…

"Maria, we do not deal with the police," Jorge informed her in a gentle voice. "And you will not be going to jail."

"But…." Maria suddenly started to cry again. "Does this make me a criminal, *Papa?*"

"Maria," Jorge leaned in closer and squeezed her body in a hug. "We are all criminals in someone's eyes, but in mine, you are a hero."

And he meant it with all his heart.

Learn more about Jorge Hernandez and his associates at mimaonfire.com. Catch up on all the news on Twitter, Instagram and Facebook@mimaonfire

If you enjoyed this book, please share it with friends or write a review:-)

Printed in the United States
By Bookmasters

Printed in the United States
By Bookmasters